DEATH WISH

REAPER REBORN BOOK ONE

USA TODAY BESTSELLING AUTHOR

HARPER A. BROOKS

H.A.B. Publications LLC

Cover Design: Covers by Christian
Interior & Formatting: Formatting by Jennifer Laslie
Editor: Midnight Library
Proofreading: Read Head Editing

For me
Because I freakin' deserve it.

CHAPTER

ONE

Do it. You have to.

I repeated the words to myself as I slid off one of my leather gloves. A man lay at my feet, clutching his chest and gasping in the middle of the dimly lit parking lot. His watery blue eyes bulged with panic as they fixed on me, and for a moment, I wondered if he could actually see me standing over him, about to end his life.

Scolding myself, I pushed away the irrational fear. Of course he couldn't see me standing here. Reapers weren't visible to the living. We came from a different plane, the other side of the veil. But still, even with that knowledge buzzing around in my head, my hand shook as I reached out to touch him.

Why was this so hard for me? After almost a year working for the Styx Corporation, I still struggled with this part. I had tried all the tricks Simon taught me during my training. Told myself I was relieving this man of his pain. Told myself it was his time to die and it had to be done. Told myself I couldn't get emotionally involved. I had been given an assignment, and I had to carry it out.

Yet, in the back of my mind was a nagging voice telling me that this man crumpled on the pavement, his newly bought groceries scattered about, was more than the picture, name, age, and basic biography on my tablet's screen. Surely he had a family who would miss him. People he loved and who loved him. Did he really deserve to die now, by a heart attack, in an empty grocery store parking lot, alone? It just didn't seem right.

One touch. That was all it took. I just had to touch him with my bare hand, and his life would be over. Just like that.

Hesitating, I glanced around. The man's Honda was one of the only cars left in the parking lot. Jumping in and out of the living world and the afterlife made it hard to keep track of the time, but from the darkness already blanketing the sky and the lack of patrons at Super Mart, my guess was that it was almost closing time. Maybe eight thirty. Pretty late to be picking up groceries, but that wasn't any of my business.

Looking at my tablet screen again, I skimmed over the man's information. Tristen James Williams. Age forty-one. Level two sorcerer. On a measuring scale of one to three, he had reached only the middle skill grade of his power.

I stopped there, knowing that if I read his bio, I might find something to squelch the rest of my nerve, like if he had children or a wife waiting for him at home.

How did Simon and the other reapers do this?

As I looked down at Tristen J. Williams, the middle-aged man—maybe a father and husband—meant to have many more years to his life, now writhing in pain, on the verge of death, my chest clenched with sympathy for him.

He had chosen a spot for his Honda under one of those parking lot lights, and the old thing flickered, making an odd sizzling sound every time it turned back on. Even in the sputtering light, the purplish-blue of his face was obvious. He let out a terrible sounding half-cough, half-gag, and my heart sank.

He was suffering.

I had to do this. I was helping him in a way, wasn't I?

Yeah, that's right. I was helping him. I had to keep telling myself that.

I closed my eyes, reached out again, and pressed my fingers against Tristen's neck. The warmth of his skin against my own was comforting but brief. In the next second, a familiar coolness crept in, as did a silence I knew all too well. No more frantic gasps for air. No more breathing at all.

Cracking an eye open, I saw his spectral form standing before me, confusion flitting across his face. Even though he was a spirit, he didn't look much different from his profile's picture or the dead man on the ground. Besides the slight opaqueness to his skin, the only differences were that he was suddenly clean-shaven and his graying hair was combed away from his blue eyes. A neater, healthier-looking version of his living self.

His gaze darted over me, seeing me for the first time. "Who are you?" he asked, a tinge of annoyance in his voice. Then he looked at his body lying by his feet. He didn't jump in horror, like I expected. He didn't even appear surprised. "What's going on?"

I tensed. Even after doing this hundreds of times, I was still terrible at this part.

Was there really a "right" way to tell someone they were dead?

I hesitated a little too long before settling for the least jarring way I could think of.

"Uh, hi there. Mr. Williams, right? Tristen?" Awful. Just awful. Maybe I needed to ask Simon for a quick refresher in my training. Six months of it hadn't been enough apparently.

Swallowing hard, I held out my hand for him to shake. "My name is Jade Blackwell, and I'm here to help you cross over. Because, well, you're dead." When Tristen only stared at my offered hand, I retracted it and quickly pulled on my glove again. "You died of a heart attack. I'm sorry. Really, I am, but I was sent here to—"

"I'm dead." It was a statement more than anything else. But again, there was no shock or grief in his eyes. Only a harshness that took me by surprise, as if he didn't believe I was telling him the truth.

Forget the fact that he was standing by his unmoving, unbreathing body.

"You are," I replied. "Dead, that is."

"Dead."

"As a doornail." I mentally slapped myself for that one, but he said nothing.

"I'm sure this all must be strange to you," I went on carefully. I didn't look like the typical grim reaper seen in the movies. There was no ominous smoke behind me. I didn't wear a black hooded cloak. No scythe or animated skeleton. Nope. Just an average-looking woman, in her late twenties, dressed for comfort in jeans and a tank, and who thoroughly sucked at formalities.

Just me.

After tucking the tablet in my back pocket, I retrieved a piece of chalk from the front one. I pasted on my best customer service smile, hoping I didn't scare him. "But as I said before, I'm here to help you cross over."

I walked to the end of the Honda and drew the circular

symbol in chalk on the blacktop that opened the spirit door between worlds. As a reaper, chalk was my best friend. Sure, I could use any kind of drawing implement I wanted to draw the door, but chalk was easy. It never ran out like ink. It never needed a sharpener, and best of all, it washed away with the rain and could be erased easily, so no risk of humans accidentally tumbling into the afterlife during their daily stroll.

When the last line and symbol was drawn, the chalk glowed orange, proving that my drawing skills were sufficient enough. The door was open. At least that part was easy. Now all I needed to do was get Tristen to hop on in. In the other side, he would go through his orientation, the one all souls went through after they passed. At least, that's what I was told. That part sounded like a lot of bullshit to me.

Because I had been next in line to be one of Styx Corp's reapers, my death experience had been different from Tristen's and everyone else's. No spirit guide and orientation mumbo jumbo for me. I didn't get the same treatment, so I didn't know exactly what happened to other souls when they crossed over. All I knew was that when they were deemed ready by whatever higher being was in charge of this rodeo, the souls were then transferred to their afterlife, where they were expected to live out the rest of their existence. That's where I lived and where Styx Corp was located, in a dimension that ran parallel to the living one, designed only for supernaturals. Humans had their own. And for those special cases, like for the murders and rapists of the world… Well, I'm sure they had their own place in Hell, too. I didn't see them again after crossing them over, and I didn't ask any questions.

"You did this to me." Tristen's suddenly hostile tone made me turn around. He stood there, body rigid, with raw hatred burning in his eyes. "You killed me."

I leapt to my feet. "What? No, I didn't." But that was a lie, wasn't it? I had killed him. Had taken his life with the touch of my hand. I wasn't going to tell him that, though.

"Put me back," he said, the edge in his tone hinting at a threat. "Now."

"I can't put you back. That's not how this works." I tried to keep my voice calm, but annoyance prickled the back of my neck. "I know this is hard for you right now, but if you come with me, everything will be explained and—"

His hand shot up, and he started mumbling, voice low and strained. His brow creasing, he began to repeat something to himself over and over.

Oh great. He was having a breakdown or something.

"Tristen…" I began cautiously and stepped closer. "Everything's going to be all right."

Whatever Tristen was trying to say, it looked like he was struggling to get it out. He kept trying, his lips moving at a feverish speed, too fast for me to read. What did come out sounded more like gibberish. Nothing I could recognize or understand. Greek maybe. Or Latin.

Wait, what kind of supernatural did his profile say he was again?

My answer came within the next second. An invisible force smacked into me strong enough to slide me backward a few feet and take me off guard.

He had hit me with some kind of knock-back spell.

That's right. Tristen James Williams. Age forty-one. Level two sorcerer. The middle grade. I'm sure if we were both alive and he had landed that hit full-on, it would have packed way more of a punch. Although powers transferred over into death, it was going to take him a little while to get used to the new state of his body and get a handle on those spells again.

For that, I was thankful. I didn't have any special abilities to match his. Whoever I was when alive made me a pretty scrappy fighter in the afterlife, but that was the only skill I had retained. Besides that, all a reaper really had was the touch of death, and that didn't work on someone who was already dead, like Tristen.

Despite my many protests, Styx Corp didn't give us weapons.

The sorcerer repeated his incantation several more times with no result, his words becoming more jumbled as his frustration grew. He shouted a couple more spurts of nonsense before finally giving up and running at me full speed.

I tried to jump out of his path, but I was too late. He tackled me onto the ground. Pain exploded as his weight slammed into me, and my head hit the pavement with an audible *crack*.

Tristen was no little guy. Technically, I couldn't die because I was dead already, but things could still hurt like a bitch. And God, did this hurt like a bitch. Colors danced before my eyes. I struggled to chase them away.

He gripped my shoulders and shook me. Hard. "You stupid fucking bitch! You put me back! You put me back now!"

Something sparked in the deep recesses of my mind, something I couldn't quite place or understand. Fear surged from it, too, my heart pounding against my ribs as if I were still alive.

"I'm going to make sure you regret doing this to me," he said through clenched teeth. "I may not be able to kill you, but how about a crushed windpipe? You talk too much anyway."

The moment his hands clamped around my throat, fury ignited, whipping through me like a wildfire. I slammed my fist into his gut with every bit of strength I had.

He rolled off me, clutching his stomach and groaning.

So much for me handling this like a professional.

I stood up slowly, my head still whirling. "Look, buddy. Wrong move. Like I told you, I'm here to help you. Not fight you. You're making this harder than it needs to be."

He jumped up and grabbed for my ankles, but I danced out of the way. He swung. I ducked and followed with an uppercut to the chin. He staggered back, clutching his jaw and spewing more curses and threats at me.

Was I really going to have to pull this guy through the door kicking and screaming?

When he came at me again, I got my answer. I spun, coming way too close to falling through the spirit door on the ground.

Shit. I had to be more careful. I shifted my weight, off-balance, and toppled forward into the Honda's rear door. Suddenly, Tristen was on me, pinning my body between his and the car. Even with his brute force, the car didn't move, not even an inch—the result of us no longer being a part of the living plane. But I felt every ounce of his two hundred and thirty pounds crushing me. Even felt the cold metal of the door against my cheek.

Shifting slightly for a better angle, I threw my elbow back as hard as I could. It connected with his ribs. As he doubled over, I pushed myself off the car and kicked him square in the stomach.

He staggered back, stopping just short of falling into the spirit circle, and teetered back and forth to keep his balance. His arms whirled like a windmill, but he managed to stay standing there on the thin edge.

The circle shimmered, as if sensing him close by.

I needed to get him through that door. But it was clear he wasn't going to go on his own.

I knew what I had to do. Not one of my brightest ideas, but it would work.

I hoped so, anyway.

Before he could completely regain his footing, I crouched low and rushed him. He tried to move, but I was too fast. We collided, all the air rushing from my lungs in one whoosh. He grabbed for my shoulders, clawing at me, trying to use my body for leverage to help himself back up, but there wasn't anything he could do.

We were falling.

He screamed.

A bright orange light flashed around us as we passed through the door. Then, there was nothing but infinite blackness.

CHAPTER

TWO

Just as my eyes adjusted to the darkness, another bright light flared, leaving me momentarily blinded. I winced against the harshness of it then blinked quickly to regain my focus. I wasn't falling anymore; I was floating. At least I thought so. Even after passing between planes multiple times, I still couldn't quite explain this part of the process except that it always made me uneasy. Good thing it only took seconds to cross over. A very terrifying few seconds.

My ears popped. The light muted and shifted to gray then dark blue, gaining more colors rapidly. Shapes appeared next, twisting and dancing as they took form. I recognized the vague outline of a large structure in the distance. A building. It was getting closer. I remembered the Super Mart's parking lot where I had opened the spirit door and pushed Tristen through. That had to be what it was.

More wobbly forms came into view. But before I could try to make sense of them, the ground rushed up to meet me and smacked against my backside hard enough to make me howl. At the same time, the night sky tumbled into place over my head.

Then, everything stopped.

Well, except my head and stomach, which both spun in opposite directions. Nausea rolled through me, and my temples throbbed. Not a pleasant combination, but one I could deal with. It was better than dry-heaving for hours afterward, which had been the result the first twenty times or so I'd done this.

The door had spit me out directly on the other side of the veil. Since the afterlife ran parallel to the living world, it was night here, too. I lay on my back, staring up at the sky. It was the same velvety black it always was, littered with too many stars and a full yellow moon. The daytime was always similar. Comfortable temperature, pale blue sky, and lots of sunshine. Mimicking the most beautiful and perfect day on earth. Completely artificial. I hated it.

When I sat up, another wave of queasiness hit, and I grumbled. For possibly the millionth time since I'd died, I wondered why I had been the lucky one to get this job. There were only ten reapers in Styx Corp. Seven in charge of crossing over all the human population and three in charge of supernaturals. Humans outnumbered supernaturals a hundred to one, hence the uneven department sizes. I was one of the three and had been stationed in the Western Hemisphere; working in North and South America, Canada, and the Caribbean countries.

When a reaper was Released from their job, either by

choice or by force, the next soul to die got tossed into line to replace them. That was what had happened to me. I had managed to win the reaper lottery.

Lucky me.

Really, I shouldn't complain. It was common for spirits to become bored of an eternal afterlife of no responsibility or problems, and so they took on work. Not for pay; money isn't needed when you're dead. Just to keep busy. I had only been here a year and understood how easy it was to fall into a cycle of monotony. I saw it all the time. Being a reaper saved me from that. And special cases—like with Tristen— certainly kept me entertained.

Speaking of the asshole sorcerer, I looked around the deserted parking lot and saw that I was indeed alone. Like I had thought, Tristen James Williams had been transferred to his afterlife orientation, or wherever new spirits went to, and I had been brought here on the other side of the door. Alone.

When he was done, he'd either be relocated to this supernatural hereafter or a Hell dimension. Depending on his behavior on earth.

And from our tussle before, I assumed we wouldn't be seeing each other again.

I rubbed my neck, remembering Tristen's hands around it, squeezing. Something had sparked in my mind then. Random twinges of feelings but nothing else. Could it have been a flashback to a moment when I was alive? Possibly.

Had it been related to the way I had died somehow? No clue.

Maybe there was no connection at all, and I was trying all I could to find a smidge of insight into my time alive. That was more likely.

Even though it had been a year since my death, I was still considered newly departed. The nine other reapers in our group had at least a century to their afterlives, so it was understandable that there were some things from my human life I was still struggling to get over. As time went on, it would get easier, or so I had been told. Things like breathing or blinking or even feeling certain emotions. They were "pesky" human habits that I no longer needed. Not to mention that for a reaper, they could greatly hinder my ability to do my job. Like my life memories, which had been completely stripped from me after my death. Years full of things and people and places, all gone to me now.

A complete mind-wipe freed me of any attachments to the living world. I understood that, too, in a way, but it didn't stop me from being a little bitter about it. I had essentially lost who I was and had been forced to start over. Left to wonder what my life was before this.

Styx Corp couldn't even give me the actual details of my death. I had no idea how or when it had happened. The first memory I had was waking up in Azrael's office. Then I had been thrown into extensive training with Simon, another reaper of supernaturals. He taught me what I needed to know to cross over all the witches, sorcerers, shapeshifters, weres, and vampires in the world when their time came to an end.

When I tried to dig a little deeper in my memory for an explanation of the strange feeling of recognition, all I got was a strange emptiness. Annoyance flared. There was no way I was ever going to get the answers I wanted. Damn memory wipe.

I spotted the building I had assumed to be the Super Mart when I was changing planes. Not a grocery store but a large library, closed now in the late hour. That made sense. There was no need to eat anymore. Since both the living and nonliving worlds mimicked each other, most of the map and landmarks were the same, but there were some modifications, like here. Restaurants, cafés, and bars still existed, but because they were places to socialize, not necessities.

Standing, I reached into my back pocket and pulled out my work tablet. Surprisingly, the thing had managed to survive another rough trip. Not even a scratch, yet my ass was sore as hell. I pressed the button, and Tristen's profile popped on screen.

I skimmed the stuff I knew—name, age, race, supernatural type—and went right to the bio. As I read, I wanted to smack myself for my stupidity.

Self-acclaimed misogynist... Known to assault his female companions... It went on to list those cases with detailed descriptions and the poor women's names. I skipped a bit. *Arrested in 2007 for battery and attempted murder against fourth girlfriend, Sarah M. Berges, but was released once charges were dropped...*

I stopped there. That was all I needed.

So much for my theory of Tristen being a family man and leaving behind a loving wife and a handful of kids.

Why hadn't I read the damn biography? It would have made things so much easier.

Sighing, I added it to my mental list of must-dos in the future.

A green light flashed at the top of the tablet, and a notification bubble came on screen with Styx Corp's company logo in the center, a circle with a man paddling a boat through some treacherous-looking waves in the center. Greek inspired, of course, like their choice of a name. A play on the River Styx in Greek mythology and the boatman who crossed over souls to the underworld, the birthplace of the grim reaper legend.

My stomach sank at the sight of the incoming message. It could only mean one thing.

I was in trouble.

Should have seen that coming. Fighting with a soul I was meant to help pass on? Not exactly the best work etiquette, but what did everyone expect? The guy started it. I was defending myself.

As I did every time I got summoned to headquarters, I wondered if there was any way I could get out of going. Pretend I hadn't seen the alert or claim I'd been busy with an assignment and had forgotten.

But as quick as the thought surfaced, it was squashed. How many times had I tried that? Never worked. Azrael then sent Simon on my tail, and being a were-creature, he was too good at the tracking part of his job for me to stay out of Azrael's grasp long. Even though he was my mentor, Simon had never disclosed what his animal side was or showed me his alternative shape, but it had to be a talented hunter because he *always* found me.

But maybe this time, I could—

A loud beeping came from the tablet in my hands, and the green light blinked faster, cutting off my thought.

"What the fuck—"

Suddenly, Azrael's face appeared, his dark hair and sideways grin unmistakable, like an alley cat facing down a cornered mouse.

"Heck," I corrected myself quickly. Cursing in front of my boss and the Angel of Death? Unwise. I had filed that one under another one of my mental lists a long time ago. A list of big fat no-nos.

"What's the matter, Jade?" he drawled, his green eyes flashing. Immortality looked good on him, permanently making him look in his mid-thirties at most. When I had first met him, I even thought him handsome, but after many trips to his office to be reprimanded, the allure faded fast. "Didn't expect to see me? Was hoping to run off again?"

I blinked. "Of course not." I faked a cough to regain

myself. "I didn't expect to see you on here. What is this anyway? Have you always been able to pop up whenever you want?"

"No. We've made some upgrades. You know, to keep with the times." He paused for emphasis and locked gazes with me. "And our employees."

So, because of me. Heard that one loud and clear. "Ah, I see," I said. "I was on my way to you. Just have to find a portal and…"

"A block down Summers Street, turn right onto Caroline. Walk two blocks. You'll see it." He never broke eye contact as he said it, only raised one brow.

So much for getting out of Azrael's summons from now on. "Got it."

"I want you here in no more than five minutes, Jade. Five minutes." The screen went black. The green light shut off, too. I waved my hand over the tablet to make sure Azrael wasn't going to just materialize again. When nothing happened, I stuck it back in my pocket.

Man, I hoped he couldn't do that whenever he wanted. Guess I had no choice now. I had to suck it up, get to the portal, and go to Styx.

I went over to the spirit door I had drawn on the parking lot's blacktop and smudged the chalk with my boot. Instantly, the orange glow extinguished, confirming the door was closed. Then, I followed Azrael's directions, walking down Summers and Caroline, and came to the portal right where he had said it'd be. It was in between two storefronts, in a small alley, partly hidden from plain view.

Portals were stationed at random points throughout the afterlife, marked with a sign and designed to help spirits travel short or long distances. Since there were no cars, trains, or airplanes, portal travel was the only means of transportation. Besides walking, that is. But since I was in

Carmel, Indiana, right now and Styx Corp was in its own dimension entirely, I couldn't reach it while taking a nightly stroll.

Like with the spirit doors, portals worked in a similar way. They were marked with an intricate symbol and transported whoever stepped on them to their desired destination.

I stood over the symbol. As the pattern glowed white as it activated, I was hit with a strong sense of déjà vu. I had been sent to headquarters so many times over the last few months, it was becoming a bad habit.

Speaking clearly, I said the two words I dreaded. "Styx Corporation."

Warm air rushed all around me, tossing my hair up and over my face. I brushed it back in annoyance as the dark alley and buildings blurred. Then they disappeared altogether, and in the next second, a giant white marble building surrounded by huge columns loomed in front of me. Like something right out of ancient Rome. White steps led to a grand entrance. Two stone-carved women statues flanked the large glass doors, one holding a baby to her naked bosom and the other with a human skull in her outstretched hands. It didn't take a genius to figure out what they represented.

Sucking in a deep breath, I trudged up the steps and went in.

The outside may have been modeled after Greece, but the inside of Styx Corp mirrored modern-day corporate America. A grand foyer stretched out in front of me, all high ceilings, straight lines, and polished marble. Brushed silver with some abstract touches made up most of the decoration scheme.

At the very center of the room, a huge metal lighting fixture hung right above a U-shaped desk. Styx's main receptionist, Maryanne, sat behind it.

The old crone fixed me with her typical piercing stare the moment I stepped through the doors.

"You can't seem to stay away, can you?" she quipped, pushing her huge glasses up the bridge of her nose.

"Hello to you, too, Maryanne," I said, not missing a beat. "Did you know that after my assignment today, I stopped at a museum and saw a couple of your relatives in their new fossil exhibit?"

She harrumphed. "You think you're so original, don't you?"

I smirked. Poking fun at Maryanne was the only upside to being called back to Styx so often. Don't let the gray hair and sweet grandmother façade fool you, either. The woman was a viper.

"Let's see if you're still wearing that grin after your meeting with Azrael." She hooked a thumb toward the hallway to the right. "He's been waiting."

All my bravado died in an instant. I really needed to stop getting myself in trouble like this. How many more times was Azrael going to give me another chance? It was very possible that I could be about to walk into his office only to be given the axe and Released.

Apprehension bubbled up as I started toward the elevators.

I didn't need to look back at Maryanne to know she was enjoying my sudden silence. I was sure I'd hear about it again once I came back down.

If I came back down, that is.

The hall was long and slender. Elevators lined the walls on both sides, all going to different departments and afterlife dimensions. My destination was the gold one at the very end.

There was no need to press the up or down button. As soon as I got close, the gold doors opened, and I stepped inside. When they closed again, the small space filled with soft jazz music.

I rolled my eyes. Sometimes I wondered if he picked the music just to fuck with me.

The elevator never moved. At least, there was no feeling of movement either up or down, but the journey itself only took a few seconds. The elevator dinged, and the doors opened again into a giant office. I stepped out. Three walls of floor-to-ceiling windows revealed pale blue skies and passing clouds, as if Azrael's office was floating in the sky.

Speaking of the man, I spotted Azrael on one of the red couches at the far end of the room. Like he always did, he wore a high-quality charcoal-gray suit, looking more like the CEO of a Fortune 500 company than the Angel of Death. No wings or halo in sight. If he did have those cliché angel features, I wasn't privileged enough to see them.

My coworker, Simon, was standing beside him, looking grave in his black-on-black attire. Like the other reapers at Styx, he was more traditional in his clothing choice than I was.

"Jade." Azrael's booming tone made me jump the way it always did. He wasn't reprimanding me or anything—not yet, anyway—but there was a power to his voice that struck me right in the gut. More than a boss scolding an insubordinate employee. As if my subconscious sensed how dangerous he could be if he wanted.

As an angel, he was on a completely different level than I was used to. He was a celestial being, after all, one of the highest and most powerful spirits in existence. Not being at least a little scared of him would be stupid.

"Come. Sit."

Both orders. Ones I knew better than to not listen to. I sat stiffly in one of the oversized chairs opposite his.

Azrael gave me another one of his wolfish smiles, which only heightened my nerves.

"You're starting to make this a habit, Jade," he said, leaning back. He draped an arm over the back of the couch. "If I didn't know better, I'd start to think you are disregarding rules on purpose."

"I do enjoy our talks," I said. The sarcasm dripping off my words was too obvious, and I scolded myself.

Keep your mouth shut, Jade. Don't be an idiot. You're in enough trouble as it is.

Simon shot me a warning look, but Azrael just laughed.

One of his perfectly manicured nails tapped the dimple in the middle of his chin. "They are entertaining, aren't they?" he mused.

Unsure if he was joking or not, I bit down on the inside of my cheek to keep my sharp tongue at bay.

There was a moment of uneasy silence. During it, I wondered why Simon had been called to this meeting, too. He hadn't been at the other ones. Were they going to throw me back into some kind of training again? Another six months?

"I'm sure you know why I summoned you here," Azrael said.

Trick question. But did I play dumb or answer it truthfully?

The way Azrael's gaze bore into mine told me his earlier playfulness was a ruse. He really wasn't in the mood.

The truth it was, then.

"I have a pretty good idea," I said. "Did the dirtbag snitch on me?"

Simon gasped, horror clear on his face.

"What? That wasn't a curse," I protested. "I learned my lesson after last time."

"Can you believe it, Simon? Something stuck." Azrael's tone teetered on a sharp edge of amused and annoyed.

Simon didn't move. His rigidness was making me even more uncomfortable, like I had missed something very important before coming.

I glanced around nervously.

Azrael shifted, resting both his elbows on his knees so that he could lean closer to me. "This sorcerer may have been a dirtbag, as you call him, but he was still a soul in our care, Jade. One you beat up before throwing through a spirit door. Am I correct?"

Another trick question, but I knew better than to answer this one.

He sighed and pulled himself up to stand. Pacing across the ornate rug, he continued. "That kind of behavior doesn't look good for us. Just last month you were refusing to cross over the shifter boy in a coma—"

"Dillion Leon Hendrickson," I added.

Azrael waved away my comment. "Yes, that one. Henderson."

Picking at my fingernails, I resisted the urge to correct his mistake again. I had an uncanny knack for remembering every person I'd ever been assigned. But even if I didn't, I'd never forget Dillion. He was a hard one to forget. At only five years old, he and his mother had been in a major car accident. His mother had escaped with just a broken femur and a few bruises, but poor Dillion had been left in critical condition. According to his profile's bio, his body wasn't reacting to any of the treatments.

I had walked into the hospital with his mother sitting in her wheelchair beside the bed, sobbing. How could I not feel sympathy for her? She was losing her child.

All I had done was whisper some words of

encouragement to him. Told him his mother needed him to get better. To my surprise, the boy woke.

Was it a miracle? Seemed like it to me.

Of course, all cases weren't like that. Dillion had been special. I doubted my words had done anything to help him at all, but from Azrael's fury later that day when I had been called into his office, I'd obviously done something wrong. Even when I'd tried to argue it was a good thing—the little boy had survived after all—he didn't want to hear it. Something about protocol, questioning his authority, judgment, and all that. Honestly, I hadn't paid attention.

"My point is, that one week you're ignoring your orders, which in turn allows an assignment to live, and today you're assaulting another. Is there no middle ground with you?" Azrael asked, pulling me back to the conversation at hand.

I couldn't ignore his use of the term "assignment" instead of little Dillion's or Tristen's names. To Azrael, even to Simon, they weren't people. They were duties, a job. That's all. Simon had told me once that it would be easier for me if I disconnected myself emotionally. How to do that? Stop thinking of them as living beings and focus on the job. Go in, do it, and get out. That's it.

It had never been that easy for me. And I'd tried. Oh, how I'd tried.

"Did you even read his profile?" Simon chimed in finally. "Did you read all details before carrying out the job? Educate yourself fully on the assignment? Like I taught you? Do you remember any of that?"

I hesitated, wondering if I should lie this time or not. "Uh… I read most of it."

"How about the part saying he had been arrested over eight times for assaulting women, serving jail time for attempted murder, and leaving one in the hospital unconscious?" Simon asked, his voice rising in desperation. "Did you read any of that?"

Dammit. I really should have read the bio. "I must have missed that part…"

Simon's frown deepened.

Azrael rolled his shoulders and tried to blow out a calming breath, but aggravation still clung to his expression. "You didn't know this, Jade, but Simon has been pushing me to give you some harder cases. He was convinced you were ready. I, on the other hand, was more apprehensive. With good reason. You can't even handle the easy assignments."

"Easy?" I almost choked on the word. Was he kidding? "Tristen tried to choke me. How was he supposed to be an easy assignment?"

"Easier as in 'with a less than clean record,'" Azrael said. "To ease your conscience some when you had to deliver the touch. My thought was maybe with a quote-unquote dirtbag, you'd feel a little less guilty when performing your *job*."

I mentally slapped myself. Simon had been trying to help me behind the scenes; he believed I was better than this, and I'd rewarded him by screwing up royally.

Guilt whirled inside me. He had been an excellent mentor. The fault lay with me. I was the worst apprentice ever.

An apology hovered on my tongue, but before I could say anything, Azrael crossed the room to stand beside Simon.

He clasped a hand on his shoulder and said, "Obviously, something has gone wrong in your training. Simon hasn't done an adequate enough job preparing you for what being a reaper entailed. It's looking like I may have to Release him."

Release? I balked. That wasn't what I had expected at all.

Simon paled, suddenly looking sick and so much smaller under Azrael's weighted touch.

I glanced between the angel and my mentor, my throat dry. "No way. He did a great job. It's not him. It's me."

Azrael ignored me. "You may have not known this, but all your indiscretions are a direct reflection on his teachings."

Chest tight, I jumped out of my seat and scrambled for the right words to defend him. He hadn't done anything wrong. He had been nothing but patient and extensive with my training. He didn't deserve to be punished because of my stupidity.

"Please, Azrael, don't penalize him. He loves his job. He's good at it, too."

For as long as I'd been dead, Simon was always the golden child in Styx Corp. He followed Azrael's instructions and considered work fun. It was something I teased him often for. Unlike me, he probably had never so much as bent a rule, let alone break one.

What had I done?

Azrael adjusted his suit jacket, his expression turning all business. "I don't want to, of course. Simon has been with Styx Corporation for a very long time. That is why I am giving you one more chance to prove his training has been effective. Another slipup like this—just one—and I'll have no choice. He'll have to be Released."

On cue, the elevator dinged and the golden doors opened. Soft jazz music spilled out, filling the dense silence in the room.

I didn't know what to say or do, so I turned around and walked to the elevators in silence. I wanted to plead Simon's case even more, tell Azrael that this had all been some kind of awful mistake and Releasing him was too extreme. But any argument died on my tongue the moment Azrael turned a hard glare on me, his green eyes glowing unnaturally.

A shiver ran through me.

"One more chance, Jade," he repeated, his voice an ominous rumble. "That's it."

The golden doors sealed shut, blocking Azrael and Simon from view, and I was faced with only my own warped reflection. It peered back at me, reminding me that his threat wasn't an empty one.

Simon's afterlife was now in my hands.

CHAPTER

THREE

Released.

    The only way to get out of being a reaper.

    When I had been thrown into this job, I had protested at first. I hated not having a choice in my afterlife. Simon had assured me everyone felt that way when they started, even him, but leaving Styx Corporation was way worse. Being Released, either voluntarily or by force, was something no one ever wanted to do.

When I had asked about the reaper before me, the one I had replaced, Simon couldn't tell me much, only that he was an older man who had been reaping longer than him. They hadn't talked much, but one day he was gone, Released, with no warning or explanation why. No one saw him again. Not in any of the afterlife dimensions. Not in Styx Corp.

It was as if he had suddenly ceased to exist.

And now Simon was facing the same fate. Because of me.

Did I consider Simon a friend? That was a good question. Did I? He was the first person, besides Azrael, I had met after my death. He had taught me the ins and outs of spirit doors and portal travel. He'd worked for six long months making sure I knew what I was doing with this reaping business, and I sure as hell didn't make it easy for him.

Besides all that, what I appreciated even more was that Simon was the only person to encourage me with anything I had struggled with. And I struggled a lot. Still did. Even now, his teachings echoed in the back of my mind, telling me it would be okay. Everyone made mistakes. I would get the hang of it eventually.

Hearing he had gone a step further and had vouched for me to Azrael only proved his kindness and confidence in me. He didn't deserve to be punished because of me. If I had known, I would have tried harder.

Azrael's threat had been loud and clear. I couldn't mess up again.

I repeated it to myself as I took the portal outside Styx Corp to downtown Fairport and opened a spirit door just outside Oh! Kay's Pastries. There were two reasons I visited the waterfront town in Virginia often. It was a city with two faces. An old-timey downtown with cobblestone roads, Navy ship museums, and grand brick-faced houses, and on the opposite end, skyscrapers, bustling streets, and big businesses that could rival New York. Not sure why, but the city had a pretty dense supernatural population, and I had been here a few times on assignments. The other times were to visit.

That brought me to my second reason Fairport was my

go-to city. My only connection to the living world lived and worked here.

Kay was a Medium. She could see and talk to spirits, hence why she could see me when other humans and supernaturals couldn't. Over the last few months, we had made a bit of an arrangement. I got rid of pesky haunts that had managed to pass through the veil and wouldn't leave her alone, and she gathered information for me, since I couldn't touch anything on the living plane.

Unlike with Simon, I didn't need to question if Kay was a friend. She was. We had met during one of my earliest assignments along the harbor. Being a Medium made her a beacon to the dead, and I had found Kay being harassed by an annoying old lady who insisted she pass a message to her son. A few quick convincing words and a cross through a spirit door solved that problem. And that became the start to an unlikely friendship.

The sweet smells of freshly baked goods and sugary icing hit me before even stepping inside the corner shop. My mouth watered, like it did every time I visited, as did the strange wave of sadness that followed from knowing I would never be able to try one of her handmade pastries. They looked delicious from behind the glass case, all bright colors and decorated with dainty accents. Macaroons, cupcakes, Danishes—anything fattening and drool-worthy, Kay made it.

Against the tall windows were a few tables and chairs, set for two with china teacups and crocheted doilies. Even the walls were painted a pale shade of yellow, reminding me of springtime. All things cutesy and innocent. Just like her.

She wasn't in her normal spot behind the counter, but that made sense because of the late hour. She was about to close for the night, so I wouldn't be surprised if she was in the back preparing tomorrow's special orders or cleaning up.

Besides me, the place was empty. The last wave of her typical college student customers must have left hours ago.

As I drifted to the curtained-off door leading to the kitchen and office, a storm of angry whispers sounded just beyond it. I recognized Kay's voice right away; it was climbing higher as her annoyance grew. The second was a male's, raspy and coming off as equally frustrated.

"Can you just leave me alone? Please? I told you I can't help you," Kay said. There was a clatter of noises, as if bowls or something metal had fallen onto the floor.

"You need to," the man snapped back. "I need to know who killed me. I bet it was Frankie, that bitch. She always said she was going to kill me, but I didn't think she'd ever have the guts to do it."

It didn't take long for me to figure out what was happening. I must have impeccable timing or something.

Speaking of perfect timing, Kay threw open the curtain at that moment and stepped through. When her gaze found me, she jumped back, gripping her chest and breathing hard.

"Jade! Christ, you have to stop doing that to me!" She shook her head, her mass of tight curls bouncing as she struggled to calm down. "We gotta put a bell on you or something. You're going to give me a heart attack."

I laughed. "Like a dog?"

She wiped her shaking hands on her flour-dusted yellow apron and glanced over her shoulder toward the curtain. "I'm sorry. I guess I'm just a little jumpy tonight. It's been…a weird one."

"It sounds like you have another pest problem."

She looked behind her again and nodded. "Can you get rid of him? I had two others this morning, but I was able to convince them to leave. This one is relentless."

Two more? That was a lot.

Contrary to what some humans believed, spirit

crossovers—or haunts—weren't common. The veil between the living and nonliving world only thinned enough for spirits to wander through twice a year, during the solstices, and since it was only the beginning of June, there shouldn't be too many spirits hanging about. Certainly not enough for three to bother Kay in one day. That was just odd.

"I'll handle him."

Walking into the back room, I almost bumped straight into the guy, who must have been just about to follow Kay into the store. He must have seen me pass through the curtain because his eyes widened.

"You're like me," he said. He was middle-aged, graying, with tan skin and a thick mustache.

"Sort of," I said, reaching in my back pocket. I took out my tablet and turned on the search feature.

"Well, get in line, lady." Anger took hold of the man's tone again. "The girl needs to answer my questions first."

I held the tablet up, snapped his picture, and waited as the database skimmed through all the deceased for a match. It only took five seconds to find out who the man was. I reviewed his profile.

Victor Martinez. Age fifty. Human. Cause of death —murder.

"You're one of those reapers, aren't you?" he asked.

I nodded as I read through his biography, took out my chalk, and started to draw the symbols for a spirit door on the side of the walk-in refrigerator's door.

"You wanted to know who killed you, right?" I asked him as the door glowed orange. "I can tell you, but you have to go back and leave the Medium alone. Sound fair?"

"I just want to know—was it Frankie? I bet it was Frankie."

I smiled. "It says here that it was actually a Will—"

"Will! That bastard! I knew they were sleeping together.

They planned this together, didn't they? To get me out of the way? I knew it."

I didn't answer, just ushered Victor toward the spirit door. Frankie and Will's motives weren't something that would be disclosed in the biography, but I wasn't going to tell him that. He could assume whatever he wanted to. What his profile did say was that both were facing jail time for his death. I passed that little tidbit along as he walked through the door, then smudged the chalk with the back of my arm to seal it shut again.

Easy.

Why couldn't all cases be like that?

When I went back into the front of the shop, Kay was counting the money in the register, head down. It took her a second, but she finally looked up, jumping again in surprise. "Jade!"

"You really did have a hard day," I said, walking over to the counter.

"You have no idea," she mumbled.

"If the other haunts were anything like Victor, I can imagine." I paused, wondering if I should bring up the real reason for my drop in. Best to just get it out and over with now. "Were you able to find out anything about me or my family?"

She shut the register and moved to the store windows to close the blinds. "I told you, Jade, it's a little more complicated than plugging your name into Google and getting an answer."

"I know." But excitement was bubbling up despite myself. "But you did find something, right? What is it? What did you find?"

She reached into the pocket of her apron and pulled out a few folded papers. I reached for them, but then remembered I couldn't actually touch them and pulled back. Kay opened them and held them out for me to read. I scanned the topmost sheet.

"Two families with the surname of Blackwell. One in Canada and one in the U.S. But I was able to find a Jade B. Well and a Jadee Black on Facebook, both in the U.S. but none of them look even a little like you. Some aren't even driving age." She flipped through the other papers, showing me the pictures she'd found of the other Jades. Even at first glance, it was obvious none of these women were me.

"Did you check obituaries around this time last year?" I asked.

She frowned. "Yes, and didn't find anyone with your name, age, or appearance. Are you sure you're from this country? I haven't checked other countries."

I shook my head. "I'm pretty sure I'm from here. A gut feeling, you know? But I guess we can expand the search to other countries. It can't hurt, right?"

"Do you have a middle name?"

"Not that I know of."

Her nose scrunched up, like it always did when she was thinking. "Are you sure Jade Blackwell is even your real name?"

Good point. If they wanted me to not remember anything from my time alive, it would make sense to change my name, too, didn't it?

My stomach sank with a heavy sense of hopelessness. The only thing I really knew about myself was my name, and now it was possible I didn't even have that.

Kay pocketed the papers and offered me a reassuring smile. "I'll expand our search to other countries. That may be all we need. Or, better yet, I'll see if Laurence can do a location spell of some kind."

Laurence was Kay's steady boyfriend for two years now. He was a sorcerer but was listed as a weaker one, a level one.

From what I'd observed, he could do a few spells, minor things only, but he was still learning.

Honestly, I wasn't sure if I trusted him with performing any magic, especially a location spell, successfully.

"Don't you need a personal object from the person to find their location? That won't work," I said. "I have nothing on this plane."

"Maybe your presence there will be enough. I can even channel you if that helps." Her brown eyes shined with sincerity. Offering to channel a spirit was big for her to offer. From what she'd explained, she'd only done it once when she was younger, and it had gone horribly wrong then. She hadn't gone too far into detail, but because of the terrifying experience, she had been too scared to try it again.

If she was willing to channel again to help me, it meant a lot.

"I'll ask him tonight," she said. "There may be something more we can do."

She was trying her best to help, but I needed to be realistic. Even if we could swing a location spell without a personal object, I doubted Laurence would be a strong enough sorcerer to complete it properly. I wasn't going to tell Kay that, though. I didn't want to be mean. I liked Laurence. He made her happy, and he seemed to genuinely care for her. They were even talking about possibly getting married soon.

"Do you know if you were a supernatural?" she asked. "What gifts you had? That may help, too."

"I have no idea." I assumed I was a supernatural of some kind, since I lived in the dimension for supernatural souls, but I had yet to see any powers hinting to what race I was. Sometimes I wondered if Azrael had put my apartment in the wrong afterlife and I was actually human. There was no way for me to know for sure, not unless I shifted into something with fur or said a successful spell at random. And none of that had happened in a year.

Supernatural origin fell under "information I wasn't allowed to know about my life" with the mind-wipe. Believe me. I'd asked.

"We'll figure it out," Kay insisted. "I'll keep looking."

Silence followed, and sadness crept in. I really didn't think finding out who I was while alive would be this hard. One time I had even tried plugging in my name in the deceased search, like I had with Victor's picture, only to come up empty. I couldn't help but feel like I was wasting my time and Kay's by making her do this for me. Maybe I would never know who I really was.

"So," she started, her tone lightening, "you look like you had a rough night, too. What's going on in the land of the dead?"

I blew hair out of my eyes. It's not that I thought Kay would understand exactly what I was going through. I wouldn't expect her to. She was not part of my world. But if anyone was going to take the time to listen to my concerns and try to empathize with me, it was her, and I appreciated that more than anything. Being surrounded by dead folks daily made Kay's humanity refreshing. It was because of those things that I wanted to tell her everything. About my assignment and Tristen, about Azrael's threat and Simon. Most of all, I wanted to ask her what I should do now.

But even if I tried telling her, more than likely, I would be censored. There was only so much information we were allowed to share with the living about the afterlife. Like most things, I had found that out the hard way.

"I've had better nights, yes," I settled with instead.

She gave me a look that told me to go on.

I sighed and tugged at my leather gloves. "I got in trouble again at…work."

Kay didn't know what I was exactly, but she did know I was a spirit and could help others cross back over into the afterlife. The specifics were fuzzy because of the restrictions. Once, she'd asked if I was an angel, which had sent me into hysterics. She couldn't be more wrong. There was nothing angelic about me.

Nope, no halo here.

"Because of my mistakes, I got a coworker in trouble." Was that vague enough? Kay didn't look confused, so I went on. "If I mess up one more time, he will be *Reloosed*."

I hesitated, hearing the strange distortion to the last word. I had been censored.

Kay's brows knitted together in confusion.

"Really?" I threw my hands in the air and glanced around the room. "*Reloosed?* I can't even say *Reloosed?*"

The censor skewed the word every time I said it, and I cursed. Apparently, Released was revealing too much information.

I shook my head. "Never mind. It's not that important." Just freaking annoying.

Kay smiled. "I'm guessing that whatever that is, it isn't good?"

I nodded.

"Does visiting me count as a mistake?" she asked.

I hadn't considered that. I visited Kay whenever I could and hadn't been reprimanded for it.

Not yet anyway.

Suddenly nervous, I moved toward the shop door. Should I leave? Had I really been that stupid to endanger Simon so quickly after Azrael's threat? With all the rules and restrictions on reapers interacting with the living during their job, like with Dillion, interacting with Kay was probably pushing some kind of boundary I shouldn't be pushing.

"Do you need to go?"

"I think so."

"Will you be able to come back?"

Honestly, I didn't know the answer to that. But I didn't want to worry her, so I forced a smile and said, "I'm sure it'll be fine. I just need to figure out some things, and I'll be back."

She didn't say anything. It didn't look like she was buying my story either.

"If any more haunts bother you while I'm gone, you have my permission to use my name as a threat. Oh, and ask Laurence about the location spell. We'll set something up next time I stop in."

"Okay," she replied meekly. "I will."

"This isn't goodbye," I told her, trying to convince myself of it as well. "I'll come by again."

She gave me a small wave, uncertainty tugging her lips into a frown.

As much as I wanted to stay, I glided through the shop door, hoping with everything inside me that I hadn't just lied to my friend and was, in fact, coming back soon.

CHAPTER

FOUR

Days passed and I hadn't gone back to Kay's shop. Why? Because I was scared. I can admit it. Azrael's threat was a constant throb in the back of my head, and I couldn't do something to hurt Simon. I couldn't do it to anyone. Like a good girl, I had concentrated on doing my job only and caused as little commotion as possible. So, when my tablet's green light began blinking rapidly as I left my apartment that evening and Azrael's face came on my screen, my stomach plummeted to my boots.

"Jade."

What scared me the most was he wasn't wearing his famous predatory smile this time. His expression was hard and all seriousness.

I tried my best to not show my worry, but I was replaying every assignment I'd completed in the last few days, wondering where I had slipped up. Swallowing hard, I pushed the panic zooming around my insides from creeping into my voice.

"What's up, Azrael?"

"I wanted to deliver your next assignment personally," he said. "Well, in a way." Still no smile from him. Not even a hint.

His words, though, were surprising. I wasn't in trouble?

It had to be pretty bad if that was my first thought every time I saw him.

"Oh?" I glanced up and down the sidewalk on Primrose Street, a few blocks down from Kay's in the living world. I had been given the choice on where to live, so of course I'd chosen Fairport right next to the harbor. The closeness to my friend only made not being able to see her even harder. There was guilt there, too. I had promised her I'd come back, after all.

"Since you've been on track these last few days and since you're in the area, I am taking a leap and giving you a bigger assignment. Something you haven't done before."

Uh-oh. Was that supposed to be a compliment? Because it sure as hell didn't sound like one. It sounded more like he was trying to push me harder, see if I'd slip up again and cause Simon's Release.

I sucked in a deep breath. I could do it. I had to. For Simon's sake. He deserved better from me.

And there was the small matter of my pride. I also didn't want to give Azrael the satisfaction of seeing me fail again. I'd prove him wrong.

As long as it wasn't another young kid, I'd be fine. Maybe I should tell Azrael that, but something told me he wouldn't see it the same way I did. He might even assign me to a child's death on purpose just to prove a point.

"I am sending the details to you now." He fixed me with a piercing look. "Get it done."

Then, he was gone. A detailed profile replaced his face.

Cole Robert Masters. Age thirty. Half-demon.

I froze. Woah. A half-demon? That was way out of my pay grade. I wasn't ready for a supernatural that strong.

Was I?

Azrael obviously thought I was. I should be flattered, and part of me was. But uncertainty reared its ugly head. Normally, Simon handled the big jobs like this. He had the experience and the skills. I was still new. And if I messed this up…

Pushing the thought from my mind, I focused on that small, fleeting bit of confidence I had left. I gripped it and held on tight. This could be my chance to prove myself—to everyone. Including myself.

My past mistakes told me to read the profile before arriving on scene. Cole Masters was a half-demon. I didn't know much about the race, except that there weren't many around because demons—just like haunts—could only cross into the living world during one of the solstices, when the veil was thin enough. They possessed men and slept with unsuspecting females to produce offspring. The babies who survived were cursed with a deadly fire power.

That's all I knew, but those were the most important parts, right?

Stay away from his fire hands. Got it.

I read the rest of his bio, but didn't find out much. It seemed a little vague, stating he lived alone most of his life and had been involved in many "underground deals." Whatever that meant. What I did think was odd was that there was no picture attached to the profile. Azrael always added a photo of the assignment. It made finding the person easier. But for some reason, he hadn't done it this time.

This definitely had to be a test.

When I thought I had gotten all the information I could out of his profile, I looked at the location typed across the bottom in bold letters. Between forty-five and forty-six Quincy Street, Fairport, Virginia. On the side street of Oh! Kay's Pastries.

Hurrying over to the front of my apartment building, I ripped the piece of chalk from my jean pocket and drew a spirit door on the bricks. My heart was beating a little too fast—especially for no longer pumping, but it was anxiety circulating throughout my veins this time, not blood. The second the symbols glowed orange, I hopped through to the other side.

In the living world, the rain came down in droves, a terrible storm beating against the old city's harbor. Wind whipped through the narrow streets and caused the waves to crash against the dock, flooding the walking paths and touristy areas. Even the lamps lining the road rattled with the gusts.

The rain couldn't touch me, but I wrapped my arms around myself anyway, still able to feel the chill and dampness in the air. Every so often, when the wind would gush, my hair would be tossed about, the elements temporarily breaking the plane.

It was weird how some things transferred between worlds and some things didn't.

Hurrying across downtown, I navigated with ease, and quickly came to Quincy Street. Oh! Kay's and a multifunctioning office building were the largest structures on the street, and between them stretched a small alleyway meant for deliveries, a quick fire escape, if needed, and storing garbage cans.

Kay's shop had the shades drawn and appeared closed, which was odd. Kay was normally open at this time. Maybe she had taken the day off? God, I hoped so. She didn't need to be around with a half-demon in the neighborhood.

I peered into the alley between her shop and the office. A shadowy figure lay on the ground next to a few turned-over trash cans. Cautiously, I crept closer.

Besides the spilled garbage everywhere, my assignment, Cole Masters, was sprawled out facedown covered in mud and God knows what else. The relentless rain soaked every bit of him but did little to wash away the stomach-turning stench of urine and rotting waste radiating from the small alley.

I glanced around. We were completely alone.

So, what was his cause of death?

I studied the profile again. It read *Head trauma. Blunt force object. Fight.*

Staring down at Cole's unmoving body again, I figured that made sense. There seemed to have been a scuffle of some kind with the mess left behind. Maybe his opponent had run off in fear of being caught by the police? Wouldn't be the first time.

Who was strong enough to take down a half-demon? Nothing was on fire, but with the storm, any remaining flames surely would have been extinguished by now.

Squatting beside him, I squinted against the darkness in search for blood. There were puddles all around but no obvious crimson coloring nearby. Not even on his clothing or jacket. He faced away from me, so if there was an impact wound, I couldn't see it.

The slight rise and fall of his back told me he was still breathing, but that was the only movement coming from him. Most likely unconscious. That would be the way to go, wouldn't it? While sleeping? Blissfully unaware.

A car passed, its headlights illuminating the alley briefly but enough to reflect against something silver near the opposite end of the lane. Small in size with a distinct L-shape to it.

A gun.

Cole's? Or his assailant's?

The profile hadn't mentioned anything about a gunshot wound.

Leaning over his body, I finally got a good look at his face.

I knew him.

Not personally. We'd crossed paths before on a few other of my assignments as the one who had murdered the men I had been ordered to reap. Not only was Cole Masters a half-demon, but he was a gun-for-hire. He killed people for a living. All kinds. Both human and supernatural. The gun suddenly fit into this scenario perfectly.

Oh man. I was in *way* over my head with this one.

Had one of his hits gone south? From the kills I had come across, Cole was a master at his job. He was neat and usually masked his kills as an accident or suicide, making sure not to leave any evidence to connect the job back to him.

But what had gone wrong this time?

I shouldn't be asking questions. That was what had landed me in a mess last time with Tristen. I needed to just carry out my assignment and not worry about anything else. No second-guessing. No meddling where I didn't belong. Azrael and Simon were counting on me to carry this out, and that was what I was going to do.

Readjusting myself, I crouched next to Cole's body again, pulled off one of my gloves, and reached to touch the side of his face. In that moment, his eyes flew open, brilliant blue orbs taken over by dilated pupils. I gasped, jerking back, and fell onto my butt hard.

Cole scrambled to his feet faster than a man should, especially a man who was hurt and had just been unconscious. His head whipped toward me, and his wild gaze roamed over my face, seeing me—really *seeing* me.

Too stunned to speak, I recoiled and jumped up onto wobbly legs. Cole's eyes followed me the entire time, and my heart banged against my ribcage, mimicking the living function. How could he see me? His profile hadn't said he was a Medium, too. He shouldn't be able to make contact with spirits.

More importantly, wasn't he supposed to be close to death?

"Who are you?" he rasped, confirming my fears.

I blinked, and in that split second, he was holding a gun in his hand and had it aimed at me.

His voice rose as panic set in. "Tell me who you are!"

I held my hands up in surrender. "Woah there. Easy now. No need to get gun-happy."

A gunshot boomed against the silence, and I winced. As expected, the bullet flew right through my form and bounced off the wall somewhere behind me before skittering across the ground. I didn't feel a thing.

"Cole? Cole Masters?" I talked fast, hoping to gain his attention before he shot at me again. "My name is Jade, and I'm here to help you cross over."

He wasn't listening. He reached into the back of his jeans, flicked the side of the gun open, and swapped out the bullets. I kept talking.

"That's not going to work on me," I said as he aimed at me again. "If you let me explain—"

Another booming shot, but this time, the bullet ripped through my right shoulder. White-hot pain unlike anything I had ever felt before exploded. The shock of it sent me reeling back and cursing. My hand flew to the wound, and to my horror, there was a hole the size of a quarter blown through my flesh above my collarbone. Black smoke emitted from it.

Impossible.

The pain ricocheting up and down my arm said otherwise. Undeniably real. The tears welling in my eyes only proved it more.

I didn't have time to contemplate what was really going on. Cole was already reloading his gun. I didn't know how he was able to shoot me, but I sure as hell wasn't going to let him do it again. Talking wasn't working. Cole was more of a shoot first, think-later type of guy obviously, so I had to come up with a different way to beat him.

Azrael was going to get an earful from me again about giving reapers some kind of weapon to aid in tough cases. There was no way for me to beat him. I couldn't get close enough to touch him with his trigger finger.

A woman's scream tore through the silence, making both of us turn. It was coming from my right, in the shop next to us.

Fear seized me, and I instantly forgot the danger staring me in the face.

The pastry shop. Kay. She was in trouble.

No longer caring about Cole and his magic gun, I sprinted past him to the front entrance. He didn't shoot at me, and even if he would've, I didn't care. Something was wrong. The sounds of commotion rang from inside, tables falling over, things being thrown. The shop was dark, but shadows moved inside. I passed through the door to find Kay on the floor, crawling backwards as a man lumbered toward her.

Nearly six feet, shaved head, glasses, wearing one of his typical geek-inspired "Wizard in Training" T-shirts from the Harry Potter movies, it was Kay's boyfriend, Laurence's, everyday look of choice. But something wasn't right with him. His posture was all wrong. Not laid back with a slight slouch. His body was rigid, as if every muscle was tight and struggling to move. Veins bulged from his neck, and his lip curled up slightly.

Was that a snarl I heard?

Kay screamed again, terror fixed on her face.

When Laurence took another menacing step forward, I called his name, forgetting he couldn't hear me. Kay did, though. Her head whipped toward me, and her eyes widened even more.

"Jade! It's not him!" she shrieked. "It's not Laurence! I don't know what it is, but it isn't him!"

To my horror, Laurence's head swiveled my way, his gaze finding me.

Kay was right. His face morphed before my eyes into a hideous creature with fangs, sunken cheeks, grey skin, and a thick, protruding brow. His eyes were the most jarring—they were an unnaturally brilliant shade of red. I blinked, and the grotesque mask disappeared. Laurence was glowering at me once again, looking as I knew him.

What the fuck is that?

I rushed over to Kay's side.

"This doesn't involve you, reaper," the thing mimicking Laurence growled. The voice coming from his lips sounded nothing like his usual calming baritone. More guttural with a thick accent I couldn't place. "Leave us."

This was definitely not Laurence.

Suddenly, the glass door behind me exploded, sending shards of glass everywhere. Kay screamed again as Cole pushed through. His eyes locked on Laurence, gun aimed directly at him.

"Xaver," Cole barked at him.

He hissed back. *Hissed.*

"I knew you wouldn't be able to stay away."

Laurence swiped at the air in warning, like an animal might with encroaching predator.

A gunshot rang out, but in a blur of speed, Laurence had leapt onto the counter. Cole's bullet missed. When Laurence snarled again, the hideous face was back with a purplish tongue slithering out. More shots, but Laurence bounced from the counter to the display case to the floor to one of the small customer tables. He moved so fast, he appeared to be little more than a blur of color and speed. Cole kept trying to shoot him, but his bullets weren't landing.

I glanced around for something I could use to help then cursed. I couldn't grab anything on this plane. There was a table behind us, and I ushered Kay behind it to keep her hidden from the beast.

"Stay here," I whispered to her. "Don't move."

She nodded frantically. I didn't need to tell her twice.

Fingers dug into my wounded shoulder, and I yelled as fresh pain shot through every nerve. Another animalistic sound before I was thrown across the room and then slid on the tile. A round of clicks sounded and then a string of angry curses. Cole was out of bullets.

Kay's screams filled my ears as the creature leaned forward, his hand reaching for her. She kicked and clawed at him. I scrambled to my feet and ran at him, then quickly slapped my ungloved hand against the exposed skin on his upper arm. There was a bright white light and a strange sizzling sound. The smell of burned flesh and singed hair hit my nose, making my stomach roil.

Laurence bellowed. As the light consumed the room, blinding me, I felt him jerk away. The loss of contact extinguished the light.

Immediately, a sharp pain spiked through my temples, and my world swayed. I locked my knees to prevent myself from spilling over.

Now wasn't the time to pass out.

By the time it took my eyes to adjust again, Laurence's distinct figure disappeared through the broken front door.

Cole rubbed his eyes to refocus them. Once he realized Laurence was gone, he ran to the door and leaned out. A flurry of curses escaped his mouth, and he punched the wall hard enough to dent the plaster.

"Fuck!" he shouted one last time for good measure and shook out his wrist. There was a glint of blood on his knuckles.

The severity of what had just happened socked me in the gut. I had touched Laurence, expecting to kill him, or whatever beast had taken him over. Not shoot white light from my fingertips. And the burning skin? That was new.

And terrifying, quite frankly.

I looked at my bare palm, expecting it to look different, but the same pale skin I was used to was there. Nothing seemed out of the ordinary.

Kay crawled out from behind the table. "Is he gone?" she asked, her voice shaking.

When Cole marched back inside, I finally got a proper chance to look at him. Even with his expression heavy with raw anger, he was strikingly handsome. Blond hair, crusted with mud, was mussed as if he had styled it beforehand with some kind of gel. A growing beard and mustache shadowed his strong jawline and full mouth, and he had a new cut across his cheek, just above another faded scar. Even with the oversized jacket on, his wide shoulders and muscular build were obvious.

If it wasn't for the cuts and bruises, I would have guessed he had a career in modeling or TV. Not mercenary work. He reminded me of a college pretty boy, not a ruthless killer.

But I had seen him shoot that gun, and he definitely was familiar with it.

"Yes. He's gone." Cole's voice was as surprising as the rest of him. A deep sound that was a bit too gravelly and severe to match his golden-boy exterior.

His blue-eyed gaze shifted to me. "What was that?"

I held up my hand and wiggled my fingers. "Oh, the old emitting lights from my fingers thing?" A too-fake laugh spilled out without my control. In that moment, I wanted to laugh and cry, and I had no idea why. But I reined my hysterical fit in as much as I could and said as calmly as I could manage, "I have no idea."

Cole's stare told me he didn't believe me, but I ignored it. It was my turn to ask questions.

"What was that thing? Laurence—"

"That wasn't Laurence," Cole interrupted. "Not entirely, at least."

Kay moved to my side, rubbing her arms. She was shaking, and every so often, she glanced at the door, as if the thing that had attacked us was due to return at any moment.

"So, you saw the weird creature face underneath Laurence's, too?" I asked.

Cole cocked his head.

I glanced at Kay, who looked just as confused.

"You know, fangs? Thick brow? Glowing red eyes?"

They both stared at me like I had just sprouted another head.

"Just me. Huh."

After a long moment of uneasy silence, Cole said, "You saw the demon within."

Now it was my turn to stare at him in disbelief. "Excuse me?"

"Not familiar with them, are you?"

I shook my head. "Never seen one in my life." Then after a second, I added, "Ugly bastards."

That won me a smirk from him.

"Laurence is a demon?" Kay peeped beside me.

"No, he's just possessed," Cole answered, matter-of-fact. Like this was the kind of shit he dealt with all the time. Totally normal.

"*Just* possessed." I shook my head. "Wait a minute. It isn't the solstice. Demons shouldn't be crossing over. That doesn't make sense."

"So you do know about demons," Cole said.

"Just the basics."

His expression changed suddenly to all seriousness, the same hard look I'd seen in the alley right before he shot at me. "Then you know your friend here is still in a lot of danger. If I'm right about why I think Xaver was here, then we need to get her somewhere safe. And fast."

"What would he want with Kay?" I glanced at my friend, and her eyes widened.

"I don't have time to explain right now. We need to go. And I need my backpack." His jaw tightened. "Xaver's going to be back, and I'm all out of bullets."

CHAPTER

FIVE

That was all Kay and I needed to know. We followed Cole out of the shop but didn't get too far because of the raging storm. Kay paused on the sidewalk, instantly soaked from the harsh rain. Glancing back at the broken glass door and the visible inside, her shoulders slumped forward, and she wrapped her arms tighter around herself.

My chest ached for her. The man she loved had just attacked her. And apparently, now possessed by a demon, wanted to come back to finish the job.

Her shop was wrecked. All her hard work, ruined. It was going to take a lot of money and time to get the place back to the colorful and welcoming aesthetic that drew customers in.

I reached out to wrap a comforting arm around her shoulder, but then I noticed my ungloved hand and stopped myself. That was definitely a mistake I would never forgive myself for. I shoved my hands in my pockets instead.

Cole led the way to the side of the shop, to the alley where I had originally found him unconscious. He walked straight for one of the knocked-over trash bins and grabbed a ripped, navy-blue backpack that had been hidden behind it.

"So," I started, spotting my leather glove on the ground. I picked it up and slipped it back on. "I have a lot of questions that need answers."

He reached into his bag, pulled out a wrapped umbrella, and handed it to Kay. She took it shyly with a nod of thanks and pushed it open.

"We need to get uptown," he said. "We'll take my Jeep. It's parked right around the corner here." As Cole began striding ahead of us, Kay and I exchanged looks. She didn't need to say a word. Her expression said everything. She was wondering if we should trust him. Honestly, I was wondering the same thing.

"What's uptown?" I asked.

"A safe house for…"

"Kay," she answered.

"Right."

Kay waited for him to follow up with his name, but when he didn't, I took it upon myself.

"His name is Cole Masters. He's a paid assassin. Which brings me to my next question. What was that thing you shot me with? How did it not fly through me like the first one?" I glanced at my shoulder again. The wound was smaller, but the skin was black around the edges and still stung.

He walked over to the mouth of the alley and peeked over his shoulder. His face was all cold seriousness, but his eyes…

A silent challenge shined in them. "I have some questions for you myself, but we'll get to all that in the car."

I didn't know if I wanted to go into a car with an assassin half-demon with weapons that could actually hurt me, and I definitely didn't want to risk Kay's life at all. But when Cole started walking down the street, we followed. Did we have any other choice really? Cole knew about demons. I sure as hell didn't. He even knew the demon's real name. Xaver. They'd seemed to have history together.

That didn't ease my nerves any, but Cole had weapons, and not just any weapons. They were ones that could wound a spirit. I didn't know such a thing existed. I believed him when he said Kay was in danger. I witnessed it for myself in how Laurence went after her in the shop. Cole could protect her better than I could. All I could do was touch the demon again, and although the lightshow had been enough to scare Xaver off before, who knew if I'd be able to get close enough to lay a hand on him the next time.

Kay stayed close behind me. She held the umbrella over the both of us. Even though the rain couldn't touch me, I didn't stop her. The gesture was heartwarming in itself. It was so...*human*. As if she considered me alive, like her. It meant more to me than she could probably understand.

Cole's Jeep was parked down a small side street. It was more on the sidewalk than on the actual blacktop. He made sure to park right underneath a sign that clearly stated *No Parking Any Time*.

The Jeep itself was a faded dark blue color and was scraped up pretty bad on the right side, as if someone had sideswiped him and drove off. The back light was broken, the canvas top was ripped in a few places, and there was a pretty big ding in the bumper. Definitely not what I expected from a notorious gun-for-hire. Killing people for a living had to earn him a pretty penny. He should have had the money to buy one of those luxury cars, or at least to fix this one up. It was ugly. Plain and simple.

He must have caught my expression because he said, "It runs fine. That's all I need."

"Right." I tried to offer him a smile, but it came out more of a cringe.

As he opened the passenger door for Kay, I phased through the back and sat in the middle seat. Cole threw his backpack near me, and when he started the car, it made a terrible sputtering sound. He quickly shut it off and tried again. A few nasty clicks and it turned over, roaring loudly.

"How do you sneak up on your victims with this monster?" I asked.

Kay glanced over her shoulder at me nervously.

Cole pulled out of the small street and whipped onto one of the main roads, lights off, despite the pouring rain. "Victims? I prefer targets. Sounds nicer to the ear."

"Whatever helps you sleep at night," I mumbled.

His reflection peered at me through the rearview mirror. "So, you said you had questions."

"And you said you do, too."

"How about we do a one-and-one kind of thing," he started. "You ask one and then I'll ask one. Seem fair?"

"But I get to go first," I said.

"Fine."

I shifted uneasily in the seat. Was it me or did it smell like wet dog in here? I didn't need to focus on that. Instead, I needed answers. There were so many questions. Where to start?

The beginning would be best.

"So, Cole, why can you see me? No other living people can, except Kay that is. But she's a Medium, so that makes sense. I've never met anyone else who can see me."

"That's a complicated one to start with," he said, his gaze

flicking between me and the road. Whatever the speed limit was, there was no doubt he was exceeding it. We were whipping in between cars on the main highway and passing others with ease. "I'm not sure I can even answer that one…" He paused. "Is what Xaver said true? You're a reaper?"

I hesitated. Kay had turned fully in her seat now and was staring at me. Should I tell them? Better yet, would the censor even let me say it? Could this end up badly for me in any way?

So much shit had hit the fan tonight, it was hard to believe I would come out of this unscathed from Azrael at all. Might as well let the truth out and get the information I wanted.

I took a deep breath. "I am…a reaper. Yes." No twist to my words. No censor. That was odd. I didn't expect it to be that easy.

"Makes sense on why I've seen you before, after some of my kills…" he mused, his eyebrow raised.

So, he'd seen me before, too.

"That makes you a spirit, which is why Kay can see you. But then, how could Xaver see you? And touch you? He was able to throw you halfway across the room."

I was wondering that one myself. Wasn't it my turn to ask the question, anyway? "I was hoping you knew the answer to that one."

"My guess is that it has to do with his demon blood," he said. "Technically, demons are from the same plane as you, the spiritual plane. Just a different part of it. Am I right?"

I nodded. Sounded logical to me.

"Then that would explain how I could see you, being half-demon myself."

Did that mean he could make physical contact with me, too?

The thought of his hands on me made a very different

feeling spike through my veins. Tangled in my hair, caressing my breasts, gripping my ass. In an instant, desire took hold and tried to run free.

I stomped down on my climbing libido and quietly told it to stay put. I definitely didn't need those kinds of ideas distracting me. Especially with so much at stake.

"Half-demon?" Kay croaked, looking paler than before. "A reaper? That's why you can get rid of all of those ghosts who follow me around?"

My throat dried. Even though I hadn't been allowed to tell Kay the truth of what I was before, for some reason, it felt as if I had betrayed her somehow. Like I had lied and disappointed her.

Two things I never wanted to do.

Cole cut in. "Being a reaper also explains why my specialty bullets affected you." When I threw him a questioning look, he explained. "They're made of pure iron and blessed in Holy Water, just in case."

"I don't understand."

"Pure iron repels spirits of all kinds. Even fairies. Holy Water is for the more demonic creatures, like demons or vamps. This way I have double the protection." He grinned.

"You seem pretty damn proud of yourself."

"I am. They've made my job much easier."

I wondered if Azrael knew about these types of weapons in the hands of the living. Bullets that could harm the dead? Not good.

Cole took the exit for uptown Fairport a little too fast, sliding me across the back seat and swinging Kay into the door.

"I hope you all are buckled in," he said.

Kay quickly grabbed her seatbelt and fastened it. There was no need for me to. My hand went right through the thing.

"I think it's still your turn technically," he said after a moment.

"Uh, yeah." I went through my mental laundry list of questions. "What were you doing in the alley before I found you? What happened?"

His jaw tightened. I could see the muscles pulsing by his ears as he ground his teeth. "Xaver."

"You got into a fight or something beforehand?"

"I've been chasing Xaver for a while. After he possessed your friend, I followed him to your shop, Kay, and surprised him. We scuffled for a bit, but he threw me against the wall. I guess it knocked me out. That's all I remember before you showed."

I wondered if he was telling the truth. His profile had said he'd been hit with a blunt object and had suffered major head trauma. Enough to kill.

Really, he could be lying, and I had no way of knowing. On the other hand, he could be telling the truth, too. What reason did he have to lie to us? I couldn't think of any at that moment, but then, I couldn't think of any reason for him to want to tell the truth either.

"Why were you following him to begin with?" I asked.

"Hey, you asked your question. Now it's my turn."

I scowled at him. He returned it with a wicked smile in the rearview mirror.

Now in the heart of Fairport, Cole turned left, deeper into the newer part of town, past high-rises and expensive storefronts. I wondered where this safe house was that he was taking us to. Was it in one of these five-star hotels?

"Why were you there in the alley in the first place?" Cole asked me, breaking the silence.

Of course he would ask the one question I really didn't want to answer. I sighed. "Take a guess."

He stopped at a red light. A herd of people crossed in front of our Jeep as the 'walk' light flashed.

Cole turned in his seat. "Me? You were there to reap me?"

I nodded. "You were my next assignment."

His expression became unreadable. Plain and guarded, as if my admission to almost killing him wasn't shocking. "But I wasn't dead. I wasn't even close to dead. Just knocked out."

"I'm just as confused as you," I said, the weight of the situation only growing heavier and more suffocating. "It's never happened before."

Once the light turned green, Cole punched the accelerator, making me jerk back.

"Shit," I said.

"We're almost there."

When I looked out the window again, I realized we had traveled to a very different part of the city. Graffiti decorated the many closed storefronts and walls. Bright neon lights flashed from both sides of the street, beckoning for patrons to come get dollar peep shows and see live nudes. Something told me that if it wasn't pouring rain, we'd see women dressed in scandalous outfits and high heels gathering on the street corners.

Uneasiness crept up my spine.

Kay finally spoke again. "Uh, where are you taking me?"

"A friend of mine owes me a favor," Cole answered. "He'll keep you safe for me while I figure this out with Xaver and Laurence."

"You won't hurt him, will you?"

"I'll try not to."

However, the severe pinch between his brows said he couldn't make any promises.

He whipped his car into a handicap parking spot along the curb and shut it off. After reaching behind him, he snatched his backpack and jumped out. I hopped out, too.

Kay struggled to get her umbrella open again, so she left it behind. The harsh rain continued to whip against her and Cole.

Cole gestured to the building in front of us. "Here we are," he said. "You'll be safe here."

Its brick face had been painted black, making the neon sign stand out even more against it. The word 'Red' gradually flickered from crimson to white and back again. Every window was covered by dark curtains, but they didn't completely block everything from view. Silhouettes of women danced in the background, shaking their asses and gliding up and down poles. Just enough to tease. Top that with a muscular bouncer beside the door, and I knew this wasn't your typical twenty-four-hour bar. This was something more devious.

"A-A strip club?" I sputtered in disbelief. "Your safe house is a strip club?"

"Not just any strip club," Cole replied with another grin. "A vampire strip club."

CHAPTER

SIX

"No. No way," I said, staring at the darkened building in shock.

That blow to the head had done more than knock him unconscious. He had lost his damn mind.

There was no way I was allowing Kay to go anywhere near there. Let alone inside.

"Vampires? Really?" Was I really having this conversation? It seemed like common sense. "They'll *eat* her. Or did you forget that?"

"Trust me," Cole said. "Andre won't let anything happen to her because of our arrangement. He owes me. He's in my debt."

"And that's enough to convince you he won't drain her

dry?" I lowered my voice to a harsh whisper, even though it wouldn't do much to prevent Kay from hearing me. She was standing right beside me, after all.

"Well, yeah."

I threw my hands up and grunted. It wasn't rocket science to know when a vampire went into bloodlust—all favors and decency went out the window. They became ravenous monsters at that point. I wasn't going to risk my friend's life to keep her safe. Where was the logic in that?

"Andre is nearly a century old," Cole went on. "He's a stickler for honor and the importance of one's word."

"Then, he has my *word* that I'll kill him without hesitation if anything happens to Kay while she's in there. Do you hear me?"

"Jade." Kay's voice was gentle, even though it wavered a bit. "I appreciate your loyalty, but maybe Cole is right."

"Listen to the girl. She's smart." The smugness in his tone made me wish I had touched his unconscious ass back in the alley. "It's a club run by vampires. Can you think of someone else who could take on a full-demon other than a vampire with a couple of centuries on him?"

He strolled toward the club's front door and gave the bouncer a knowing wave. The brooding man stepped aside for Cole, and he nodded for us to follow.

Looked like I didn't have a choice.

When we walked through Red's door, I glanced at the football player of a man standing there and noticed that his eyes scanned over Cole and Kay but never found me.

So, I was still invisible to the world. At least most of it. Was Cole right, and it was a demon thing? He was the first half-demon I'd ever reaped.

I'd have to ask Simon once I got back to Styx.

A knot formed in the back of my throat at the thought of Simon and Azrael. I must've broken a dozen rules tonight, getting involved in this mess. Not including the fact that I had failed my assignment with Cole. Once Azrael figured out that he had never passed through the spirit door to his afterlife, he'd be looking for me. He might even send Simon after me—that was, if Simon hadn't been Released already because of this.

Shit. This was bad. My tablet was probably flashing with all kinds of notifications from Azrael. But I'd do damage control later. Something big was going on here. Cole hadn't even been close to dead when I had shown up to reap him. I may have been scolded before for questioning Azrael's assignments, but things weren't adding up.

The sudden appearance of haunts and a big-time demon *before* the solstice? Not normal. Once I made sure Kay was safe from Laurence—or Xaver—I would hike my tail right back to Styx Corp and tell Azrael all about what was going on. He had to have another celestial being or whoever to handle these sorts of problems.

This was way out my league. That was for sure.

My only hope was he understood my involvement and wouldn't hold Simon accountable for any of it.

Kay stayed close to me as we entered the club. I slid my right glove half off, just in case things went south. The burning white light was still a mystery to me. I didn't know how to use it again, but hopefully if the situation arose, my body would know what to do. If not, I could still kill someone with my touch.

Just another thing I'd have to bring up to Azrael and Simon. Did either of them have magical glowing fingers? No other supernatural had the power that I knew of, so if this was actually my supernatural side finally showing itself, I had more questions instead of answers.

Nothing was making sense here.

We stepped into a giant, dimly lit club tinted in pulsing

red lights. To the far right was a stage where a woman in the tiniest black frilled bikini swung on a pole to the thumping bass of music. A fully stocked bar lined the opposite wall, and tables, some with poles and dancers and some without, took up a majority of the floor space. All what you would expect from a shady club. But what was shocking was that unlike those other dirty establishments, Red was exceptionally clean with expensive and modern décor. Everything was either red, silver, or black and had straight lines. Sleek and sexy.

Vampires were a complicated group, but the basics were this: Vampires were high on the supernatural hierarchy not only because of their strength, speed, and near immortality. They were feared mostly for their involvement in organized crime. Only three bloodlines carried the vampire gene and could gain another life after dying once, and every were-creature, sorcerer, and witch knew them. The Perez, DeMonte, and Omari families had their hands in drugs, prostitution, money laundering, and any other kind of illegal dealings you can think of.

To top it all off, they all hated each other.

A flash of movement above the main floor caught my eye, and when I glanced up, I saw cages hanging from the ceiling with young girls dancing inside them. And I said young for a reason. They didn't look older than twenty.

Gross. I knew age was irrelevant to vampires, but still—yuck. Some of these girls looked like they were supposed to be in high school.

"I don't know about this, Cole," I whispered to him. "There has to be somewhere else we can take her."

He threw me a sideways glare. "I wouldn't bring her here if I didn't think this was the safest place she could be right now. Vamps can put up a good fight, and they're extremely hard to kill."

As much as his attitude irritated me, he had a good point.

Vamps were pretty much immortal, since killing them was limited to beheading, complete blood loss, and fire, but even with those facts, my stomach still clenched with uncertainty. Even if Kay was a Medium, she was still mostly human. I couldn't help but feel like we were throwing her to the lions and expecting them to keep her safe from the bears.

A shadow passed along a wall of tall glass windows on the second floor. The slight tint in the glass made it hard to see any faces, but it was obvious someone was not only watching everything happening on the floor below but was very interested in the three of us as well.

I didn't like this one bit.

Moving closer to Cole, who was eyeing the bar with a hungry look, I said, "I think we're being watched."

Cole followed my gaze to the windows. The shadowy figure had disappeared.

"It's probably Andre," he said. "He should be down in a minute."

Andre, huh? I guessed that was who we'd come to see.

"Who are you talking to?" a smooth male voice whispered near my right ear, making me jump.

When I whipped around, I gaped at the beautiful man standing so close to me that we would have brushed against each other if I were alive. His pungent cologne filled my nose enough to burn and make my eyes water. Appearing to be in his mid-thirties, he had long blond-brown hair, elegant, pointed features, and an old-world air about him with a face that could rival royalty. Those dark eyes of his, though, passed right through me. He couldn't see me either.

His closeness was unnerving. It was almost as if he could sense me here.

I was just being paranoid now. Too many weird things happening lately.

"Andre, there you are." Cole's body tensed, and his grip

tightened on his backpack's straps, all indications that these two weren't exactly the closest of friends.

Great. And I was about to leave Kay with this man.

Andre straightened, his gaze traveling over Kay, who was trembling, and then to Cole.

"I hope you're not here for business," he said, a tinge of a French accent creeping into his voice. At that moment, I had a pretty good guess what family he was from. DeMonte. They controlled most of Northern Europe from what I was told. If I were a betting woman, that was where I'd put my money.

"No, not business exactly. Even with all your enemies, none have called me to take you out." Cole grinned. "Yet."

"Surprising…" This time, the vamp turned toward me, and his brow furrowed slightly.

"Cole," I muttered between barely open lips, "why do I feel like he can see me, too?"

He gave his head a short shake, just noticeable enough for me to know to keep my mouth shut.

"I'm here to collect the favor you owe me," Cole said, pulling Andre's attention away.

"Ah, that." Andre crossed his arms, his expression turning bored. "Yes, well, I am in your debt. So what would you like from me?"

"I need you to protect this woman here. Her name is Kay."

"Protect her?" Andre asked, suddenly interested. "From?"

Cole's gaze hardened. "I don't think that's any of your business."

"I think I should know what it is that could come crashing through my door at any minute. It seems more like common courtesy than nosiness."

"It's always nosiness with you, Andre."

For the first time since we'd come, Andre laughed. "This is true."

"It's Xaver," Cole said after a tense moment. "He possessed an amateur sorcerer and came after the girl."

"Of course this is about Xaver. Isn't it always?"

Cole clenched his jaw, a tight muscle in his neck twitching.

Andre ignored him. "I guess my next question is how Xaver got over here in the first place? Without the solstice—"

"That's what we're trying to figure out," I said, but then remembered I wasn't part of this conversation.

Cole shot me a look before repeating my words for Andre to hear.

"I hate demons." Andre winced as if he had tasted something sour. "Everything is too complicated with them. Too messy. Honestly, Masters, I don't know how you do it. Even as a Halfling."

"I'm not a Halfling," Cole snapped back. "Not yet, anyway. Why do you think I'm trying to get out of it?"

I hesitated. Get out of it? Get out of what, exactly? Being a half-demon? That was impossible, wasn't it? They were born by a demon father and a human or supernatural mother. It was in their DNA. A person couldn't just get out of it or wish it away. It didn't work like that.

Andre rolled his eyes. "You're wasting your time. I've told you this before. There's no way to lose your demon. It's impossible. Frankly, how you've lasted this long without the beast taking over completely is a miracle in itself."

Cole ignored that. "Can I count on you to keep good on your promise or not?"

Andre walked over to Kay and circled her like a tiger stalking his prey. After a few turns, he said, "What is she exactly?"

"Huh?" Kay paled. "What am I?"

"You're a supernatural of some kind. I can smell it in your blood. But not a common one. I can't quite place it."

"She's a Medium," Cole answered, annoyed.

"Ah, that's it." He mused. "It was familiar but unfamiliar at the same time." He turned to Cole again. "How long do you suspect she has?"

"What the fuck is that supposed to mean?" I barked at Cole, who flinched.

"What do you mean?" Kay asked, her voice high with panic.

"Yeah, what do you mean?" Now I was getting pissed. Cole had said Kay could be in danger. The entire part of bringing her to this "safe" house was to protect her from Xaver coming back for her, but from the way they were talking, you'd think something had already happened. Like the damage was done.

My heart hammered in my chest. What could Xaver want with Kay? He possessed Laurence to get to her. That was obvious. The only thing I knew about demons was that they possessed supernaturals to bear children.

Ice raced down my spine as the realization hit.

"Kay, when was the last time you and Laurence *did* it?" I shouted, unable to control the volume of my voice.

Her head whipped towards me. "Uhhh…" Her cheeks reddened.

She was never the type of person to talk about such personal things like her sex life, but right now, it was crucial I knew.

"Was it any time recently?"

She didn't answer, just looked grim.

"Kay!"

"After our date the other day," she choked out.

"Oh shit."

If Xaver had possessed Laurence then and had seduced her, that meant he had picked Kay to be his next victim and the mother of his child. And that meant her fate was sealed. Victims never survived the birth of demon children.

Never. Some didn't even last through the pregnancy.

Andre was watching Kay with a mixture of confusion and interest.

"You don't think…" Her hands flew down to her stomach, still flat and showing no signs of a demonic baby within. Horror flashed across her face. "Oh my God!"

Then, her eyes rolled back and her body crumpled. Cole snatched her shoulders before she hit the ground and tried to get her back to her feet, but her head fell forward.

Shit. Shit. Shit.

Andre watched the scene pensively, appearing more amused than worried. "Well, Masters," he began, turning to Cole with a widening smile, "I think it's safe to say this nightmare of yours has just begun."

CHAPTER

SEVEN

After we made sure Kay woke from her fainting spell and Andre gave her some water and a bit of food, Cole and I left the club. Despite my protests, Kay promised me she was okay. That was enough for Cole, but for me? I'd touch and kill every single one of those vamps if they decided to make a snack out of my friend.

Released or not. I didn't care.

Panic clawed at my insides. Realistically, she could have passed out from shock. Or, it could have been the demon baby she was carrying.

Stop. Let's not sign her death certificate yet.

There was a chance she was fine, right? Maybe Xaver hadn't gotten a chance to…

Acid coiled in the pit of my stomach, telling me I knew the truth deep down. Lying to myself wouldn't help anything.

Was there any way to tell if she was definitely carrying a demon's baby? Some kind of supernatural pregnancy test or something?

"Why did Andre think Kay was pregnant?" I asked Cole as we walked back into the storm. "It was as if he knew it right away."

Cole hunched his shoulders as the rain pelted him. "It's probably something to do with her blood. He might be able to smell it on her."

"Like a dog?"

He snorted a laugh. "Even for a vamp, Andre definitely can be a bitch."

As Cole climbed into the driver's seat of his Jeep, I searched the street for a private, covered place to draw the spirit door and cross over. I had so much to do next; it was overwhelming. First, I had to get back to Styx Corp and tell Azrael what was going on with the spirits and demons. I couldn't forget the mistake of Cole being labeled as a reaping assignment without being close to dead. He'd want to know that, too.

More importantly, I had to find out whatever I could about demons and their offspring. If Kay really was impregnated with a half-demon baby, there had to be a way for us to reverse or stop it. Like I had told Cole, I didn't know much about demons besides the basics, but even I knew demons were too powerful, even as babies. Mothers weren't known to survive the births.

Of course, death didn't scare me. I was used to it by now. But Kay was my friend, the only one I had made after crossing over myself. She was the only connection I had to the living world besides my job, and I didn't want to lose that.

Did that sound selfish? Yes. But it was true. I had to figure out a way to save her from this. I owed her that much.

After a few minutes, I realized Cole's Jeep was still parked in the same spot. He rolled down the window and stared at me.

"Are you getting in?" he asked.

"I wasn't planning on it." Our dealings were done—at least for now. Kay was temporarily safe from the demon, Xaver, in the vampire club.

Cole shrugged. "I just figured you wanted to find a way to save your friend."

"I do," I replied. "Of course. That's why I'm heading back to Styx to find out all I can about it."

"Styx?" His brows knitted together in confusion.

I froze. I had just released the name of something critical to the spirit world and unknown to the living one, and the censor hadn't morphed my words again to hide it.

Not a good sign. I would have to mention that to Azrael, too.

"Er—I should go." Reflexively, I grabbed the tablet out of my back pocket. I must have had dozens of messages from Azrael or his secretary, Maryanne.

But when I checked the screen for the familiar flashing light in the corner, all I found was darkness. No notification bubbles or lights anywhere.

I frowned.

After pressing the new Contacts tab on the menu bar, I found Azrael's face first on the list. I clicked the green call button and waited.

A soft ringing sounded.

It rang and rang, but the screen stayed black.

"Everything okay?" Cole was suddenly by my side, and his closeness made me jump back.

I shoved the tablet back in my pocket before he could see anything. "Yeah, but I should go."

When I looked up, a dark figure dressed in black from head to toe, stood on the street adjacent to ours. His bald head gleamed in the hazy streetlights.

Simon.

I raced across the street.

As I approached, his eyes widened. It wasn't until I got closer that I realized it wasn't me he was looking at but something behind me.

"Jade," he whispered. "Why is that man following you?"

Skidding to a halt on the sidewalk, I glanced over my shoulder to find Cole calling my name and waving to get my attention. He paused as a car passed before crossing the street.I cursed under my breath. Really? Come on now.

Simon stiffened, his exposed right hand clenching just in case.

"I can explain," I began, but then realized I really couldn't. I had no explanation as to how Cole could see me. "Sort of."

But then that made me think—could Cole see or touch Simon, too?

"Jade, you can't just go running like that," Cole said between gasps of breath. "I don't like chasing people."

I lifted a brow. "You chase people for a living."

"Touché." His gaze searched the space in front of me, where Simon stood straight-backed and nervous. Then, he turned back to me. "Why did you come over here anyway?"

So, he couldn't see Simon. Just me.

There went the theory about demons being able to see spirits because they dwelled on the same plane. Right out the window.

"Uhh…"

"He can see you?" Simon blinked rapidly, the seriousness of the situation finally hitting him. "Oh no. This isn't good."

"Tell me about it," I grumbled under my breath.

"What?" Cole asked, confused.

I rubbed my forehead with an exasperated sigh. "Can you give me a few minutes?" I asked him.

"Uh, yeah. Sure. I just figured you'd want to come with me to figure out this thing with your friend. I know a guy."

"Of course you do. A werewolf this time?"

His grin brightened his entire face. Even with his wet hair stuck to his forehead from the rain, he still looked breathtakingly gorgeous. "No, a human."

"Fabulous." I glanced at Simon and then turned back to Cole. "Just give me a few. I'll be right back."

Not waiting for an answer, I sped-walked down the sidewalk and turned into the closest alleyway, gesturing for Simon to follow me. He did.

When we were alone in the darkness of a side street, Simon spun on me. "What is going on here? Explain."

"A lot has happened..." Not sure how powerful a half-demon's hearing was, I made sure to keep my voice on the low side. "I'm as confused as you are."

Simon just stared at me, and even though he didn't say a word, I could almost hear his thoughts. He had to be thinking the same thing I was—how did I always manage to get myself into trouble like this?

Wish I knew. It was like the stuff followed me.

Trying to offer him a small smile, I said, "I'm glad to see you're still here though."

Seeing him meant two things. One, he hadn't been Released. Yet—I reminded myself. After this catastrophe, who knew.

And two, Azrael must have sent him to fetch me. So, my boss must have had some idea of what was going on around here.

His expression turned grave, and with Simon's sharp

angular features, it wasn't a comforting sight at all. He looked more like one of those Renaissance statues in museums, the ones that always look like they're staring directly into your soul. Judging you. "I've come to find you because something's happening at Styx Corp. Something not good."

Uh-oh.

"The building is empty. Completely deserted," he said. "Azrael is gone."

My stomach dropped. "Gone? Just poof? Vanished?"

He nodded slowly. "I tried looking for him."

Tracking him, he meant. Simon's most useful talent. And if he couldn't find him, then Azrael was really gone.

"He's a little more difficult to get a read on, though, being a celestial being."

"Do you think something's happened? Like he's been kidnapped or something?" I asked, although I couldn't imagine that the Angel of Death could ever be forced to do anything he didn't want to do. But I didn't understand that part of the spiritual world, and now, I wasn't sure I wanted to know.

"I don't know," Simon replied. "All the dimensions are locked down. No one is around to give the reapers any instructions. We are all still getting assignments pinged to our tablets from somewhere, but there's no contact with anyone at Styx. I ran into Constance and Victor in the lobby, and they're just going to keep to their work until Azrael notifies them."

Constance and Victor were reapers in charge of human spirits across the seas. They've been doing this gig for way longer than me and were known for not pushing any buttons. So, I wasn't surprised they were just going to keep their noses buried in work until things calmed down.

Me? I wanted to know what the heck was going on. From the look on Simon's face, he was dying to know, too.

I hadn't gotten any more notifications on my tablet. I wondered why that was.

"Maybe Azrael got some kind of special orders from the man upstairs? Or team, or whatever it is above him calling the shots?" I suggested, trying to offer myself some kind of reassurance that everything wasn't actually going to shit. Maybe there was a logical explanation to it all.

Simon didn't seem convinced, though. "An empty Styx Corp. and missing Angel of Death, and now the living can see you? Does that sound like a coincidence to you?"

"Only Cole can, as far as I know," I said.

"Cole…" He pondered his name for a moment. "You've been interacting with him." It was more a statement than a question.

"I didn't really have a choice. He was my last assignment, and…it didn't really go as planned."

"Jade…" His voice took on a more scolding tone.

I held my hands up for him to let me explain. "I found him downtown passed out. As I went to touch him, he leapt up and attacked me. He wasn't even close to dead. Not at all."

Surprise captured Simon's face. "What? That's impossible. Maybe he was meant to have a sudden death, like an aneurysm?"

"His bio said a fight, death by a blunt object. Nothing about a sudden death. I figured someone at Styx had made a mistake."

"They never make mistakes." Simon shook his head frantically. "Never."

"Well, maybe there's a first time for everything. Besides, I didn't really have time to think hard on it because he started firing his gun at me. He could see me, and I have no idea why." I touched my shoulder where Cole's special bullet had hit. The hole was gone, but the skin was still puckered and pink. "And his bullets actually made contact. They hurt like a bitch."

Simon's stunned silence said it all. During our training sessions, he was always the calm and collected one. Even through all my stupid mistakes and panicky moments, nothing seemed to surprise him. But now, the horror and fear in his face was unnerving.

If he didn't know what was going on, then we were in trouble. We all were—both the living and the dead.

Simon gripped my shoulders. Tight. And looked me right in the eyes. I swallowed hard.

"Jade, you need to listen to me. Whatever is going on, you need to stay out of it and stick to your work. Keep your nose clean. Azrael must be fixing whatever is going on behind the scenes, and that means when he comes back, he needs to see that we were able to function without him. You need to lose this Cole guy and keep to your reaping assignments. Don't go wandering. It can be dangerous for everyone, not just you. Especially if he can see you and hurt you. If things get worse, he may try to come after us all." He paused. "Maybe that's why Azrael wanted you to kill him. Maybe you should—"

"I'll lose him," I blurted out. I couldn't kill Cole, not yet anyway. Not when he knew so much about Xaver and could possibly know a way to save Kay. "When Azrael comes back, if he wants me to kill him then, I will. For now, I'll lose him."

Simon's hands fell back to his sides. "Good." He glanced at the alley's entrance to make sure Cole wasn't peeking around the corner. He wasn't. "Remember what I said. Stick to your assignments and stay low. If I find out anything else, I'll message your tablet or come find you. Okay?"

Was that sadness in his eyes? And worry? My heart clenched. Man, Simon was probably twice my age, and over the last year, I hadn't seen him as anything other than my instructor, but now, seeing how concerned he was for me, I realized I was worried for him too. He had always been there for me when I needed him, especially when being a reaper was too hard for me.

There were so many things I wanted to tell him. I hadn't mentioned the censor being on the fritz, or anything about the demons and haunts crossing over. I wanted to ask him if he knew anything about what Kay's predicament could mean, too, but that would mean admitting I had been talking to a living supernatural for a year, and I wasn't ready to do that yet.

Besides, I could predict his answer. Just like Azrael, Simon wouldn't approve at all and would say the same thing he had about Cole. I would have to stop seeing her and completely disconnect from the living world, with the exception of my job, of course. I had been the one to break that rule from the beginning.

If Cole really did know someone who could save Kay, then I would meet them. It was best to leave Simon out of this. I wasn't sure why, but I felt like what had happened to Kay was my responsibility anyway. I was going to have to fix it.

Simon took out a piece of chalk from his breast pocket and turned to the brick wall. When the symbols were drawn, the ring glowed its familiar orange-red. Before stepping through, he looked at me one last time. "Stay safe, Jade."

"You too," I muttered.

He walked through the spirit door and disappeared. Then the glow extinguished as he smudged the chalk from the other side, sealing it closed. I made sure to scuff the chalk, too, with my boot—an extra precaution—before walking back to the sidewalk.

To my surprise, Cole was still standing at the corner, his arms wrapped around himself as the rain continued to pelt him.

As I got closer, he spotted me and smirked, and for a second, my heart fluttered awake again. There was something about him that made my body react without thought. Not only was he a half-demon with the ability to manipulate fire, he was a highly skilled mercenary with an arsenal of weapons that could actually hurt me. My gut was probably warning me that this was a bad idea. That could be why. Fear. Trepidation.

"All better now?" he said, without a hint of annoyance that I had made him wait in the wind and rain without any real explanation.

"Yeah…" I replied, a little hesitant. Simon's warning was a constant buzz in the back of my head, but I shook it away. "So you were saying you had another contact that could help us figure out what's going on with Kay and how to save her?"

"I sure do. When you've been in this business as long as I have, you tend to make friends."

"Let's be clear—friends like Andre? Because he didn't seem too excited about doing this favor for you."

Cole shrugged. "He owed me. He didn't have a choice, really. But no. This friend isn't like Andre."

We walked back across the street toward his Jeep. I took one more look at Red before hopping in the passenger seat, hoping I was making the right choice by ignoring Simon and putting myself deeper in this mess with the dangerous Cole Masters.

But I had to. For Kay. I owed it to her.

CHAPTER

EIGHT

The ride out of town was just as nail biting as the trip in had been. Cole was one reckless driver, swerving around corners and pedestrians, ignoring red lights, flying down the highway. I might be dead already, but that didn't prevent me from holding my breath whenever he did something daring.

A few times, Cole glanced over at me and smiled. He was thoroughly enjoying the torture.

"Come on," he said as he switched lanes a little too quickly and without a blinker. "It's not that bad."

When I went to reply, I realized my teeth were clenched so tight I had to pry them open. "Let's just say your driving makes me wonder if there's any way I could die again," I said. "Where are we going anyway?"

"It's a bit of a drive. Not too far, just not in the immediate city."

That told me no information.

"His name is Wyatt. He knows everything there is to know about the supernatural world. If there is anyone that knows a way to help your friend, Kay, it's him."

"I thought you said he was human," I said.

"He is."

A human that knew about supernaturals? That seemed like an accident waiting to happen. From what I knew, supernaturals worked really hard not to involve humans in their lives. Since they were much smaller in numbers, it was a way to keep them safe. Humans had a nasty habit of wanting to destroy things they didn't understand instead of learning from them, and if they ever discovered that there were people with outstanding abilities, you could bet they'd either try to eradicate them or control them. And that was something the supernatural community would rather not risk.

I didn't blame them either.

Humans were better living in ignorance. It was safer for everyone.

"I'm surprised other supes haven't gotten word of this and tried to off him." And I was. You'd think to protect their secret from spreading any further, supernaturals would track this man down and kill him. I mean, if it were me, and my life was at risk because of a human, I wouldn't be able to say I would think any differently.

"How do you think we met? I protect him when he needs it, and in exchange, I get whatever information I want, whenever I need it." Cole grinned, and a dimple appeared on his right cheek. It made him appear more innocent than he really was. Definitely not like a man with a deadly fire power, demon blood, and who had probably killed more people in a week than I had in my year as a reaper.

I couldn't help but wonder if there was a matching dimple on the other side.

Don't get too caught up in how sexy he is.

Even though the voice in my head was right, it was hard not to look his way and stare a little. He was wickedly good-looking. Maybe it was the danger element, too. It only added to his model appearance. But I had to remember that if he wanted to, he could do some damage, even to me. Although I didn't think he could *kill* me again, I didn't want to find out what he could do.

That made me slide off my left hand's leather glove. Just in case I had to quickly reach over and touch him to protect myself.

Cole noticed the move, and his smile faltered. "Don't trust me, huh?"

"Should I?" I said. "A couple of hours ago, I found you in a downtown alley and was about to just do my job, and you shot me. A crazy demon tussle and vampire club later, I'm in your Jeep heading to God knows where. I don't know anything about you besides that you're a half-demon, your job choice, and your name. So, you'll have to forgive me for being cautious."

"No, I completely understand," he said. "I haven't lived this long in my line of work by being trusting." He whipped the steering wheel suddenly, jerking the car in and out of the lanes.

My hands instinctually shot out to the dashboard to brace myself, but when they passed right through instead, I grunted.

Cole snorted a laugh. "Just make sure you're careful with those hands of yours and don't accidentally grab me."

"Maybe if you didn't drive like a lunatic, I wouldn't have to brace myself so much," I replied.

There was a moment of silence.

Cole shifted in his seat, sitting straighter. Then he put both hands on the wheel and flexed his fingers. "Why didn't you kill me when you found me?" he said. "There in the alley?"

His question surprised me. "What?"

"It's your job, right? As a reaper? I was your next assignment. But you didn't kill me."

"Like I said before, you shot me."

"So, you still plan on killing me?" Even when asking this question, he didn't appear nervous. More like he had been wondering about this for some time. Ready for it.

Now it was my turn to smile. "Maybe."

He laughed, and that adorable dimple appeared again.

Who knew what would happen after things settled down and Azrael came back. He may want me to carry out my assignment and cross Cole over. Actually, the more I thought about it, the more that was very possible. Especially if he found out he could see me and we had made contact. With the censor gone, he already knew too much about the spirit world and what my job was. Azrael wouldn't like that at all.

As for right now, I needed Cole to save Kay, so I couldn't off him yet. He was the only contact I had to the living world and its information—besides Kay, and she was a little indisposed right now. He knew people who knew things. He had been tracking down the demon who had possessed Laurence. He had the tools I didn't. For now, I had to work with him. What came after was a mystery.

"So…" he began, flicking off his windshield wipers. We had come out on the other side of the storm. "What's it like to be a reaper? What does that entail exactly?"

I should have expected him to ask that type of question

one way or another, but still, it hit me strange. After a year of working mostly in secret and with the censor blocking me from sharing anything with Kay, it felt weird to have someone know what I really was. Let alone discussing it openly. Like it was as normal as being a cashier or elementary school teacher.

I *killed* people for a living.

But then again, so did he.

I still wasn't sure how much information I should reveal to him, if any at all. The fact that he knew I was a reaper and was sent to kill him was dangerous enough. Like Simon had said, he could decide to track us down someday.

I was careful with the words I chose. "I suppose it's like yours, but without all the fancy guns and bullets. Oh, and the money."

"You just get a deadly touch and light beams shooting from your fingertips?"

"I already told you, I have no idea how or why that happened. It's a first for me."

"Maybe it's a power from your life before?" he pressed. "Were you a supernatural before you died?"

Okay, that hit a nerve. Of course, he wouldn't know that the erasing of my memory after death was a sore topic for me, but damn if it didn't make annoyance flare. I drew in a deep breath. "I don't know honestly. Any memories of my life before death were erased. It's part of the gig."

"Oh." He made a face, as if realizing he'd made a mistake in asking. Were my facial expressions that obvious? Probably. I had a hard time keeping my feelings off my face.

"Besides," I said, "I don't know of any supernaturals that can do that."

"The only thing I could think that would be close is a witch. Some kind of light spell?"

Interesting thought. But no other powers had shown

themselves during my year dead, and I had never heard of light spells repelling demons like it had with Xaver.

Instead of answering him, I switched the conversation onto him. "What about you? A half-demon using guns? What about that fire manipulation? Seems pretty cool."

His hands gripped the wheel so tight, the leather squeaked and his knuckles popped.

It seemed someone didn't like talking about who he was, either.

He was quiet for a while, even slowed the Jeep down to twenty miles per hour over the speed limit instead of forty. Then he muttered, "The fire stuff isn't all it's cracked up to be. Believe me."

At the last minute, he swerved onto an exit ramp and slammed on the brakes to take the curve slower. The Jeep reared up on two wheels for a breath-taking second before readjusting, the tires screeching loudly. Cole didn't even blink.

"You said you knew the basics about demons, but I'm guessing you don't know that the fire power we're cursed with is corrupting. Meaning, every time it's used, the more of the demon takes over the human half. It's why I trained with weapons."

"Shit. Really?"

He nodded. "Most half-bloods lose themselves to the demon side pretty early on. Then they're recruited back to Hell. I've been able to dodge that by barely using that part of me. I'd rather not have it at all."

That's when I remembered what Andre had said back at Red about Cole being on a useless mission to get rid of part of him. "That's why you were tracking down Xaver tonight? To ask him to expel the demon in you?"

"Not exactly," he replied. "It's not as easy as 'asking' for a cure. I've been hunting for a way to get rid of my demon half for years."

"No luck, I'm assuming?"

His entire body stiffened as we pulled onto a two-lane main road and he was forced to slow down even more. Wherever we were, the area reflected more of a small southern town with a one-pump gas station and an auto repair garage on one side, and a Waffle House that needed some major repairs to its roof and parking lot on the other. Every hanging stop light blinked yellow, as if the rules of the road were really up to the drivers instead of the law, and every car on the road was a different color pickup truck.

"Have you tried an exorcism?" I asked.

"That only works with possession. Like with your friend's boyfriend." He frowned. "I am close to finding the answers I need. Closer than I've ever been before."

"How about other spirits? Can you see them? Haunts?"

"Like ghosts?" His brow rose. "No, I can't. You're the first and only dead thing I can see. Besides other demons, but they're technically my kin, so..."

"Our previous theory about you and Xaver seeing me has been officially squashed, then."

"Damn. You're right."

The sky above the trees in the distance brightened to a fiery pink as the sun began to ascend. I glanced at the dashboard clock. Five forty-five in the morning. "Is your friend going to be pissed that we're about to wake him up so early?"

"Probably. But he's used to it."

We drove over a hill, and at the very bottom, Cole drifted the Jeep onto the shoulder. The trees and sudden bend in the road made it hard to see anything besides forest, so when he turned right, I thought we were heading for disaster. Instead, we careened down a dirt road that was so buried in the woods, tree branches scraped the sides of the car, making a terrible screeching sound that grated on my nerves.

It was a long, winding trip. The deeper we got into the forest, the less sunlight was able to peek through, giving the feeling of nighttime darkness again. Cole flicked on his high beams, but all I could see were the tire tracks that we were following and more and more trees.

Then we came up to a tall chain-link fence that stretched deep on both sides. Barbwire lined the top and along the bottom, and a thick keylock sealed the gate closed. It was an intimidating sight.

"Either he's trying to stay hidden way back here or he's trying to keep people away," I said, reading the posted signs. One read *No Trespassing* and the other *Beware of Dog*.

"I'd say a little bit of both." Cole threw the Jeep into park. "Wyatt doesn't particularly care for people."

He opened his door and stepped outside. It was hard to see him in the darkness, but I could just make out his figure striding over to the gate and hear the jiggling of the chain and lock. Then there was a loud thud and a snap. The squeal of the gate being pushed open ripped through the silence of the early morning.

The angry bark of a large dog echoed farther down the dirt trail.

When Cole climbed back into the car, I shifted in my seat uncomfortably. Anxiousness started to rise up. But I couldn't let it get the best of me. Especially if I was about to enter into a dangerous situation. There were too many unknowns.

The car lurched forward, and we began our trek again.

"He gave you a key?" I asked him as the Jeep bumped along. The holes and mud were worse on this side of the gate, and I couldn't help but wonder if that had been done on purpose as another deterrent for trespassers. If Cole's car hadn't been an off roader with four-wheel drive, there was no doubt that we would have gotten stuck in one of these pits.

"Not exactly."

The forest opened up finally to a large lot. The barbed wire fence encircled a rusty double-wide trailer, several unattached storage boxes, and discarded pieces of scrap metal. An old Buick sat farther off. Even though it was partially hidden behind tall grass, it was obvious the vehicle had been used for parts since it sat on only its axels, the tires and hood having long been removed.

This place looked more like a junkyard then a person's home.

On the porch, a massive German shepherd barked wildly as we approached, spit flying from its jaws.

I must have gasped or something because Cole said, "Don't worry about Angel. Once she gets to know you, she's a sweetheart."

My brows shot up in disbelief. "A-Angel?" I sputtered. "Really?" There didn't seem to be anything angelic about this beast. The name had to be chosen ironically.

Cole stopped the car in front of the trailer and cut the engine.

"Does she like you?" I asked.

He chuckled. "Nope. Not in the least. But I'm working on it."

Oh boy.

Suddenly, the trailer door flew open, the rickety thing crashing against the siding so hard it sounded like a gunshot. Or maybe it was an actual gunshot, because the first thing to come through the door was the deadly end of a sawed-off shotgun, followed by a man dressed in complete cowboy attire. Right out of one of those old western movies. Wide-brimmed hat, grey hair spun into two braids, a scruffy beard, and skin like tanned leather with a permanent scowl etched into it, all the way down to the dirty plaid shirt, ripped jeans, silver belt buckle, and boots.

This had to be Wyatt. Forget Virginia. This guy looked like he should be in the heart of Texas.

With determined fingers fixed on the trigger of his gun, he pointed the barrel in our direction, and uttered the two words that made my heart jump into my throat.

"Sic 'em, Angel."

CHAPTER

NINE

It didn't matter if I wasn't alive. Having the double barrel of a shotgun pointing in my direction was unnerving.

I ducked out of reflex, but Cole did something even stranger. He shoved his hands between his seat and the center console and pulled out a big slab of dried beef jerky. With the other hand, he rolled down his window. The moment Angel leapt for the door, he chucked the meat like frisbee across the yard. The dog was off running in the next second, sights now trained on the treat.

"See," Cole whispered, his rising and falling chest revealing that he was more scared than he let on. "We have a love-hate relationship."

My heart pounded in my chest. I didn't mind dogs. Even better—puppies. Puppies were cute. They were snuggly. All they wanted were kisses and love. What I did mind were massive beasts with sharp teeth that were trained to kill on command. Angel was no angel, that was for sure.

As Cole reached for the door handle, he leaned close to me and whispered in a rush, "By the way, Wyatt doesn't know what I am, and I would like to keep it that way."

I blinked, a little stunned. "What—why?"

He opened the door and quickly jumped out of the car. "You'll see. Oh, and be careful where you step." He slammed the door shut before I could press for more.

Sometimes he was really irritating.

I got out, too, looking from Angel, who had found the jerky in the brush by the fence and was munching it, to the cowboy Wyatt, who still hadn't lowered his gun. Every time Cole moved, the barrel followed him. I never thought I'd ever be so thankful for being invisible to the living.

Some friend Wyatt was. Where did Cole find these crazies?

Cole's hands shot up into the air, and his shirt pulled up, revealing a strip of pale, muscular midsection, lightly dusted with blond hair. If this were any other time, I may have bit my lip and admired such a beautiful specimen, but I became a little distracted by what rode on his hips, a concealed belt fully stocked with bullet cartridges, two handguns, vials of Holy Water, and a sheathed dagger. He was packing in more ways than one.

"Wyatt," Cole called out as he approached the porch. "It's just me."

Wyatt's gun never wavered. "You broke my gate's lock again," he shot back. His voice was abrasive and raspy, like sandpaper scraping against metal. Harsh.

"I'll buy you another one," Cole said, glancing my way, a silent signal for me to stay close behind him.

Wyatt's stare hardened. "You owe me six already."

"I'll buy you six next time I come by, then. And a twelve-pack of beer. How does that sound?"

That made Wyatt lower the gun, but his glare never eased. "I want the one Sean got me that one time." He smacked his lips. "Somethin' Bastard. Somethin'—"

"Sean?" I whispered, more to myself than anyone else.

"His son," Cole mumbled, his lips barely moving.

"Somethin'… Somethin'…"

"Arrogant Bastard?" Cole offered.

"Yes, that's it. Expensive. Tasty. None of that cheap piss water stuff."

Cole's hands lowered back to his sides. "Arrogant Bastard. It matches you."

He climbed up the porch steps and clapped Wyatt on the back. Wyatt, though, didn't relax much.

A prickle of warning raced up my spine, and I whipped around to find Angel sitting behind me, her ears perked up in curiosity and her tongue running over her lips from her recent snack. I froze, afraid to move.

The animal was staring right at me, but the ferocious beast I had seen before was gone. She cocked her head to the side, as if she were only confused by me.

I wasn't surprised Angel could sense me here. It was unclear how much of me she could actually see, but she definitely knew I was here, in front of her. I found out fairly early during my training that animals were much more sensitive to the dead than humans were. They could track my movements.

Ever get freaked out when a dog or cat stares at nothing? Well, you should be. More than likely, you have a spirit.

A sharp whistle rang out, jerking Angel's attention back

to her master on the porch. Cole was staring at us with wide eyes.

"What is with you, girl?" Wyatt called. "Come here."

Her head jerked my way one more time before running to the trailer. As she and Wyatt walked into the house, Cole stayed behind for me to walk over.

"What the heck did you do to her?" he whispered.

I shrugged. "Nothing."

"She saw you?"

"I think so."

"It's taken me years to get her to not take a chunk out of my leg. Hence the jerky. That's the only thing that seemed to work for me."

I shrugged again.

Cole touched the door, but before he walked in, he paused. "Oh, and as I mentioned before. Be very careful where you step. If you see any markings on the floor or walls, do not touch them."

What did that mean?

Again, before I could ask more, he stepped inside.

I was beginning to believe he was doing this on purpose.

When I passed through the door, I stopped short. I knew trailers weren't the most spacious of homes, but this one was packed in tight by boxes, books, and papers stacked on top of each other from floor to ceiling. They were everywhere.

To my left was a small kitchenette, but the hoard had even stretched into there. Scrolls were shoved into the kitchen cabinets instead of food, and more boxes crowded the counters. To the right was a living room area, which was the most congested. A small path had been made from the door to a desk and a battered old armchair. Overpacked shelves lined the walls behind them, blocking a fairly big window. Actually, the more I looked around, the more I realized how dark the space really was. Every window had been covered, either by a heavy shelf or by plywood boards.

He was clearly trying to keep someone out.

Or some*thing.*

Besides the dingy interior, layers of dust on everything, and not-so-pleasant smells of cigarettes, mildew, and old books, this place could be a librarian's wet dream.

Or nightmare. The disorganization would probably drive them crazy.

Wyatt collapsed in his armchair and reached into his front shirt pocket for his pack of cigarettes and lighter. Angel curled up at his feet; this was their obvious routine.

Cole sidestepped carefully through the small pathway, and it was then that I noticed the strange markings spray painted on the carpet. He tried not to make his movements conspicuous, but I saw them. He was avoiding the marks, stepping around them as gracefully as he could manage.

The symbols on the floor were foreign to me. They reminded me a bit of the ones that made up the spirit door and transportation portals, but the details were hard to see completely. Most of them were covered by the piles of junk, but if Cole was doing his best to avoid them, there had to be a good reason. I would have to ask him about it later.

I mimicked his movements, following as close to the wall as I could so I didn't touch the marks.

"Where is Sean?" Cole asked, glancing around the room. I guessed the bedrooms in this place were off the kitchen and maybe Sean was in one. I wondered if they were as tightly crammed as everywhere else.

Wyatt puffed on his cigarette. "He ran out to town. He should be back soon." His scowling expression turned more suspicious. "Let's cut the shit, Cole. Why are you here bothering me again?"

"Straight to business. It's one of the many things I like about you."

Wyatt rolled his eyes to the ceiling. "Yeah, yeah." He took another deep draw of his cigarette.

Time to cut the bullshit, as the old man had said.

"I ran into Xaver." They were four simple words that to anyone else would have meant nothing, but by the way Wyatt's eyes flew open and he half choked on his next puff, he knew exactly who Cole was talking about.

He sputtered and coughed for a minute as he struggled to regain his breath. When he finally did, he stubbed out the cigarette and moved to the edge of his armchair. What was even more surprising was that the grimace was gone and a grin sat in its place. "You found him?"

"You really didn't believe I would?"

"Hell no, I didn't. Xaver isn't some Halfling Hell minion. He's a full-blood."

That was the second time I had heard that word. Halfling. First by Andre and now Wyatt. And the way Cole's lip curled up in disgust each time he heard it made me think it wasn't just some typical nickname.

More like an insult.

"I told you not to doubt my skills," he grumbled.

Wyatt ignored him. "Did you kill the bastard?"

"Er—"

There was the glower again. "Some skill."

"Things got…" Cole paused, choosing his next word while glancing over at me. "Complicated."

He could say that again.

"It's a good thing I didn't pay you to kill him," Wyatt said. "It would have been a waste of money."

"If you had, then you bet he would have been dead. Money is a great motivator."

Wyatt huffed in disbelief.

"Here's the thing. I ran into Xaver last night. Without the solstice."

Wyatt's brows shot up, and before Cole could utter another word, he pushed himself off the chair and walked over to one of his overloaded shelves behind the desk. After skimming the spines of the old books, he chose one and pulled it out. Opening to a random page, he grumbled something as he read it over.

Cole kept talking. "He possessed a woman's boyfriend over in downtown Fairport. A sorcerer. And was after the girl—a Medium."

The sudden snap of Wyatt closing the book made me jump. He cursed, tossed it onto his cluttered desk, and moved to another pile of leather-bounds by the armchair.

Angel's eyes stayed locked on me, and she whimpered softly.

As Wyatt flipped through another book, he muttered, "A Medium would be a prime target for a victim."

Victim. Worry twisted in my gut. It only solidified how much trouble Kay really was in.

He continued, "Depending on how strong this Medium's gift is. But they are not only rare, they're the middleman, so to speak, between our world and theirs. The living and the dead. It makes sense Xaver would want her. She can most likely survive long enough to produce his offspring."

I winced. The fact that the first thing he went to was Kay being pregnant with a demonic baby made me want to throw up. Wyatt and Cole knew more about demons than I did, and if they both were thinking the same thing, then odds weren't looking in Kay's favor.

"Is there a way to confirm it?" I asked, but then realized only Cole would be able to hear me. Oh, and Angel, whose head perked up at the sound of my voice.

Cole repeated my question to Wyatt.

He picked up several more books and flipped through their contents. Finally, his finger stopped midway down a page, and he nodded in satisfaction. "Well, yes and no."

"What the heck does that mean?" I said, my nervousness getting the better of me.

"Explain," Cole told him.

"A demonic pregnancy can be confirmed by the sudden death of the mother or the evidence of a speedy gestational period."

"Speedy what? What the hell does that mean?"

Cole threw me a look, and I clamped my mouth shut.

"So, there's no way to tell for sure without waiting," Cole added.

"Unfortunately. But by then, it could be too late. Has she shown any signs of a demonic pregnancy? High temperature? Fainting spells? Weakness? Expanding stomach?"

Fainting, yes. But I figured that was just from the shock of it all.

From Cole's thoughtful expression, he was considering the same thing.

"There has to be some way to know for sure without waiting," he said. "Some kind of test."

"A demonic pregnancy doesn't show up on a typical piss-on-a-stick pregnancy test," Wyatt shot back. "Since the gestation is only three months compared to the normal nine, we should know for sure within a couple of weeks. She should be showing by then. You'll just have to hope she survives even that long."

I let out a slew of curses. Only three months? Kay was in some serious shit.

And I had to help her.

The sound of a car pulling up grabbed everyone's attention. Especially Angel's, who leapt up and raced to the door, knocking into Cole and almost sending him toppling over. She didn't bark, though.

"That must be Sean," Wyatt said. "She knows the sound of his truck."

A door slammed. I walked over to one of the boarded windows and peered between the gaps in the boards. A young man, probably in his early twenties, was looking over Cole's Jeep with brown paper bags in his hands. He must have recognized it because he shook his head.

As he dug into his pocket for his keys, my eye caught movement behind him. A dark ghostly figure stretched across the ground, out of the shadows of the surrounding woods, and my heartbeat sped up. It was as if it grew from the darkness. Then another emerged from the right part of the forest, moving toward the trailer. Toward Sean, who appeared oblivious to their presence.

Slowly, the moving shadows grew and solidified, pulling themselves off the ground and taking shape. Like I had seen on Laurence with his possession, their faces were twisted and mangled, with protruding brows, glowing red eyes, and lipless mouths, but unlike the full-demon, these creatures had no distinct shape to their bodies. They were constantly changing forms and shifting as they moved.

"Uh, Cole. We have a problem," I said, my throat tight.

In the next second, he was at my side, peering through the small space of the window, too. His body tensed.

After yanking one of the guns from his belt, he started loading it.

"What? What is it?" Wyatt's panicked voice came from behind us, followed by the distinct click of his shotgun being loaded again.

Angel barked furiously at the closed door. Every hair stood up on my bare arms.

"Sean's here." Cole gripped the door's handle. There

wasn't a hint of fear on his face. Instead, I saw determination and a bit of excitement. This was his area of expertise after all. "But he's not the only one."

"What are those things?" My voice rose with my fear. Whatever the answer was, I knew it couldn't be good. "More demons?"

Clicking the safety off his gun, Cole turned to me, and for a second, I could have sworn his blue eyes flashed red. Like Xaver's.

I jumped back, unsure of what I really saw. My insides froze over.

When he spoke again, his voice was deeper, more ominous. Almost like an animalistic rumble.

He only said one word.

"Halflings."

CHAPTER

TEN

Halflings.

That's all he said, but the word sent a chill through my very being.

"*Those* are Halflings?" But wait… Wasn't Cole a Halfling, too? He certainly didn't look like a ghostly creature with a contorted face and needle-like teeth. The red eyes—I must have imagined it in my moment of panic. Now, as I looked at him, they were as blue as the Caribbean Sea. Nothing menacing or scary about them.

His grip on the front door tightened; he seemed to be straining to not open it and run out guns blazing.

"You should stay here, Jade." Even though his voice was low, still that strange rumble, there was no doubt Wyatt had heard him. And besides, he must have looked pretty silly staring at the empty place in front of the window so intently. Wyatt either likely knew something was up or figured Cole was off his rocker. "You don't know how to take these things down. Leave it to me and Wyatt. When Sean gets to the door, let him in. Make sure he locks the door behind us."

One, how the hell was I supposed to *make sure* of anything if Sean wouldn't be able to hear or see me. And two, I wasn't some helpless damsel here. I could not only defend myself, I could fight.

"So, I'm supposed to just leave this up to the boys, then?" I said with a roll of my eyes. "Of course."

His entire body shook. No, vibrated, right in front of me. Was it from the mounting annoyance I could see in his gaze, or something else? I really wasn't sure.

"You don't understand," he said in a rush. "These are Hell-dwelling Halflings. Fully corrupted by their Hellfire power and then dragged back to Hell to do nothing but obey. Mindless puppets who will stop at nothing to carry out their orders. *Nothing.*"

I stared at him for a second as his words sank in.

"But aren't you a—"

"Not like me," he added in haste, then grumbled, "Not yet anyway."

That spoke volumes in itself. So, if Cole tapped into the demon half of him by using his fire gift, it would turn him into one of those…*things.* He'd be dragged off to Hell, forced to live out the rest of his damned existence as a demon's minion?

Tough break.

Now the need for guns and magic bullets made more sense.

"I still have my weird glowy hand," I said finally. "It worked on Xaver. It should work on his babies, too."

"Can you guarantee it'll happen again?"

"Uh…"

He shook his head. "We can't risk it."

"But they can't hurt…"

The rest of the sentence died on my tongue. Could they hurt me? It was getting harder to keep up with who could see me and who couldn't. Xaver had tossed me across the bakery like a sack of dirty laundry, so it was possible the Halflings could, too. Especially since they had demon blood in them.

God, this was getting complicated.

"They may not be able to hurt you, Jade, but they can certainly drag you back to Hell with them."

I stiffened. That was a horrifying thought.

Why had I complained about my boring afterlife before? I certainly had my hands full now.

After a long second, I gave him a firm nod in understanding, and he threw the door open. It crashed against the trailer's exterior in a loud bang. Wyatt rushed outside after him, Angel hot on his tail. Gunshots along with the dog's ferocious barking rang out in the early morning silence.

I peered through the gap in the window again. Two more demon Halflings had joined the fight. The young man named Sean scrambled up the porch steps in the chaos, spilling the contents of his bags all over the ground.

"Get inside and barricade the door!" Cole demanded, seizing Sean by his shirt and half-throwing him toward the trailer. A second later, Sean burst through the door, cursing.

"Are you kidding me?" he gasped as he locked every one of the six deadbolts on the door. "That's it. Pop's going into a nursing home. I've had it."

When his gaze drifted my way, he paused.

A strange wave of energy passed over my skin, raising the

hairs on my arms. Something zipped up my spine, and like when I had used my light power, my temples throbbed.

But only for a second. As fast as it had raced through me, it was gone.

What the actual fuck was going on with me?

I glanced at Sean to find him staring, his eyes large saucers compared to the rest of his face. His entire body trembled.

"Oh shit," I breathed.

He leapt back so far, he crashed into a leaning pile of books and boxes, toppling over with them as they fell.

"Wh-Who are you?" Face pale, he scrambled to stand again, but only knocked over another stack of his father's stuff.

"No way. You can see me, too?" I threw my hands up in defeat. "Really? *Really*?" I shouted to the ceiling. Another living person could see me. This was getting ridiculous. "You've got to be kidding me!"

When Sean finally stood again, he looked around the room wildly and reached for the closest object he could find. Obviously, it was a book. He hurled it at me.

I didn't move—shouldn't need to. But when the book smacked into my chest and pain radiated from where the surprisingly dense thing hit, I gasped in surprise. As if it hit something solid, it clattered on the floor in front of me.

I froze, not sure what I had just seen or even felt.

Sean was just staring at me, waiting for me to do something. Attack him. *Something*.

Instead, I examined my hand. It appeared like it always did to me. Without thinking, I reached out, and my hand collided with the rough surface of the two-by-fours covering the window.

Rough. Jagged.

Ow. Splintery.

I stared at my finger, now with a nice chunk of wood sticking out of the tip and a droplet of blood welling up.

Blood.

My blood.

Oh.

FUCK.

More gunshots exploded from outside, jarring me back into the chaos unfolding around us. A piercing howl resounded, followed by Angel's ferocious barks.

I couldn't just stay in here. I had to do something.

Wait. If I could bleed, maybe I could die. Again. Should I hop in and help, put myself at risk?

I shook my head, pushing away those thoughts. There was no time to debate this. I knew death. It didn't scare me, and people were in danger.

"Do you have a gun?" I asked Sean.

He stayed planted in place, too stunned to move.

I groaned. "Sean—that's your name, isn't it? Sean?"

Not even a nod.

"Look, Sean, I don't have time for this. I need to help Cole and your father."

"Y-You appeared out of nowhere." He gasped, his chest heaving. "Just materialized out of thin air!"

Another carnal shriek blared from somewhere near the house's boarded window. More shots. My head fogged at the thought of the two men dying outside while I was stuck in here, dealing with this deer in headlights.

"I'll explain later," I snapped, knowing full well I couldn't. I needed him to focus on my words first. "I'm a friend of Cole's. I won't hurt you."

Whatever was going on, it had made me suddenly solid on this plane. Maybe that meant I could manipulate a weapon, too.

"I can help them." I held out my empty palm. "Do you have a gun?"

He held out a shaky finger, pointing to the fireplace mantel. Under a slew of papers was a cigar box. I ran to it, shoved the crap off the top, and opened it. A dirty-looking revolver sat on a velvet pillow.

Still a little unnerved that everything I was touching wasn't going right through my grasp, I fumbled with the cool metal as I checked the chamber for bullets. It was loaded.

Problem was, I'd never handled a gun before.

Not that I remembered anyway.

Yet, the moment I held the revolver in my hand, a twinge of familiarity vibrated through me. Like before, when the sorcerer, Tristen, had wrapped his hands around my neck. That same unsettling shiver ran from my head to the tips of my toes.

Damn, this was getting weirder by the second. And I didn't like it.

Sean was watching me with a mix of apprehension and fear as I went to the door.

"Grab yourself a weapon. Something to defend yourself if this gets bad. And lock the door behind me."

His wide-eyed expression said it all.

"Do you understand?"

He said nothing. Only remained frozen in place.

I didn't have time for this.

I kicked open the door and rushed outside where the sudden commotion was such a contrast to the silence inside, I recoiled for a second.

In the center of the front yard was a giant crater, a gaping hole that was so deep, I couldn't see the bottom from where I stood on the porch. If there was a bottom, that is.

Remembering what Cole had said about the Halflings dragging people to Hell, I swallowed hard.

Two Halflings had Cole pinned against his Jeep, snarling in his face and chomping on his arm until he released the gun. All he had were his fists to beat off the beasts. Wyatt was crouching behind the tireless Buick tucked deep in the tall grass, trying to reload his shotgun with fingers that were slick with blood. A jagged gash marked his forehead, spilling more blood into his eye.

A third Halfling was crawling his way on all fours, making sniffing and huffing noises as if it were catching his scent but without a nose.

These things were ugly S.O.B.s.

Wait there had been four. Where was the—

A vicious growl came from above me. I whipped around just in time to see the blackened creature leap off the trailer's roof and hurl itself at me.

The size of a large animal, maybe a Great Dane or a small bear, the weight of it surprised me. Especially for a ghostly shadow half-demon. It certainly was more ferocious than any dog, though, even Angel. It snapped its yellow-stained jaws at my arms and neck as it tried to swat my gun away with its claw-like fingers.

Those sharp nails slashed across my forearm, sending pain like fire through my muscles, and I gasped. It was the kind that took your breath away, and I hadn't felt pain like this in so long. I definitely didn't miss it, either.

Knowing it was trying to disarm me, I clutched the gun even tighter and bucked my body to dislodge the thing from its place on top of me. After getting one arm free, I whipped the gun across the monster's face, gaining another horrid squeal from it. But it was distracted enough for me to spin and throw it off my back.

At the corner of my eye, I spotted Wyatt firing another shot at his encroaching Halfling. He hit his mark, right where the heart *should* have been, but instead of it doing much damage or even slowing it down, the bullets only threw him back a few feet. More of an annoyance than anything else.

It stalked toward Wyatt again. He fumbled to load another round.

I guess Wyatt didn't have any of those magic bullets in his guns, like Cole did.

Turning toward the Halfling on the floor, I aimed at its head and pulled the trigger. The bullet hit, but just like with Wyatt's shot, the creature only bared its teeth at me and growled.

Not good. I was going to have to get a hold of one of Cole's weapons to really make a difference in this fight.

As my foe started to climb back to its feet, I spun and kicked it back down. Then, I sped down the porch toward the Jeep where Cole was still struggling to bat away his demons.

Just before I reached him, though, there was a flare of reddish-yellow light and a rush of heat that blew my hair back and stung my eyes. I skidded to a stop in time to see both Halflings fly back, black smoke billowing from their already blackened bodies and the smell of burnt flesh filling the air.

Cole's head whipped toward me, finally sensing me standing there, and what I saw scared me more than anything I had ever reaped. Red glowing eyes—as red as the embers of a fire—stared at me without any hint of recognition at all. His breaths were so ragged, his shoulders and chest heaved from the effort, and his skin appeared gray, sickly almost, as if he'd been deprived of water for days.

"Woah, Cole." I couldn't help it. The words came out on their own with my shock. "Are you okay?"

He blinked, staring at me, as if he were seeing me for the very first time.

Beside his feet was the loaded gun with spirit-repelling bullets, though. Exactly what I needed.

He clenched his hands into fists, and they glowed red.

Uh-oh. Was I really going to have to fight him, too?

I held my hands out in surrender. "Cole, it's me. Jade. We're on the same side, buddy. Why don't you extinguish those bad boys, and come back to earth here with me. We're on the same side."

His head cocked, studying me.

Wyatt's gun went off behind me again, making me jump.

Shit. He was going to run out of bullets soon.

I didn't have time for this.

As I snatched the gun off the ground, Cole's hand clamped around my wrist. His touch was searing, and I screamed, launching my fist for his face. The moment my knuckles met his cheek, white light erupted from my palm, sending him sprawling back into the Jeep hard enough to break the glass. He landed in a heap by the tire.

Suddenly, it was as if someone had plunged a spike through my temples. Gasping from the sharpness of the pain, I rested a hand on the hood of the car. My vision blurred, and I blinked rapidly to prevent everything from going black. Heat climbed up my neck, along with the threat of losing consciousness.

Was this going to happen every time I used this new power? It seemed like my reaction afterward was getting worse.

I gave myself a hard slap on the side of my face. Anything to urge my mind to stay present. Slowly, things came back into focus.

A chorus of half-demon wails filled the air, their jaws extending in an unnatural way. All at once, they rushed at the hole in the center of the yard. The two Halflings that Cole had been fighting leapt over the Jeep, no longer interested in

Cole or me, and dove headfirst into the pit, followed by the one stalking Wyatt and the fourth I had clocked in the head with my boot.

The moment the last one disappeared, the ground filled in where it had been missing until the hole was completely gone. The grass, the rocks, everything was there, undisturbed, as if there wasn't an opening to a Hell dimension there a second ago.

Not sure if the danger was completely over, I sank to my knees beside Cole and gave his face a light tap.

"Cole, wake up." I slapped him again, a little harder this time, and his eyes fluttered open. The same cool blue color I was used to.

"J-Jade?" he stammered then groaned. "Oh shit, my head." He rubbed the back of his head and looked at his palm, no longer glowing with fire but now wet with blood.

"Oh, sorry about that. But you went full evil on me," I said.

"I did?" For the first time, there was genuine dread on his face. "Did I hurt anyone?"

"Just a couple of pissed off Halflings."

He glanced around. "Where did they go?"

"Hopefully back to whichever Hell they crawled out of, never to return."

"How...?"

I waved my hand at him. "Magic light fingers again."

"Ah." That's when he noticed the glass all around him from his shattered window. He looked up and cursed.

"Sorry about that. That was me, too."

He grabbed the side mirror and tried to haul himself up to stand.

It must have taken a second for my words to register, but when they did, his eyes widened. "Wait. You? How?"

Articulate, wasn't he?

"Would you be surprised if I told you I have no idea?" I said.

His gaze fell to my hand, still gripping his gun. An ugly-looking burn mark, pink and raised, wrapped around my wrist from where he had grabbed me. My other arm, which thumped and throbbed like it had a heartbeat, hung lifelessly at my side. Blood dripped from the Halfling's claw gashes.

He gasped. "You're bleeding."

"A lot."

"You're…solid?"

"I-I think so."

"How? Why?"

I blew out a breath. "You keep asking me questions I can't answer. I have no idea. It just…happened."

"Is this a reaper thing?"

What did he think? We were given some kind of textbook on these things after death with all the information I could ever need, and tested on it? *Reaper 101* or *Reaping for Dummies*? That's not how this worked.

"It's never happened to me before," I explained. "I am going through it at the same time as you are."

He scratched his chin in thought. "Does this mean you're alive now?"

I paused, my heartbeat speeding up. But was it really beating this time or just mimicking an action it remembered from a past life?

Staring at my arm, still throbbing and bleeding, I marveled at what I was feeling and seeing. The pain was more intense than anything I had experienced in the last year. And the blood—I couldn't remember the last time I had seen blood, my own blood, coming anywhere from my body.

I was aware Cole was staring at me, saying nothing, but I didn't care how stupid I looked. The more I studied my cut-up forearm, my burned wrist, and the gun still firmly in my grasp, the more hope bubbled up, even though my common sense said there was no way. What I was seeing and feeling— it had to be in my head.

I drew in a deep breath, filling my lungs to the point of pain with actual warm, morning air, and then released it too fast, choking a little at the end from the unfamiliarity of it.

As I sputtered and struggled to suck in another breath, I couldn't help but smile.

Could it be true?

Was it even possible?

Could I really be...*alive*?

CHAPTER

ELEVEN

I didn't have time to ponder the question long, because the hot barrel of a gun singed the skin on the back of my neck. At the same time, Wyatt's gruff voice barked, "Don't move or I'll blow your head off your shoulders."

The sting of the overused gun—I felt it. It hurt, like someone stabbing my neck with a poker that had been lying in a burning fire.

It was real, and I felt it.

But again, I didn't have time to revel in it because then came the sudden severity of the situation crashing down on me. Wyatt could see me. He thought I was a threat because he didn't know who I was. And he was about to blow my head off.

"Wyatt... I know this all seems weird now, but I'm not one of those Halflings."

He jabbed me again with the barrel, making me wince. "How do you know my name? Who the fuck are you?"

"Woah." Cole pushed himself off the Jeep, hands up. "Put the gun down, Wyatt. She's a friend of mine."

The gun left my skin, and from the corner of my eye, I could see it now hovering over my shoulder, pointed at Cole. "And who the fuck are you? Or what are you, I should say."

Oh shit. He must have seen Cole use his Hellfire.

"All this time you've been one—one of those things? A demon?"

"Yes and no. Wyatt, please. You have to let me explain." Cole's calm voice and demeanor were way better than my own. My body was shaking, and I couldn't seem to make it stop.

"All this time..." A bit of disappointment leached into Wyatt's tone, but it was quickly replaced with anger. "All this time! I let you in my home! You played me!"

The gun's safety clicked off.

Would I be able to disarm him faster than he could fire the thing? Time to check my skills.

I whipped my elbow up, hitting the gun's barrel into the air at the same time the loud boom sounded and a plume of smoke exploded from the end. Startled, he let go of the weapon—better for me because I didn't want to hit him to make him drop it. He was still an old man after all. A ruthless and persistent old man, but one nonetheless.

When I snatched the gun before it reached the floor and dispelled the empty shells in one swift motion, Wyatt stumbled back, eyes wide. I could hear Cole's "Wow" from behind me.

I grinned. Whoever I was while alive, I must have been interesting. Maybe I was part of the S.W.A.T. team or a ninja.

Glancing over my shoulder at Cole, I said, "I told you I could fight. But no, you wanted to leave it to the boys, right?"

A smile lifted his mouth. "Feel free to prove me wrong again in the future."

I'd have to remember that.

The clatter of the trailer's door opening had us all turning that way.

"Pop!" Sean was on the porch, looking relieved to see us all alive and the Halfling creatures gone. "Jesus Christ, Pop! I can't keep doing this! I'll have a heart attack before I'm thirty."

I held out the shotgun for Wyatt to take. "Let's go back inside, and we can talk this out. Figure out what's going on."

Wyatt's gaze danced between me, Cole, and the gun, as if he were debating which would be the best option. He did nothing else for a long moment, but then, he reached out hesitantly and wrapped his fingers around the barrel.

"I would suggest not trying to shoot me again," I said with a smile, but it fell the moment I realized how intimidating I may have looked. I quickly added, "Let's just go inside before those things come back."

Wyatt nodded, and to my surprise, made no move to reload the gun or shoot us. We all walked up the porch and went back inside. Immediately, Wyatt pointed to the armchair and gave Cole a hard look.

"Sit," he said. "You owe me answers."

Cole threw me a sympathetic look and then stepped over the many boxes and papers to the armchair in front of the desk.

Behind me, Sean locked the door. "Pop, what's going on?"

"Shut it, Sean. It seems our old friend hasn't been completely honest with us all these years."

When Cole tried to shift himself in the ripped chair, his body didn't move. It was as if he were pinned to the seat by an invisible force. A spray-painted circle with obscure symbols marked the carpeting under the chair.

Some kind of magic binding Cole to his spot?

I moved toward him, but his gaze snapped to me in warning.

"It's a demon trap," he explained to me. "Meant to keep demons confined to one place."

No wonder he wanted me to avoid the other spots like the one on the rug. Even though other symbols sprawled across the floor, who knew what they were capable of—what any of these other weird squiggles and loops across all the boarded windows and wallpaper were capable of. Hopefully they were just for protection and nothing painful. Like sending someone straight to a Hell dimension.

"So, it's true. You are one of those...those *things*," Wyatt spit.

Cole shook his head. "I have demon blood in me, yes. But I am not a full-blood. I'm a half—"

"A Halfling," Wyatt finished.

He grunted. "No, I'm not."

"He's still before the full corruption," I said, making Wyatt's furious glare whirl on me. I'm sure Cole didn't need my help with the explanation. I certainly didn't know him any more than these humans did, but I couldn't help myself from wanting to help him a bit.

"Do you have the Hellfire?" Wyatt asked, his hand tightening on the gun. "Is that what I saw before?"

Sean's breath caught, as if he couldn't believe it. "No way, Pop. He's saved our skins too many times. A demon wouldn't. That doesn't make sense."

Cole glanced away, ashamed. "I do have the Hellfire. But I work very hard not to use it."

"Impossible." Wyatt wasn't having it.

"I've lasted this long without going full Halfling minion,

haven't I?" Cole said. "Those creatures outside… They aren't me."

"You'll get corrupted. They always do."

Cole's expression hardened. Determined. "I prefer guns."

Wyatt didn't look convinced. "All your interest in finding Xaver makes sense now."

Cole tried moving again in the chair, seeming uncomfortable.

When all his pulling and tugging didn't work and he was still stuck in place, he sighed heavily. "I need the cure. To save Jade's friend…and myself."

There it was. His motivation for helping me. The truth behind it all.

I didn't know why it hurt to hear, but it did. Maybe I was madder at myself for not seeing it sooner. In hindsight, it was the obvious answer to why he would be going through so much to find Kay a solution.

He didn't want to help Kay. He wanted to help himself.

He was using me.

Fury bubbled up from somewhere deep within. For him and my own stupidity.

Sean's calm voice snapped me back to the present. "We've been through every book and scroll. There is no cure. We've told you this."

"There is one! There has to be," Cole said, his blue eyes wild.

He'd become obsessed. But did I blame him, really? Find a cure or become one of those disgusting shadow creatures? Yeah, I'd pick cure, too.

That didn't excuse him for trying to secretly use me to do it.

"And who is she?" Wyatt snapped, gesturing my way.

I hesitated. Guess it was my turn for the interrogation.

"Another one of your demon pals?"

"Does she look like one? Come on, Wyatt. Don't be an idiot."

"She was in the trailer when I got here. I saw her…" Sean rubbed his shoulder nervously. "She just appeared. Materialized out of thin air. The wards didn't work on her."

Wyatt turned back to Cole. "Was she here the entire time? Why couldn't I see her? Is this a trick?"

I cleared my throat. Nothing like being talked about as if I weren't right here in the room. "Can I explain this part? I mean, it does pertain to me, and I am still here. I'd like to be included in this conversation."

Cole's knitted brows and pinched mouth said he didn't think that was a good idea, but I ignored him.

"My name is Jade Blackwell. At least I think it is anyway." Why did I even say that last bit? I wasn't going to go into the specifics of why I wasn't sure who I was. I would just confuse them even more. After clearing my throat again, I continued, "I'm a reaper. Meaning I'm not alive." Again, no magical celestial censor obscured my words, so I guessed I was still free to talk about the spirit world.

"We have spirit wards written around the house, too. It should have repelled you," Wyatt shot back. "You're lying."

"I don't know why they didn't," I said honestly. "But things are a little more complicated than even that. Things in the spirit world are a bit of a mess. And now, my friend Kay, a Medium, has been more than likely impregnated by this Xaver fellow, and I need to find this cure to save her life. While being attacked by these demon Halflings, I suddenly solidified, and you all can see me. I don't know what that means exactly. It's never happened before."

"Are you alive now?" Sean asked, seeming intrigued.

"I honestly don't know." I held out my still bleeding arm. "That's a good sign, isn't it?"

Wyatt, though, didn't seem convinced. "And you and Cole

are friends?"

"More like working associates I would say." But that title didn't even fit, especially after finding out he'd been using Kay's situation to his benefit. "I was assigned to kill him and help him cross over as part of my job, but it turned out he wasn't even close to dead."

"Sounds like a setup," Wyatt replied.

"Or a mistake."

"Do they make many mistakes in the ghost world?"

"Uh… Not usually."

Wyatt's crinkled face crinkled up even more.

"Like I said, things are a little crazy right now."

"A reaper…" Sean started, rubbing the dark stubble on his chin. "Is that what that emblem means? The one on your upper…"

I glanced down at the tattoo on my upper left breast, over my heart, clearly visible with the simple tank top I wore. I'd always had it—at least for as long as I could remember. It was a symbol, kind of like the ones painted on the trailer walls, but it reminded me more of something out of a classic painting, with swooping curves and elegant swirls. More delicate than the harsh circles and straight lines in, say, the spirit door design. At least I thought so anyway.

I figured it was something I had gotten during my life that had carried over to death. A rebellious teenage act, maybe? Or an invitation into a club? It was pretty—that could be why I had got it too. Just 'cause. I never thought too much about it.

"No. It's just a tattoo," I said.

Sean pressed his lips together into a hard line. "I feel like I've seen this before."

My eyes widened. "What? Really?"

He nodded. "I've seen it before…" He glanced at Wyatt. "Pop? Any ideas?"

Finally, Wyatt put his shotgun down and leaned it against the wall. He walked over to me and looked me over with a scrutinizing eye. I stole a glance at Cole, who shrugged.

After a long, tense moment of this older man staring at my chest, saying nothing, I interjected, "Look familiar to you, too?"

"This part here—the main structure with the stem-like middle with the branches—looks very similar to the symbol for rebirth in the ancient Celilian texts."

"Three hundred BCE texts, or first century CE?" Sean asked.

For someone who hated his father's involvement in the magical, Sean sure knew a lot. I guess after growing up with it around for so long, it wasn't too surprising.

"Three hundred BCE. And they are scrolls, not texts. There is a difference."

Sean snorted. Semantics he obviously didn't care about.

Sean turned back to staring at my chest and studying the tattoo. "I can see what you're saying about the rebirth symbol, but there's something else, though. I've seen this symbol before just like this. As it is. I know I have."

Wyatt squinted as he focused on the tattoo. He hovered his finger over my skin without touching and outlined the more complex part of the tattoo, near the middle. Even though he didn't touch me, I could have sworn my skin tingled around the thing. I shivered, disturbed by the feeling.

"I don't know, Sean," Wyatt said. "I don't think I've seen it before, and I've seen everything."

"What does it matter?" I said, placing my palm over it. I was growing tired of all these men staring at my goods. It was uncomfortable. "I'm sure it was just something I did before I died. Maybe there was a discount off tattoos at the shop I had gone to or something."

"You don't remember?" Sean asked, surprised.

I shook my head. "I don't remember anything from before my death."

Sean hesitated, looking suddenly sad. "Is it like that for everyone that passes?"

Was he thinking of someone in particular? From the sorrow clinging to his gaze, it seemed that way. I knew that look well enough to recognize it. Sean had lost someone he loved dearly.

Hopefully I could reassure him a little.

"No, just me," I replied. "Well, just reapers really. We have our memory stripped. It makes our jobs easier."

Relief washed over his face instantly. "That makes sense." Then he gave me a shy smile. "A reaper, huh? That's probably one of the few supernaturals Pop doesn't have many books on. How would you feel about us picking your brain? I would like to find out more about the afterlife."

"It's not all peaches and cream. Believe me."

"Oh, really?" Concern passed over his expression again.

"Not like that. It's mostly because it's boring." I sighed. "Like when people retire… Things get repetitive. No excitement because there's no challenge. Everything is blissfully mediocre. Most people like it, but me? Not so much. Even with my job, things get monotonous."

"Ah…" Sean rubbed his chin again. "I'd love to hear more. Maybe we—"

"I hate to interrupt," Cole threw in. "But if Jade's friend is really pregnant by Xaver, then we are on a deadline, and I'm still stuck in this trap. Can someone let me out of this thing, please?"

Wyatt and Sean exchanged looks. They didn't know if they could trust him, and honestly, I wasn't sure either. I'd only known the guy for a day, and I was finding out more things every minute. I couldn't even vouch for him.

"Guys, it's me. I've known you for years," Cole said,

seeming to grow desperate. "Come on, Jade. Back me up here."

I shrugged. "I think you're handling it well enough."

His gaze narrowed on me. "Okay, I get it. You're mad at me, too. I deserve that."

Damn skippy.

"I owe you an explanation, too—"

"Wait…" Sean said suddenly, his eyes widening with recognition. "I know where I've seen your tattoo before!" He rushed out of the room in the next second, leaving us all in stunned silence.

Wyatt went to the hallway and shouted after him, "What are you doing? You know not to go in there! Sean! Not your mother's room!"

Mother's room. So, Wyatt was married. I couldn't imagine any woman who would be okay living in this clutter and dust, but there was someone for everyone, wasn't there? A lid for every pot? And Wyatt was a special pot of strange.

Then came my next question—where was Sean's mother? She must have been out for the day if she hadn't come out during the Halfling attack. That was lucky.

There was a bang, like a drawer closing too hard, and then Sean emerged again, pushing past his father with a small box in hand, maybe the size of a shoebox. It was difficult to see what it was made of—wood? It was too old and dirty to tell, caked in dried mud or sap or something else disgusting.

"Here." Sean gasped, almost tripping over a pile of boxes as he barreled back into the living room. "Here. This is it."

"Sean…" Wyatt warned. "What is that?"

Sean thrust the box at me. "See? There. There it is. It's the same symbol."

I peered down at the box, and my heart dropped into the pit of my stomach. He was right. On the top of the crusty-looking box was the same design as my tattoo etched into the wood roughly.

"W-What is this?" I asked, my voice trembling. My chest was suddenly so tight, breathing hurt. It was the first time I'd seen anything resembling my tattoo, and here it was, the very thing that could give me some hint to who I was.

A quick glance at Wyatt's weighted expression revealed two things: he didn't like that his son had ruffled through his mother's things, and he had completely forgotten about this box.

"We don't know exactly." Sean shot up as he tried to rein in his excitement. "It's something my mother found during her travels. She was a self-made anthropologist of sorts."

"That's a nice way to put it. She would have liked that one," Wyatt said with a sad smile.

Oh. So she was dead.

Sean's interest in the afterlife was because he had lost his mother.

"We never could get this thing open." Sean dug his fingers into the dip along the edge and pulled to show me he wasn't lying. It didn't budge. "We don't want to destroy it, either, because it's a piece of history, you know? That's what Ma always said, anyway. Out of everything she'd collected, it was her favorite piece."

He smiled, but it was a heavy one, full of unexpressed pain and grief. "It's definitely the same symbol though."

"Yeah, it is." I reached out and ran my finger over the dirty cover along the rough edges of the design.

From within the box, there was a loud pop. It startled Sean enough that he let go of the box, but I was quick enough to snatch it as it fell. The moment my palm connected with it, there was a flash of white light, and the lid sprung open, as if whatever was inside couldn't be contained any longer.

As if it had been meant just for me.

CHAPTER

TWELVE

I t was my turn to almost drop the box. I fumbled with it for a few seconds, trying to hold on, and as I did, something fell out and flopped onto the floor.

I bent down and picked it up. It was rough and dry between my fingers, but almost as thin as a piece of paper.

Turning it over, I noticed the strange cluster of symbols painted onto one side. Maybe not painted, exactly. The ink appeared to have sunk deeper into the paper. But wait—what were those? Wrinkles? Hairs?

My breath caught. This wasn't paper. It was skin. Either human or animal skin.

I dropped it again, my stomach coiling in disgust.

Sean was quick to scoop it back up. "What is it?" he asked and flipped it over to the written side.

"Skin," I choked out, wondering who in the world would use someone's skin as a writing implement. Even as old as it seemed to me, wouldn't wood or leaves be efficient enough?

His lip turned up in repulsion, too, but he didn't half-throw the thing like I had. Just examined it further.

"These symbols seemed to be tattooed also. And look, there's yours at the top."

He pointed at the one matching the mark on my chest, and I stared at it in disbelief.

That was weird.

"Let me get a look at it." Cole continued to struggle against the magical restraints of the demon trap on the armchair.

"You shut up," Wyatt barked at him.

Cole let out an aggravated sigh. "Come on, Wyatt. You know me. You've known me for years."

"That's what makes this feel more like a betrayal," Wyatt snapped.

"Pop," Sean began, more calmly. "If he wanted to kill us, he's could have done it many, many times."

Cole smiled. "He's right. I could have."

I rolled my eyes. From the anger still on Wyatt's face, it was clear Cole wasn't making his situation any better for himself.

"I don't like the demon part of me. I want to get rid of it. You know I've been trying to find Xaver forever."

"What is that saying? 'The enemy of my enemy is my friend'?" Sean said.

Wyatt's eyes narrowed—an old man stuck in his ways.

As much as I didn't trust Cole, I couldn't deny that I was going to need his help to get Kay's cure. Especially if that meant confronting Xaver or more Halflings again. My weird magic light fingers had saved us before, but now that I was bleeding and breathing, things were more complicated. Those blessed bullets and guns would come in handy. He wanted my help for some reason, and I needed his.

Guess we were stuck together.

"If it makes you feel better, you can hold your gun," I suggested to Wyatt. "If he tries anything, I won't stop you from blowing his head off."

For the first time, Wyatt's lips split in a grin. His teeth weren't the straightest and they were tinged yellow from decades of what looked like a bad smoking habit, but it was nice to see him get some joy out of something. Even if it was the thought of murdering Cole if he turned on him.

Without hesitation, he snatched his shotgun, walked over to the armchair, and scuffed the demon trap markings on the carpet just enough to break the magic. Before Cole could even rise to his feet, Wyatt had his gun cocked and aimed at Cole's noggin.

I didn't know why exactly, but I admired this old man's gritty spirit and toughness.

He took no shit. From anyone. And I liked that about him.

Ignoring Wyatt's gun and threatening glare, Cole strode over to us and reached out for the piece of skin. Hesitantly, Sean handed it over.

"Do you recognize any of these marks?" Cole asked, holding it up for Wyatt to see with ginger hands. His eyes were wide with excitement, as if we had just stumbled across an ancient map leading to El Dorado and its treasure. "I've never seen them before."

Wyatt lowered the barrel a smidge. "Again, they seem similar to the language in the Celilian scrolls, but not enough for me to decipher any of it. At least not now. Maybe if I studied it, I could come up with a general idea."

"And how long would that take?" asked Cole.

"Two weeks maybe? If I worked all night and day and ran off nothing but that beer you owe me and Red Bulls."

"Two weeks!"

"Hey, I have all these books to reference." He swept a hand toward the mess of papers, boxes, and shelves cluttering his living room. "And I don't know if you've noticed, but I'm not exactly a spring chicken anymore."

"You have Sean to help."

"Oh no." Sean shook his head frantically. "I'm not getting mixed up in this mess. I've sworn off the supernatural. It only leads to trouble, and me getting hurt. My ankle still isn't the same from the last problem you dropped at our front door."

Cole's grin widened.

"Besides," Sean went on, "I'm trying to get Pop out of this stuff. He needs to retire."

Wyatt snorted at that. "I'll retire when I'm dead."

Knowing a good deal about the afterlife and what kind of person Wyatt was, I severely doubted death would be enough to stop him from getting involved in supernatural business.

"Can I see that again?" I asked, taking the piece of skin before Cole could even answer. I pushed down the bile rising in my throat at the weird feeling of dried, mummified skin against my palm. Even though most of the color had faded to gray, there was still a pinkish hue to it in some places. God, I hoped this was from some kind of animal, like a pig, and not from a human. Either way, please let the poor soul to have been dead before having his skin ripped off and written on.

My throat burned as more stomach acid clawed to the surface.

I had to suck it up. There was something going on with this box, something about me. Not only did it have the same marking on it as my tattoo, but Sean had said it had been sealed up for decades and then it had popped open just for me? That was more than just a coincidence.

Scanning over the strange, branded symbols, a twinge of recognition hummed through me. But this was my first time seeing these scribbles. Wasn't it? The more I stared at the symbols, the more my temples pounded. I tried to search my memory for any recollection of the box and came up empty, except for the painful pinching behind my eyes.

The longer I stared, the greater the pain got. Digging deeper and deeper into the pit where my memories were once stored was excruciating, but just as I was about to give up, the shapes readjusted and moved to form words—words I understood.

I could read it.

"It's a list," I thought aloud, amazed that I had even known that much information. "It's a list!"

Cole's face lit up with excitement. "A list of what?"

I kept staring at the symbols. The words sprang up from my darkened memory, like little balls of floating lights, guiding the way into my past. Giddy at the find, I almost squealed with joy. "Something about the four elements being needed…to save a damned soul? Does that make sense to anyone?"

"Holy shit." Cole balked. "Could this be it?"

"Let's not get ahead of ourselves," Sean said, his voice calm and collected.

I glanced between the men. "What? Did I miss something?"

"Cole thinks this is the cure he's been looking for."

"You're shitting me." Finally, Wyatt lowered his gun. The faster he spoke, the more his southern accent came out. "You're telling me the demon cure was sittin' in my wife's bedroom all these years? Just sittin' there, underneath her socks and T-shirts? In this house? It's not supposed to exist."

"It would explain why so many things have been trying to

get into this trailer," said Sean. "It could be something they've wanted."

"Not because of the other thousands of spells and enchanted talismans I have stored away in here?" Wyatt replied.

"That, too. It certainly doesn't help your case any," Cole said.

"And this is why I want you to retire." Sean threw his father a hard look. "Normal families don't go through this kind of shit. Other families worry about who's bringing what to Thanksgiving dinner, not when's the next time an all-powerful demon will be blasting through their door."

Wyatt waved the comment away. "Those families are boring as sin. The people in them don't even want to be part of them."

"But boring is safe."

Boy, was Sean wrong. I could tell him that from experience. I mean, look at what I was involved in now. My boring afterlife led me here, and none of this was safe. It could be fate or just bad luck, but this kind of stuff sought you out.

"So what does the list say? What do we need?" Cole was so close to me now, his warm breath tickled the side of my neck and shoulder. His shaking fingers hovered over the skin in my hands, as if he were about to snatch it any second and run off with it.

"Uh…" Scanning the list again, my focus readjusted, and the symbols changed to actual words I knew. "The Holiest ground. Breath of life. Hell's fire. And damned blood. Whatever that means."

"The elements," Sean said. "The ingredients are based on the four elements. Earth, wind, fire, and water."

"Water? Did I miss something there?" Cole asked.

"The blood," I replied with an eye roll.

"My blood?"

"Or Kay's. I guess."

"Well, that's easy enough. At least we have one item on the list right off the bat."

Something told me it couldn't be *that* easy.

I passed the piece of skin back to Sean. "The Holiest ground…like a church or graveyard?"

"That would make sense," he answered. "I can't believe you can read this. I've never seen this language before."

Wyatt stroked his white beard in thought. "Yeah, not this exact language."

"I have no idea how I can." I was just one big ball of mystery, wasn't I?

There were other things scribbled in the corners of the list, but before I got a good look at them, Cole snatched it from Sean's grip.

"So Holiest ground…" Cole repeated. "I know plenty of cemeteries and churches. There has to be fifty in this town alone. We can just scoop up some dirt—"

"But it says 'The Holiest of grounds,'" I cut in. "How do we know one of those are the Holiest of grounds?"

"She's right. It can't just be any cemetery dirt," Sean added.

"Well, what makes a cemetery 'Holy'?" Cole asked.

"A few things," Wyatt chimed in. "Being blessed by a man of the church, prayer, Holy Water… All religions have their things, but the principle is always the same."

"You'd think the Holiest ground would be one of the oldest, too, right? The one blessed the most or the longest," I said.

"That's true. The age certainly wouldn't hurt."

"Old-ass cemetery. Okay, still easy." Cole ran his shaky fingers through his hair. "Two out of four."

"I'm not sure that'll be it." Sean glanced back down at the writing.

The more I thought about it, the more I knew Sean was right. It couldn't be that easy. This was supposed to be the cure to a demon's cursed blood. If it were that easy, Halflings wouldn't be such a problem, now would they?

Think, Jade. You live in the afterlife and work for the Angel of Death. You should know something about this.

Maybe my tablet had something to help me out here? As I reached for my tablet in my back pocket, I paused, remembering the piece of chalk in the front of my jeans—the piece of chalk that allowed me to hop between the living and nonliving world. I pulled it out, an idea forming. Wouldn't the Holiest of times or places be when the dead and the living collide? When one could cross into the other freely? Like when the veil was at its thinnest?

"The solstice." The words burst from my lips as the realization hit. "Maybe the blessed earth needs to be collected during the solstice, when all worlds are aligned and demons, spirits, whatever can cross over?"

Cole's eyes widened. "She's right. That would be considered the Holiest of nights."

Sean and Wyatt exchanged looks and then nodded.

"It is when all supernaturals are at their magical peak, too. It makes sense," Wyatt said.

Cole sighed, seeming annoyed. "So old cemetery, on the solstice…"

"We've got a few days till then," I said.

"What are the oldest towns in this state?" Cole whipped out his cell phone and began tapping on the screen. "Fairport's harbor was used during the Revolutionary War to bring in supplies and for trade even before that. It has to have one of the oldest cemeteries in the country there."

I wasn't surprised. Fairport was full of history. It was one of the reasons why I loved it so much.

"Looks like we're off to Fairport, then," Cole said. "And while we're there, do you think you guys can figure out what the other two ingredients are? That way we can track them down as soon as possible and test this thing."

Wyatt gave Cole a hard look, likely not impressed by his pushiness.

"Please," I made sure to add, and tacked on a sweet smile for good measure. "My friend needs this to save her life. I know she doesn't have much time, and honestly, I don't know if she will last the full three months. I need to get this to her as soon as possible."

Not to mention this was the first real clue I had to my life. I needed to know how I was connected to this demon cure and what the symbol on my chest actually meant.

Wyatt's cold gaze flickered between me and Cole. After a long moment, he said, "Obviously my wife was interested in this for a reason...and I am curious about it." He snorted, seeming to convince himself. "Fine. I'll do it. But on two conditions."

"A-Anything," Cole sputtered, grinning.

Wyatt locked eyes with him and jabbed his finger at Cole, like a father scolding his disobedient child. "No more secrets, for one."

Cole held up his hands. "Done."

"And that beer." Wyatt's voice became even more serious. "The expensive kind I told you about, remember? Lots of it."

Cole's head fell back as his laughter exploded. "You got it, you arrogant bastard."

CHAPTER

THIRTEEN

"I feel like I should apologize or something for not warning you more," Cole said as he swung the beat-up Jeep onto the main highway back toward Fairport. After being in the middle of the Halfling fight, the clunker was vibrating and whining suspiciously the faster he accelerated. I gripped the door handle, thankful I was able to touch things in the living world now instead of being tossed around like before. Even though I hadn't eaten an actual meal in over a year, I could feel something roiling in my stomach, threatening to come back up.

"Wyatt is an…interesting character," he added. "But he knows his shit. So does Sean, as much as he tries to keep out of it."

I swallowed hard, forcing whatever was fighting to creep up back down. "I don't need an apology for him. I liked Wyatt. He's a tough cookie, and I can respect that."

"Then why do you look like you're mad at me for some reason?"

"Resting bitch face syndrome?"

He snorted a laugh. "Is that really a thing?"

"I have been told I have an extreme case by others. I'm not the friendliest-looking person apparently, and I don't mind it."

"I thought that was just part of your badass reaper façade," he said, and that sly smile of his returned.

Heat rose to my cheeks, and I looked away, scolding myself for such a schoolgirl reaction.

We sped past cars and some angry-looking drivers. One even flipped me the bird.

"I will admit I was a little pissed when I found out you were using me and my friend Kay's predicament for yourself."

"Ah, so that's it." He rubbed his chin. "I knew there was something bothering you."

I shook my head. "It doesn't matter though. We both want the same thing. We will help each other get the things on the list for this cure and that's it. Then we'll go our separate ways."

"What about you and this new 'being alive' thing?" he asked.

"Not sure." And I really didn't know what was going on with me or even how long it would last. "Who knows if this is all temporary."

"Maybe this is you leveling up as a reaper or something. Special powers?"

I hadn't thought about that. But the idea bubble was quickly popped when I realized no one else working for Styx Corp had magical glowy fingers or could hop between dead and alive. Not even Simon, and he was Azrael's shining star.

No, this was all new. And strange.

Of course it was happening to me.

"I don't think so," I said quickly. "Nothing special. It's just my luck."

I sighed, and Cole slid me a sideways glance. "Why don't we pick up some food? Breakfast?"

Had I heard him right?

"Sausage, eggs, toast? Coffee?" he said, making sure I understood what he meant. "We have a few days before the solstice. Until then, we can work on the other parts of the cure on our end, get some sleep, and maybe visit your friend and make sure she's okay."

My stomach made the strangest sound at the mention of food, like a raptor waking from a long slumber. Cole's brows arched.

Before heated embarrassment could crawl up my neck, I shrugged it off. "It's been a while since I've eaten actual food."

To my surprise, he laughed. "I could have guessed. How long?"

"A year."

His eyes widened. "A year without coffee?" He snorted. "I wouldn't have survived."

"Food isn't necessary when you're dead," I reminded him. "We have a few restaurants and bars in the afterlife, but it's not the same. There's no need to eat or drink. It's more of a social thing."

"Hmm... I don't know how I feel about that. I love my breakfast foods. Can eat it any time of day."

"I suggest you don't die, then," I said.

"Easier said than done."

"Since you were on my assignment list for reaping, I would say so."

He laughed again, smacking the steering wheel with each wheezy breath in. "You got me there."

After a moment, he said, "So...breakfast? I know a pretty decent place downtown. It's pretty hipster-y with its clientele, but if you can get past all the college kids and teens, the food is tasty. Portion sizes are huge, too."

I was shaking my head no, but my stomach made another animalistic sound. "I was thinking about going back and seeing if there's been any word there about what's going on." Which reminded me about my tablet. I pulled it out and tapped the dark screen. Still no notifications from Azrael or Styx or even Simon. Nothing. Not even an update to my reaping list. Cole Masters was the last name for my assignments and the only one without a little check mark next to it. I wasn't sure how I was going to explain that one, but I'd figure it out once this entire thing with Kay was fixed. Just another thing for me to worry about later.

The weight of all my unanswered questions pushed against my shoulders. Things must still have been crazy at Styx Corp, and with no updates from Simon, the itch to return back to Styx and see what was up was overwhelming. I was completely cut off on this side of the portal. It was unnerving.

After clicking the screen off again, I slid the tablet in my back pocket.

"You're going to go back?" Cole asked, glancing at me. "Are you sure that's a good idea?"

Why would he care if I went back or not?

"I feel out of the loop. Maybe I can find out some more information about all these demon attacks and influx of haunts before the solstice. Maybe someone knows something about the box we found and the demon cure, too."

His lips pressed into a hard line.

"What?" I asked.

"What if you can't get back? You said it yourself you were breaking all kinds of rules by not reaping me and by being involved with the living like this. What if you get reprimanded or something and aren't allowed to come back?"

He had a point. I hadn't thought about that.

I guess I had been lucky Azrael hadn't tried to contact me through the tablet. If he got ahold of me and didn't like what I had been doing over on this side of the veil, worst case scenario was I could be Released. Then there was no coming back at all.

Cole was right. I couldn't risk it. Without the cure, Kay was as good as dead, and I couldn't do that to her. I had to stay in the living world, at least until Kay was safe. Then I could receive any consequences Azrael wanted to dish out to me. *If* and *when* he came back.

"I guess I'll stay, then," I said but then quickly added, "for now."

He grinned. "Breakfast it is, then!"

The diner was located in a small, refurbished church, with tall, stained glass windows, pew booths, and a service counter where the altar would have been. As Cole had said, the place was crawling with young people. Only a few older patrons sat at the counter, chatting happily with the waitstaff there, but for the most part, the clientele were twenty-one years old at most.

It made me feel really old.

We sat in a booth by one of the stained glass windows. The light streaming in painted the table and wooden floor in beautiful patterns of ruby and violet. I couldn't stop staring at the high ceilings, gold pillars, and angelic sculptures decorating the space.

A half-demon and a chaser of death in an old church? The irony.

"Jade." Cole's voice snapped me back to the present. He stared at me over his menu. When I looked up, I noticed a young woman—our waitress, I assumed—waiting patiently with a pen and notepad in her hand.

"Do you know what you want?" he asked.

"Oh." Truth be told, I hadn't even picked up the plastic-covered menu. Hadn't even glanced at it. Frazzled, I just said, "I'll have whatever he's having."

"Are you sure about that? It's a lot of food," Cole said.

"Yeah, what the hell." I handed the waitress my menu. "You bragged enough about this place. Might as well."

"Thanks, Jill." Cole winked at the girl as he handed her his menu.

She smiled before walking away.

I rolled my eyes. "You come here that much, huh?"

"More than an assassin probably should."

The way he said it—so nonchalantly and no worry of being overheard by others—made my hair stand up on my arms.

He laughed. "We aren't known for staying in one place for too long, if you can imagine, but there's just something about Fairport that always brings me back. I'm not sure why."

I could relate to that. I loved this unexciting city. Not quite sure why, either.

Glancing around the diner again, I lowered my voice, unlike him. "Aren't you not supposed to be in here? A demon in a church? Why aren't you bursting into flames?"

"That's a myth." He waved the comment off. "Although, I've never seen a fully corrupted Halfling or a full-blooded demon in one, so I'm not sure how it works for them." After a second, he added, "Although, I probably should say that I don't visit many churches either. Besides this one, of course. So, who knows."

I sputtered a laugh.

"What?" he said, smiling. "The idea of me burning to death a funny thought to you?"

I shrugged. "Maybe."

"Ouch. And here I thought we were beginning to be friends."

I paused, unsure how to respond. I wasn't sure why, but the word 'friends' threw me for a loop. Maybe it was because the one friendship I had ended up in this mess. Not that I blamed myself for Kay's attack, but I did feel like I could have done more to protect her from it.

Besides, Cole didn't strike me as friendship material. More like "I'll use you until I don't need you anymore" type of person, and that was just from knowing him for a day. My assumptions could just be because of prejudices from his career choice, or even his bloodline. Or it could just be my gut telling me to beware. All were very possible.

"Speaking of friends…" he began slowly, calculating, as if he had set himself up this question all along. "I've been wondering why you're doing all this for the Medium girl? This doesn't have to do with you or the afterlife, really. So why get involved?"

I eyed him suspiciously. "As you said, she's my friend."

"Well, yeah, I got that, but I have friends I wouldn't die for."

"And I'm sure you have some you would."

"She's one of those, huh?"

I nodded.

He leaned back in the booth and crossed his arms, waiting for me to continue.

I sighed. "She was the first friend I made after my death. Even though interacting with the living is forbidden, and I couldn't really explain to her what I was because of the… *rules*, but we clicked somehow. And when I was going through some real hard shit with my mind-wipe and not

153

knowing who I was in the beginning, she was there. She's always been there."

It was true. All of it. I had my fair share of breakdowns at the beginning of my reaper job. It had been hard for me to accept what had happened to me and what had been taken away, but having Kay to talk to had always been the lifeline I needed to keep me sane—that one thread, one remaining connection, I had to the living world. And I wasn't ready to give that up yet. I wasn't sure I'd ever be ready.

"She's too nice for her own good, you know what I mean?" I said. Sometimes I even felt like I didn't deserve her company.

"Oh yeah. I got that from her, too."

"But in a good way," I made sure to add. "You don't find people like that every day."

"I know what you mean."

"We ended up making sort of an arrangement," I said. "I help her get rid of any harassing haunts, and she helps me search for who I was when alive."

"Why do you care so much about your life? That part is over with obviously. Might as well move on."

Wow, he sounded a bit like Simon there for a second. He at least wouldn't have been so blunt with his wording, but the idea was still the same.

I glanced out the stained glass window, the tinted glass painted the street and sidewalks outside in beautiful shades of color.

"Sorry, did I hit on something I wasn't supposed to?" Cole asked with genuine concern in his tone. "I didn't mean—"

"No, no, you're fine." I rubbed my lips together, searching for the right answer to his question. "Honestly? I don't know why I care so much... I want to move on. I do. It would make things so much easier for me, but I just *can't*."

The need to know who I really was before my death was

like a constant ache in my chest I couldn't shake. It was difficult to explain—even to myself sometimes—but without knowing, I couldn't be whole.

I couldn't be *me.*

"Hey, I get it," Cole said after a long moment. "We all have our things. If anyone can understand chasing a seemingly impossible dream, it's me."

I traced the tabletop's line pattern with my fingertip to avoid his gaze. "Yeah, guess so."

We remained quiet until the food came. I was shocked by the heap of pancakes, sausage, and scrambled eggs on my plate. Cole didn't even flinch. He started shoveling the food down the moment the plate touched the table. I, on the other hand, didn't know where to begin. It'd been so long since I'd touched real food, but the smell of smoky pork and buttery pancakes was enough to make my stomach growl loudly. *I might not be ready to eat real food, but my insides were saying something completely different.*

I cut into a sausage link first and put a small chunk into my mouth. A rainbow of flavors exploded on my tongue, causing a flickering in my memory with every bite. Ravenous hunger hit me like a blow. I cut another piece and shoved it in my mouth before even swallowing the first. Again, that same tingle of familiarity signaled in my brain, still too far away to place but close enough to make me want more.

Another delicious bite, another dip into the past.

"Woah there. Slow down," Cole said. "You're going to choke if you keep that up."

He pushed the mug of black coffee toward me. "Why don't you drink something to wash that down?"

After taking the cup, I chugged a big gulp of the burning, bitter liquid so fast, it scalded the back of my throat. I coughed, spitting some of it back up.

Cole handed me a napkin, and I took it and wiped up my shame.

"I probably should have mentioned it would be hot," he said sheepishly. "Maybe you should try some cream and sugar, too." He pushed the cream container and some sugar packets toward me.

I smiled, even though my cheeks were burning from embarrassment. "Thanks."

"I told you the food was good here."

The way he was staring at me, with his small side smile and his blue eyes sparkling as they searched my face, made my breath catch. Sure, I'd been hit on by my fair share of scumbags. Even in the afterlife, guys will try anything to get in your bed, and I'm ashamed to admit that it worked for some. But none of them ever looked at me the way Cole was looking at me now—like I was some prize he couldn't wait to win. A goal, a challenge, something he had wanted to claim for a long time, and now that it was sitting in front of him, he'd do anything to get it. It made a shiver race down my spine.

The familiar *blurrrinngg* of a cell phone sounded. Cole whipped his out of his pocket and answered before it could ring again. "Sean, what's up? Did you find out anything?"

I couldn't hear Sean on the other end, but from the pleased look on Cole's face, Sean was telling him things he wanted to hear.

He waved his hand to the passing waitress, Jill, and mimicked writing with a pen. She handed him the one from her apron pocket with a flirtatious smile, but he snatched it and began scribbling on a napkin without even noticing. She scowled and walked away.

"How confident are you that this is it?" Cole said to Sean. There was a moment's silence. "That's good enough for me."

More words from Sean that I couldn't hear, but I was

assuming it had something to do with the things we were going to find. Wyatt and Sean must have found something else out during their research.

"Do you think Marla's still open?" Cole's lip turned up in disgust at her name. Another "friend" of his, I was guessing.

"No, no, don't call her. I don't want her to know I'm coming. She'll never let me in."

But then he glanced up at me, and a slow, calculated grin lifted his lips. I could see the devious idea as it was forming in his mind.

"But…" he drawled, "she doesn't know Jade."

Oh no. What was he getting me into now?

Eyes glittering with the same mischief and determination as before, he hung up the phone.

My stomach flipped with uneasiness. Right then, I decided that I didn't like that look after all.

Not in the slightest.

CHAPTER

FOURTEEN

"What was that all about?" I asked, my nerves showing themselves in my shaky tone.

Cole was all grin. "Wyatt and Sean were able to find another object on the list. The air element. It's a rare herb, almost extinct nowadays, with some kind of complicated name that translates into the Breath of Life. Seems easy enough."

"Go on," I pushed him, knowing there was more to the story that he wasn't telling me.

At least he lowered his voice this time. We didn't need the mess that would follow if a human overheard. "There is a magic oddities shop here downtown run by a witch named Marla."

"Another friend of yours?" I mixed a sugar packet into my coffee and added a little of the cream. After a quick stir, I took another big gulp. Much better.

"Not even a little. She hates me."

Hmm. I wondered why.

"The name of the shop is Divine Magic," he said. "Have you ever been there?"

I shook my head, but remembered the little corner store a few streets over from Kay's. "I've passed it many times, but I've never had any assignments there. The windows are always covered, like it's closed. I don't think I've ever seen people going in or out of there."

"Since it's close to the solstice, she may be doing appointments only. It's her busy season for the magical folk. The front of the shop is a front for tourists mostly. Candles, incense, fake relics, and earth stones. A wannabe's dream. But for the real sorcerers and witches, the powerful and rare stuff is in the back under lock and key, and that stuff can get nasty."

"And you think she carries this herb we need," I added.

"If anyone has it in this state, it's Marla. People travel from all around to visit her shop. She's made quite a living for herself."

"And that's where I come in I'm guessing? If she hates you, I have to be the one to get the herb."

He leaned back in his chair and crossed his arms. "You're quick."

I shrugged. "It's common sense. She hates you, so that leaves me." I took another bite of my food. I couldn't help but notice that Cole hadn't touched his since his phone call. Too preoccupied now? "Do you have money for this herb? It must be expensive if it's so rare—*if* she even has it, that is."

His right eyebrow arched. "Oh, don't worry about that. We won't be paying."

"Stealing?" My voice rose, and I quickly dropped it when a couple nearby glanced our way. "You want me to steal this thing? Are you out of your mind?"

"If I know Marla, she's not going to just hand it over willingly."

"What if we pay for it?" I asked.

"How much money do you have in your bank accounts?" When I didn't respond, only blinked at him dumbfounded, he said smugly, "That's what I thought."

"Hey now. I've only been breathing again for a couple of hours. What's your excuse? Does the mercenary business not pay well these days?"

He crossed his arms and met my stare head-on. "It pays. But I haven't been taking cases for a few months."

"Nobody to kill?"

His expression was unamused. "I've been busy chasing down Xaver. Took up a lot of my time." He shook his head and sighed. "Look, it doesn't matter. Even if I had been keeping up with my current clientele, Marla would claim this powerful herb is priceless. I'd be in debt for my entire life. Maybe not just money-wise. Marla also collects favors, and that's something you just don't want to get involved in."

"So stealing it is our only option, you're saying," I replied.

"Unless you want to sell your soul to the she-devil," he said.

My soul was already sold to Styx Corp, pretty much, by no doing of my own. If I ever could get out of my job without being Released—some kind of cosmic loophole I had no idea about—I definitely didn't want to be in debt to anyone ever again.

My shoulders slumped. "Stealing it is, I guess."

"Good. I'm glad you're on board." He reached into his pants pocket and pulled out a wad of money as big as my fist. As he thumbed through the bills, I noticed they were all hundreds. He slapped one on the table and stood. "Come on. Let's go."

A hundred dollars for a twenty-dollar breakfast, at most? When I raised my brows, he smiled broadly.

"What?" He laughed. "Just because it's been a slow couple of months doesn't mean I don't still have a good savings."

Cole parked his beat-up Jeep a few streets away from the Divine Magic shop. It made a terrible puttering sound when he threw it in park. I was about to say something about putting that hefty pocket change of his into something useful, like fixing up his car, but I held back. It took a lot out of me to keep my mouth shut, but I did it. Go me.

On the way over to the shop, we discussed the plan. I was to go inside, act like a tourist, and browse. I had to somehow get behind the counter to the back room without Marla seeing me and grab the herb. That part would have to be all me, and I was going to have to be creative. Marla would know I wasn't a witch like her right away since all magic wielders can sense the magic in each other, and I was bone dry in that department. So I couldn't just ask her about the herb outright. She'd know I was up to something.

I was going to have to be clever.

And of course, Cole would be sitting pretty in the getaway car, waiting for me to come out. Lucky bastard.

The storefront was smaller than Kay's with a single curtained-off window and door. Anyone could miss it walking by if they hadn't been looking for it. As I walked up to the entrance, I was surprised to see the sign hanging from the door turned to *Sorry, We're Closed*.

Now what?

But before I could turn around, movement in the shop behind the sign caught my eye. A short woman with a housewife-type bob and friendly smile opened the door to me. She was a full foot shorter than me and looked more like the president of the PTA with her ruffled pink blouse, jeans, and matching costume jewelry than a powerful level three witch. I don't know what I had expected Marla to look like… Maybe a Hansel and Gretel type hag? Definitely older than the woman in front of me now. She couldn't be any older than forty. Thirty-five if I was feeling nice.

"Hello!" she chirped with a board, straight smile. "You must be my ten o'clock."

My eyes widened. I still had to get used to this whole people-being-able-to-see-me thing.

My first instinct was to say no, but I swallowed it. I needed a way to get in, and this was it. An appointment.

I nodded.

"Come in! Come in!" She ushered me inside, like an old friend welcoming me into her home for tea. "I have your order all ready for you."

An overwhelming cloud of different scents hung in the shop, coming from the variety of perfumed incenses and displayed candles for sale. The smells were so powerful, the inside of my nostrils burned with every breath in. On tables and shelves, there were neat displays of colored stones claiming to bring good luck and fortune, crocheted scarves and purses, and different types of handmade metal jewelry. Even a designated section full of flavored teas to help with everything you could think of—from curing a hangover, to making one's hair grow, to even helping with fertility or erectile dysfunction—sat by the front table and register.

The shop screamed tourist attraction, catering to humans with an innocent interest in Wicca or pagan-based religions. The fact that Divine Magic was actually run by the most powerful type of witch around who sold dangerous and actual magical relics and trinkets to the highest bidder in some kind of magical black market was completely hidden behind this frou-frou façade.

It was a clever cover-up. I'd give her that.

Marla walked behind the counter, but before she could step behind the glittery curtain, where I assumed the real magical items were stored, she gave me a pageant-like smile. "I assume Mr. Johnson will be transferring my payment directly, like usual?"

That took me aback a little, but I kept my surprise off my face. Mr. Johnson had to be an alias, right? Like John Smith or Jane Doe. The name seemed too generic for the circumstance.

If I were in the dealings of stolen magical artifacts, I wouldn't use my real name either. It was easier to fly under the radar that way. So whoever this Mr. Johnson was, he had obviously had many transactions before with Marla by the way she spoke about him. If Marla assumed I was one of his associates meant to pick up, I had to play the part. But at the same time, not say too much to reveal myself as an impostor.

I had to be cool and collected, yet find a way to get on the other side of that curtain without getting my ass blasted by an energy bolt or whatever other spells this witch had up her cardigan's sleeves.

"He has everything handled." I made sure to say it firmly, like I knew what I was talking about. Truly, Mr. Johnson could have been a little old man in need of some medical herbs for his dying wife and paid in pesos. There was no way for me to know really, and I wasn't planning on sticking around long to find out what Mr. Johnson's dealings were really about anyway.

Marla's grin widened, seeming happy with that answer.

As she stepped into the back room, I got a glimpse of what lay beyond. A closet-sized space with about half a dozen shelves, all congested with different jars, challises, and rolled-up scrolls. Some dried plants hung from the ceiling, and for a moment I wondered if one of them could be the

Breath of Life herb I was looking for, but would someone really store something so rare and desirable out in the open like that? Not if they were smart, and Marla—although far from a stereotypical witch—didn't strike me as stupid. Especially if she had survived in this business this long.

Nothing else in the small back room appeared spectacular or alarmingly dangerous. The items stored in there didn't even seem hard to get to if I wanted them, to be honest. It was all pretty lackluster, like Marla herself. Unexpected. Innocent.

Deceiving.

That had to be it. It had to be staged. Or maybe even an enchantment to make it appear ordinary to deter robbers. It was very possible the room was booby-trapped, too. If Marla was really a level three witch, like Cole claimed, I wouldn't be surprised if she had pulled out all the stops to protect her hoard.

As I crept around the corner, a tingle of magic caressed my skin. It froze me dead in my tracks. I wasn't a witch by any means, so if I was able to detect magic at all, it meant Marla had laid out some powerful stuff to protect her precious back room. Just as I'd predicted.

So that meant strolling in there and taking Marla off guard enough to knock her out, or grab what I needed and run. Neither was the wisest of plans. But hell, I had known that the moment Cole had thought of it back in the Jeep. Outsmart and out-magic a level three? I should have known better.

"I'll be right there!" Marla's voice echoed from somewhere beyond the curtain. Even though the room had appeared small, she sounded farther away, only confirming my suspicions of magic being involved.

I hurried back to the safe side of the counter. Had I triggered some kind of invisible trip wire to warn her I was close? Probably. It was time to abort mission and regroup. I needed to get out of here before raising too much suspicion and let Cole know this wasn't going to be as easy as he assumed it would be.

Turning around, I noticed two large shadows moving on the other side of the shop's door.

My breath caught. Mr. Johnson's actual associates? Oh shit. I was about to be found out.

Just as the door opened and the bell rang to signal a customer, Marla's trill came from behind me, making me jump.

"Oh! I'm sorry, but we're closed today for appointments only." Nothing in her tone indicated fear or even the slightest bit of concern—the confidence in her abilities coming through. "We will be open at regular time on Saturday, if you boys would like to come back."

Boys? The two men filling the doorframe as they took turns stepping into the shop had definitely passed puberty decades ago. Even though they were dressed in black suits, their sizes and muscular builds were obvious. Very intimidating and here for a reason.

These had to be Mr. Johnson's real friends, but Marla didn't seem to think so. She didn't even blink when they ignored her warning and stepped farther into the store.

"We have an appointment," the bald man with a shiny gold tooth said. "At noon."

Marla and I glanced at the grandfather clock against the wall, which read ten twenty.

"We're early," the other man said, his voice low and scratchy, like a longtime smoker.

Marla's face changed to annoyance. "Appointments are made for a reason." She sighed, turning to me. "I'm truly sorry about this. There's a certain way I like to run my business. Organized and professional. But I can't control if someone decides to be late or early, now, can I?"

I eyed the men again, who were both staring at me intensely, as if they knew something about my reasons for being here. My heartrate sped up as I wondered if they were going to out me, but I told myself my fears were all in my head. If these two weren't really from Mr. Johnson's and had a later appointment, there was no way they could know who I was or what I was here for.

"It's okay," I told Marla. "We're almost done anyway, aren't we?"

Marla held out a purple velvet bag closed with a drawstring. I took it, surprised by how light it was in my hand. I didn't know what I was expecting exactly, but I'd have to check out what was really in the bag later. Once I was out of here and out of harm's way.

"Please tell Mr. Johnson it was a pleasure, as always. And I hope to do business with him again."

"Of course." I offered her my attempt at a polite smile, hoping it didn't come across as too forced. She didn't seem to notice though. With the bag in hand, I strode past the two large men, feeling their eyes on me the entire way, and walked out the door. For some reason, the jingle of the bells sounded louder this time. Like a warning.

All in my head.

Pushing it from my mind, I rushed down the sidewalk a few blocks, to where I knew Cole was parked. I was relieved to see the Jeep was still there, still running, with Cole sitting in the driver's seat. His face lit up when he spotted the purple bag in my hand.

I hopped into the car, and before I could even settle in, he pulled out and sped down the street.

"You got it." He laughed. "Damn. I can't believe it. I admit

I didn't have much faith in you, but I have no shame saying when I'm wrong."

That may have stung in another situation, but I hadn't had much faith in this plan working either.

"I got something, but it's not the herb we need."

"What?" He slammed on his brakes at a red light, propelling me forward. "What's in the bag, then?"

"Not sure." I set it on my lap, about to tug at the drawstring, but Cole's hand shot out to stop me.

"Woah. Wait a minute. Marla gave you a bag with some kind of magical object, and you have no idea what it is?"

"Well…yeah. Things didn't exactly go as you said they would. As I predicted."

"Don't open that," he snapped. "Not yet at least. We'll bring it back to my motel and check it out there. That way if things get out of hand, we'll have some room to defend ourselves."

"Defend ourselves?" My brows rose. "What the heck do you think is in this little bag? It barely weighs anything."

"You don't know Marla. A small bag like that can contain thousands of trapped angry souls or some kind of ancient deity imprisoned for centuries and wanting revenge."

"Why would Mr. Johnson want an ancient deity?"

He glanced at me as the light turned green. "Mr. Johnson?"

"Like I said. Things didn't go as planned in there." I proceeded to tell him about my introduction to Marla and what I had witnessed in her store. The magical booby-trapped back room and her noon appointment showing up early. He was quiet until I finished, even driving slower than usual down the downtown streets.

"I don't know a Mr. Johnson," he said finally. "It has to be an alias."

"That was my thought."

"Well, at least we accomplished something. We know where our herb is and what we're going into now. A magically protected room we can plan for."

"I hope this plan is better than your first," I said.

He grinned. "It will be. But nothing will happen until night. We'll go back then, when Marla is gone and the shop is closed."

"We're breaking and entering now?"

"Do you want to save your friend?"

"That's a stupid question," I shot back.

He shrugged. "This is what we need to do to get the herb. The herb is for the cure, and the cure will save her."

"I know. I get it. I know what has to be done, but that doesn't mean I'm not going to complain about it the entire way."

He laughed. "I wouldn't expect anything less."

CHAPTER

FIFTEEN

Cole zigzagged throughout the downtown city streets until we made it to the outskirts again, where a few family-owned motels lined the highway exit. Of course, he pulled into the most rundown-looking one in the area, which was set underneath the underpass.

He parked in a spot in front of the office. The *No Vacancy* sign glowed red in the window.

"A real five-star joint, huh?" I said, getting a big whiff of urine and sewage coming in from the broken Jeep window.

"It's not too bad." Cole grinned. "Once you get over the strolling prostitutes, drug deals, and occasional roach."

"Roaches! You're kidding."

"I never saw one, but you can only assume," he said. "But I'm barely here. It works fine for a quick nap and shower while I'm in town, and then I'm off to work again."

I wanted to bring up the subject again of why a well-known and well-paid mercenary was staying at a roach-infested motel, but I kept my mouth shut. Not my business, I reminded myself.

"I'm right here, in room two." He opened the door and climbed out.

I did the same and followed him to the door.

"Greg?"

A stranger's voice and throat clearing made us both whip around. Leaning out of the office door was an unshaven man wearing a stained guinea tee and an unpleased look on his face. His gaze drifted to me, and it took me a second to remember I could be seen now. And that "Greg" was really Cole.

"Follow along," Cole muttered, his lips barely moving at all. Then he gave the man his brightest smile, like they were long-lost friends. "Leonard! What's goin' on, man?"

The man named Leonard glanced at me again but with suspicious eyes.

I was about to ask him what his problem was, but the sudden arm wrapping around me made the words die in my throat. My first instinct was to grab for it, twist it hard, and elbow the person in the gut, but the moment Cole's scent—a mixture of the morning's coffee and worn leather—filled my nose, my heart skipped a beat or two.

Every muscle tensed as he pulled me to his side and said, "This is my girl, Danielle. Sweetie, this is Leonard. He helps me out whenever I'm in town and need a place to stay. He owns this place."

I looked up at him in disbelief. Even though his *follow along* echoed back in my head, I couldn't stop my face from showing my feelings.

Sweetie? Really?

Despite Cole's friendly smile, I could read the warning in his blue eyes. I forced myself to look at Leonard again. He was still staring at me intently, like he didn't believe Cole's story one bit.

"You know the rules, Greg. If you're bringing a"—he paused, searching for the right words—"a lady friend for a few hours, then you need to pay for the extra occupant for those hours."

A few hours? What did this guy take me for? A hooker?

That's when it hit me. That was exactly what he thought I was. A lady of the night.

My anger came hard and fast. I leapt forward, wanting nothing more than to punch the asshole square in the nose for such a remark, but Cole's hand was quick on my upper arm to stop me. He tugged me back, making me stumble into his chest with a loud "oomph." Before I could shove away, his mouth was on mine, and the moment I gasped, his tongue pushed past my lips for a breath-stealing kiss.

It was so unexpected, I didn't know what to do. My head screamed for me to fight him off. Hit him. Something. But instead, my body melted into his arms as he pulled me in closer and his hand cradled the side of my face. My mind fogged, and for those few moments, I was completely lost to this world. It was like I was passing through the spirit door again, hovering between planes, my stomach doing somersaults as it tried to determine which way was up.

The sound of Leonard's forced cough had Cole pulling away. Without missing a beat, he said, "We're visiting her mother, who lives in the city. Isn't that right, hon?"

My heart was hammering in my chest, but Cole's voice was smooth and convincing, spinning his lie like a spider's web.

I felt myself nodding in agreement, too, feeding into it even more.

Leonard's expression relaxed a bit.

"If it's really a big deal, we can go to Monty's place next door. I'm sure he still has rooms for the night."

A vein popped out of Leonard's forehead as he gritted his teeth. Cole had obviously hit some kind of sore spot. Monty must have been a rival motel owner. The competition.

"No, no. Don't worry about it. I'm sorry for assuming…" He glanced at me. "I'm truly sorry. I didn't mean to offend you, if I did. We just get some shady characters around here sometimes."

My mouth opened to curse him out, but Cole's grip tightened on my upper arm. "It's okay," I mumbled instead.

"Great!" Cole said, gently steering me toward the motel room labeled 2. "You know I don't care for Monty's mattresses. No support for my back."

Leonard smiled broadly, revealing a few missing teeth. "That's because he stuffs them with newspaper."

With a quick wave, he ducked back into the office and closed the door.

When I turned back to Cole, he had his finger to his lips, telling me to stay quiet. With a quick swipe of a plastic key, we went inside the motel room.

The décor of the place was very simple and very…brown. One king-size bed with a beige and brown patterned quilt, tan walls, and an ancient box TV on an equally brown wooden dresser filled the small space. Like something out of a seventies' sitcom. It was plain but functional and surprisingly clean. I had expected much worse.

The moment I heard the door click shut and Cole flick the lock, I spun on him. So many things were bubbling up inside me, I was about to explode. And I pretty much did, the words spilling out of me in a jumbled rush.

"A hooker? A hooker! He thought I was a hooker?" I gestured to my simple clothes—dark jeans, a tank top, boots, only accessorized by my leather gloves. No neon fishnets. Not even a speck of makeup on my face. "Do I really look like a hooker?" When he opened his mouth to respond, I cut him off. "Wait, don't answer that."

Cole crossed his arms.

That only fueled my annoyance. "And you—" I stepped toward him, pointing. "That kiss! What the heck was that about? You... You..."

The slow spread of one of his sexy smiles stole the rest of my sentence. The memory of his lips on mine sprang up again, and instantly, my anger extinguished, leaving me gaping there like a fish out of water.

Cole casually waved my accusatory finger away from his face. "I had to make it convincing. I didn't expect you to get so flustered."

I paused.

I *was* flustered. But why? I wasn't sure. That kiss may have taken me off guard, but it shouldn't have had me gushing like a teenager. Maybe it was because, deep down, I had wanted that kiss to happen, but not exactly that way. Or maybe I was disappointed in myself for not being able to control my body's response to his touch. No man had ever made me feel so out of sync with myself. And I didn't like it.

"You have to know what to do and say to get what you want in my line of business. Got to be a quick thinker and an even quicker shooter."

I rolled my eyes.

"Well, you can't just go around kissing people. That's not how this works."

He took a step closer to me, his body a breath away from mine. Close enough for me to smell his intoxicating scent again. "Really? Because I was under the impression that you enjoyed it."

I swallowed roughly, trying to keep myself composed. Trying but failing.

Man, he was gorgeous. Breathtakingly handsome but with a rugged, dangerous quality that made my heart pound.

"Or was I wrong?" Without waiting for an answer, he leaned in and captured my mouth again. Unlike last time, this kiss was hard, full of passion and urgency, as if he had been wanting to do this for a long time.

My own desire surged, and instead of resisting, I gave into it completely, matching his movements equally. My hands snaked behind his neck and tangled in his hair.

No longer holding back, Cole's arms came around me and cupped my bottom, half picking me up to press me against the wall.

I missed being alive. I missed being able to feel another person's body against mine. It had only been a year, but so much had happened in that past year with Styx Corp and my reaping that it felt more like a lifetime.

Cole's hand traveled along my thigh and guided it over his hip. That's when I felt him, all of him, pressing against my jeans, ready and willing to take that next step with me.

Was I really about to do this? With a person I had just met and wasn't even sure I trusted fully?

A strange vibration against my thigh made me hesitate. Cole did, too, pulling away from our kiss and glancing down at my jeans.

Confused, he stepped back and let me down.

I reached into my pocket and pulled out the velvet pouch

I had gotten from Marla. Even in my hand, it trembled, as if something inside were trying to get out.

Cole stared at it. "What the heck?"

"Should we open it?"

He pulled one of his concealed guns out of his belt, cocked it, and pointed it at my hand. "Okay, ready."

"Woah, woah!" I shouted, holding up both hands. "Let's not get trigger happy now. It could be harmless."

Cole's eyes hardened, turning all business again. "Open the top and toss the bag onto the bed. Quick. If anything jumps out, I'm shooting."

The bag still shook in my palm, but I did as he said, pulled the drawstring, and threw it onto the bed in the same swift motion.

A little yellow pebble popped out and rolled halfway across the bedspread. I rushed over and snatched it before it fell onto the floor and under a piece of furniture, never to be seen again.

"What is it?" Cole asked, his gun still hovering my way, aimed and ready.

Standing, I studied it between my fingers. That was all it seemed to be—a rock the color of amber with a cloudy swirl in its center. A precious stone, maybe?

"It's just a stone or gem of some kind," I replied. Harmless, just like I'd thought.

On cue, the bag vibrated again, skidding across the bed some.

Cole approached it cautiously, finger still on the trigger of his gun.

Dozens of colored marbles erupted from the small pouch, covering the quilt, and spilling onto the floor. To my surprise and horror, they continued to flow out, quickly coating the dingy carpet in shiny stones.

"What the…" I tried to dance away but was soon standing

in a pool of marbles. They were everywhere.

Finally, the last tiny ball popped out and clattered onto the floor with the rest.

I stared at the velvet bag, now empty, sitting at the center of the bed. How did something that could sit in the palm of my hand fit *all* those stones? There had to be thousands of them.

"What was that about?" I breathed, still unsure about what I had just witnessed.

Cole burst into a fit of laughter, his shoulders bouncing from the force of it.

"Oh, I'm glad you think it's funny. Our room is covered in these little balls!"

When he could finally catch his breath, he said, "Leave it to Marla to pull something like that."

"What? Was this supposed to be a practical joke or something?"

He gestured around the room. "Whoever this Mr. Johnson is, he's obviously pissed her off. She got him what he paid for, which is obviously the bag, but she added a little extra for a bit of revenge. Very Marla-esque."

"So, the bag is what this Mr. Johnson wanted?" I repeated as Cole picked it up, turned it upside down, and shook it a bit. Nothing else came out. "It must be charmed to hold more than its size."

"Exactly. Must have been a pricey item since it requires some powerful magic."

A person could hide anything in there. I wondered if something as large as a car could fit. If so, you could carry an entire vehicle in your back pocket. That was incredible.

I walked over to Cole and snatched the bag out of his hand.

"Hey!" he protested.

"Marla gave it to me. It's only fair."

He raised an eyebrow.

"Could come in handy later."I tucked it back into my pocket as Cole holstered his gun.

He moved toward the small bathroom. "I'm going to take a shower. Maybe you should grab some sleep since we have a busy night ahead of us." He paused, smirking. "Or…" he drawled, "you can join me…"

My stomach flipped at the thought, but I shook it from my head and snorted a laugh instead. "Nice try." My smile grew anyway. "I'll take the bed."

"If you change your mind…" He gestured toward the bathroom. "You know where I'll be."

"Goodnight, *Greg.*"

Cole laughed. "Goodnight, *sweetie.*"

In the early morning darkness, we jumped into the Jeep and made our way back to Divine Magic. A thick fog clung to the cobblestone streets, and with the glow of the gas lamps lining the sidewalk, downtown Fairport looked more like a scene from a Jack the Ripper movie than anything else.

Like before, we parked a couple of streets away from the store and walked the rest of the way. Upon first inspection, Marla had locked up for the night, even pulled the curtains closed in every window.

"Are you ready for this?" Cole whispered as we swung around the back of the old brick building. "You remember the plan?"

I nodded. "Keep on my toes. When the trap triggers, if it's something physical coming at us, let you handle it with your magical bag of tricks and big, bad guns." I gestured to the backpack in his hand. If it wasn't for the loaded gun in his other hand, he looked just like a college pretty boy off to visit his parents for the weekend. "Anything spirit-related is my responsibility with my..." I pulled out my handy-dandy, super deadly piece of chalk and waved it at him.

Before we left the motel, I had tried making a quick spirit door to see if I still had that power in this state, and luckily everything worked. I could make the door open if I needed to, so at least we had that going for us. Everything else, though, was up in the air.

"And if anything surprises us, we'll have to wing it," he added. He rummaged through the front pocket of his bag and pulled out a rusty, ancient-looking key. Intrigued, I watched him hold it to the door's thick padlock.

There was no way a medieval key was going to fit into a modern lock that was three times smaller than it. But somehow, Cole pushed the key in, twisted, and the lock popped open.

I stood there, shocked.

Cole glanced at me, smiling. "Enchanted key. Can open any lock. Even ones locked with magic. A handy tool in my line of work."

My eyes widened. "How did you manage to get your hands on that?"

"I did some work for a level three sorcerer and accepted it for payment."

Funny how he said "did some work" like he'd mowed his lawn or tinkered with his car. Not killed someone.

"If you have the ability to open any lock, why do you keep breaking the one on Wyatt's gate?"

His grin was slow and deliberate. "I like busting his chops."

Cautiously, Cole pushed open the door all the way, revealing the back room behind the counter, exactly where we needed to be. The space was small, dark, and lined with crowded shelves.

The air shimmered slightly, revealing the magic at play. I was hoping it was just a mirage spell, only meant to take the appearance of something else and distract an onlooker. But if Marla was as devious as Cole said, there had to be a more dangerous trap waiting for us beyond the door.

Cole put the key away, slung his backpack over his shoulder, and held up his gun again before stepping inside. I followed close behind.

The room appeared to be just big enough for the two of us at first, but to the left, the wall of shelves shifted before my eyes, revealing a hidden space behind it, also covered in different jars, dried plants, and sacks full of God knows what. And a small shrouded figure lying in the center of the floor, not moving.

A shiver of foreboding shot down my spine.

"Are you seeing that? There's someone back there," I whispered to Cole.

He nodded. "I wouldn't be surprised if Marla has someone locked up back here." We approached the hologram wall cautiously. It was difficult for me to imagine that Marla, who looked more like a soccer mom than a dangerous witch, would keep prisoners locked in some back room, but I'd helped a lot of people cross over whose personalities didn't match their appearances.

I mean, look at Cole.

Better yet, look at me.

When we passed through the bewitched wall, magic caressed my skin, making goose bumps rise. Like stepping through a waterfall or spiderweb.

I tried to shake the strange feeling off as we crept closer to the person lying soundlessly on the ground. Cole's gaze swept the shelves, his hand steady on his weapon just in case another trap tripped. I couldn't take my eyes off the figure.

When I spotted the mousey brown bob and pink ruffled

collar peeking out from underneath the carelessly tossed, blood-soaked blanket, my chest constricted.

It was Marla.

She was dead.

CHAPTER

SIXTEEN

As a reaper, I knew death, and Marla was most certainly dead.

Walking around her unmoving body, I took in the pool of blood underneath her chest, her blouse that I had thought as PTA mom-ish only hours ago now shredded into strips and stained red. Three deep slash marks raked from her stomach to her sternum—claw marks, like from an animal.

Shit, was that a part of her intestine peeking out from one of them?

Fear gripped me.

I swallowed the bile creeping up my throat. I'd seen many deaths in my year as a reaper. Some more gruesome than this. But for some reason, knowing I had just interacted with Marla only hours ago and now she had been gutted from chest to belly button made uneasiness stir inside me.

What animal could have done something like that?

Maybe it wasn't an animal but some kind of creature.

A supernatural creature.

My thoughts shot back to the horrifying Halflings crawling out of the Hell hole on Wyatt's property. Their gray scaly skin, soulless eyes, and pointed teeth were things of nightmares. They had claws, too, didn't they? But why attack Marla?

My stomach dropped at the idea of possibly leading those hellions straight into Marla's shop and causing her death. This could be my fault.

Cole came to my side and let out a deep breath. "You're thinking it, too, aren't you? Halflings. This looks like their work."

He pointed to a smear of blood that left a trail out of the back room, toward the main shop. "She wasn't killed here, though. She was dragged here afterwards."

I nodded slowly, my mind not really grasping what he was saying.

"Marla's a tough cookie. She wouldn't go down without a fight," he said.

"But if she was ambushed…"

"That's the big question, now isn't it?"

A loud crash sounded in the main shop, followed by a guttural, unnatural snarl.

Cole held up his gun, aiming it at the beaded curtain separating the two rooms.

Shadows jumped on the other side. Not just one either. Many.

Dread crawled up my spine. "I think we're going to find the answer sooner rather than later."

Cole gripped his gun tighter, although his face was smooth of any fear. I tried to imitate his composure, but my insides were trembling. I stepped behind him and held out my hands, hoping whatever I had done back at Wyatt's trailer would work again here.

More crashing and glass shattering.

Slowly, a shadow elongated in the corner near the door until it formed into a skinny, stick-like leg, reminding me of some kind of mutant spider. Then the shadow stretched to form another. Then another. Until one of those hideous Halflings stepped into the back room, his head swiveling our way instantly.

I held my breath.

When its eyeless gaze rolled over us, unseeing, I didn't move. The magic concealing the back room seemed to be confusing it enough to conceal us, too. Every muscle tensed, and beside me, Cole was just as rigid.

The creature lifted its head, and its slit for nostrils flared open slightly as it sniffed.

Its head whipping our way, it let out a piercing screech and charged.

"Get ready!" Cole shouted, shooting at the Halfling. It scurried up the shelf to avoid the bullet. Cole shot again and nailed it in the shoulder. The skin sizzled, and it fell to the floor screaming.

But the victory was short-lived, because in the next second, more of the shadowy creatures were sliding through the beaded doorway, their transparent forms appearing like drifting smoke at first before gaining depth and revealing their truly horrifying features.

Oh shit. We were in deep trouble here.

The moment they solidified, they came at us, crawling over each other in a frenzy like something out of a horror film.

There was no way I was going to be able to get close enough to touch one of these things without getting hurt myself. Why did Cole get the gun? I needed one.

A rain of gunfire. He hit a few right off the bat, the smell of sulfur and burning rubber filling the enclosed space. But the ones that managed to break through uninjured rushed at us full force, leaping off the shelves and knocking over jars.

Glass shattered everywhere, spilling different pungent liquids and other ingredients.

The largest Halfling leaped for Cole. He shot at it but missed as it landed on top of him, toppling him to the floor. He held open his snapping jaws just inches away from his face.

I was about to reach for him to help, but needle-like nails dug into my calf and tugged back hard. I slammed onto the ground. Pain ricocheted throughout every muscle, and I couldn't stop the scream from leaving my mouth.

Suddenly, I was being dragged across the floor. The creature holding on had a hunched back, its spine protruding through its thin, blackened skin, and a mouth that was too wide for its face. A true thing of nightmares.

I grabbed for the Halfling's taloned fingers, all the while praying the white light would reappear and blast the bastard back to Hell.

The moment I made contact, a flash of blinding light exploded from my palm, consuming the room entirely.

A wail of pain sounded, and when the light dissipated, the creature I had been clashing with was gone.

Gone. Poof. Just like that.

Vaporized? Or just transported somewhere else?

From the shriek, I would put my money on the former.

I stared at my palms again. Like the other times, they appeared completely normal. Nothing that could hint at having super demon-zapping powers, but I'd take it. Anything that would help me survive this madness.

Before I could revel in my upgrade, I was smacked in the head by a pain so excruciating, my vision blurred. My entire body convulsed from the shock of it, and my world tilted. I cried out as the room began to disappear.

"Jade!"

Cole's shouts were the only thing keeping me grounded. I hung onto consciousness by a thin string. Warmth pulsated through me, engulfing me, but instead of a soothing feeling, it left me perspiring and sickly. It seemed like my body's reaction was getting worse and worse with every use of my new power. Maybe I was tapping into something I wasn't supposed to. Something too great for me to control.

When I found Cole, he was wrestling with the same Halfling, doing everything he could to avoid its teeth from sinking into his neck. His gun lay feet away, lost during their fighting.

I struggled to my feet. When another jolt of pain ricocheted through my skull, tears prickled my eyes. I took several deep breaths and forced myself to stand just as another half-demon lunged for Cole.

Ignoring my body's protests, I ran at it on wobbly legs and tackled it to the ground. We both fell with a *boom,* and I swore the ground shook underneath us. My fighting style definitely wasn't the cleanest or most precise, but damn was it efficient.

The massive creature bucked wildly, like a spooked horse, and in its thrashing, managed to land a kick to my stomach. All my breath shot out of my lungs in an instant, making me sputter and cough.

The beast whirled on me, fangs bared.

Clenching my fist, I sucker punched it straight in its already unhinged jaw.

Again, when my hand made contact, the light appeared, drowning the room in brightness and making me wince.

Then nothing. The Halfling had disappeared.

As expected, the punishment for unleashing the power struck me next, doubling me over. It was as if dozens of tiny little hot knives were poking into my brain over and over, and barbed wire raked through my gut.

When vomit rocketed up my esophagus, I didn't fight it. Everything in my stomach spilled onto the floor.

Yep, eggs, pancakes, sausage, and coffee. It was all there.

I wiped my mouth with the back of my hand.

The scurrying of claws retreating sounded, and when I glanced over my shoulder, I spotted the other Halflings fleeing to the shopfront and hopefully to whatever hole they'd crawled out of.

Cowards.

I didn't have much time to ponder what was happening because a guttural growl came from behind me, snapping my attention. Cole's arms wrapped around the same Halfling's neck. The one he'd been tossed around by before. This time, Cole dragged it back to the floor with him, trying his best to pin it in place with an elbow in the throat.

The thing found an opening and flipped around at the last minute. It seized Cole from behind and sank its claws dangerously close to his jugular.

"My gun," he choked out as the Halfling sank its teeth into his shoulder. Blood poured out, staining his jacket red. "Get my gun!"

I scurried across the room, but when I went to snatch it, my fingers passed right through the metal.

A boulder sank into my gut and hardened.

I grabbed for the gun again, but my hand couldn't grab hold.

"No, no, no, no! Not now!" My voice climbed in my panic. I couldn't be a spirit again. Was this some kind of sick joke?

How was I supposed to help Cole? I grabbed desperately at the gun, hoping that somehow the magic turning me from ghost to alive would switch again.

It didn't. I couldn't make contact with anything in this world.

Cole and the Halfling rolled across the floor, fists flying and claws slashing. Blood spilled out of the new wounds on Cole's arms and chest, but he kept his grasp tight.

"What are you doing?" Cole shouted as the two tussled. "Shoot, dammit! Don't just stand there! Shoot!"

"I can't! I'm not alive anymore. Something's happened."

"Do *something*, then. Use your touch!"

Everything still ached from the last time I had unleashed the light, and the burning in my throat from throwing up told me next time I used it may make me really regret it.

The Halfling let out a hair-raising snarl.

"DO IT!" Cole's strangled cry had me rushing toward them.

I slapped my hand onto any piece of exposed skin I could find on the creature, which ended up being his shoulder.

Whiteness erupted from my fingertips, blanketing the room.

A loud gurgling cry rang out. But not from the Halfling. It was Cole's voice.

Withdrawing my hand, the light diminished. The demon was gone, like the others, but Cole was on the floor, groaning and with his eyes closed. Every muscle twitched underneath his skin, and the pungent smell of burnt flesh and hair wafted past my nose, making me gag.

Before I could come to his aid, the spiking pain pierced my temples again, bringing me to my knees beside him. This time, though, I was expecting it, and I gritted my teeth as invisible spears drilled away at any remaining strength I had left. When my stomach spun, I took deep breaths in through my nose and out through my mouth to prevent myself from retching, all the while telling myself I had to get through it. Squeezing my eyes shut, I rode out the pain and bouts of nausea, everything spinning around me.

When the waves of pain lightened enough, I opened my eyes and stared at Cole still writhing on the ground. Fresh wounds covered his face and neck, along with a blistering red rash all over his exposed skin.

Guilt weaved throughout my chest, constricting. Had I done that?

I reached out to touch him but stopped myself, remembering I had fought bare handed. Patting my jeans, I found my leather gloves in my back pocket. I quickly slipped them on.

What could I do to help him? I had no idea. I hadn't known the light would hurt him like this. Like one of the Halflings.

What was I supposed to do?

"They'll be back," a familiar female's voice called.

When I looked over my shoulder, Marla's spirit stood there, staring at me and Cole with a look of complete disappointment. She was dressed in her frilly pink blouse and tailored pants, like before, and her hair was perfectly curled. If it wasn't for the slight transparency to her form and the deceased body at her feet, it'd be hard to tell she wasn't really alive. She was a strong presence. Even in death.

"Of course you two couldn't come just a couple of minutes earlier and save me from those..." Her lip curled up in disgust. "Beasts."

I didn't know what to say besides, "Sorry."

Arms crossed, she glanced down at her body and shook

her head. "I had so much more to do in my life. So much more money to collect. What a waste."

Cole moaned again, his breathing growing shallower.

She sighed heavily. "So, you work for Masters, huh? Not Mr. Johnson." When I didn't reply, she added, "You know, he's not going to be too happy when he realizes he never got his package from me. He paid good money for it—not that any of that matters to me anymore."

I had bigger issues to worry about than a secretive Mr. Johnson and his underhanded dealings right now. Whoever he was.

"What are you exactly?" Marla asked, tilting her head to the side and studying me.

I stood slowly, locking my knees before they could buckle again. "I'm a reaper."

"I did sense something off with you when you came into my store but couldn't place the magic." She paused, as if what I was took a second to actually sink in. "A reaper. Like the grim reaper?" She glanced down at her body again, and a visible shudder ran over her ghostly form. "I guess it's really over for me, huh?"

"I'm afraid so," I said. "I can help you cross over, though. It's my job."

At least it was anyway.

"I just need your help," I quickly added.

Her eyes rolled dramatically, and she *tsk*ed me, like a mother might do to a child. "Of course you do." Glancing at Cole, who had gone completely still for the moment, she sighed. "Some fryda aloe with bikket seeds should help with the burns and speed up the healing. You can find them…" She pointed across the room where there were broken shelves and spilled jars all over the floor then grimaced. "Somewhere over there."

"Thank you. But that wasn't what I'm talking about."

Her eyes narrowed.

"We're looking for an herb called the Breath of Life—"

Marla's widening eyes and gasp cut my sentence short. "What could Masters possibly need that for?"

"It's for me, too. Well, for my friend. She's been attacked by a demon. We think the herb can save her life." I didn't want to give her too much information, just in case it hurt my chances. Especially since she didn't particularly like Cole. If I kept her focused on me, maybe she would be more willing to help.

"And Masters thought I had it?"

I nodded. "He said if anyone was going to have it, it was you. You're the best at all things magical."

She squeaked a laugh. "He'd be right about that," she said. "On both accounts. I have the herb. It is one of my most prized possessions since it was extremely hard to get ahold of. Actually…"

"What?"

"Two men—the ones who cut our meeting short—asked about the herb, too, after you left. I thought it was strange. Not many people know about it. But I didn't give them too much information or even hint that I had it. They just left after that."

"When did the Halflings attack you?"

Could they be connected?

"The moment I closed the store…" She hesitated, wringing her hands together. "You think those demon things were looking for it, too?"

"That's what I'm guessing."

"But why?"

Should I tell her the reason?

"Cole thinks it could help cure him of his demon side. Make him human."

"He's still chasing that crazy dream of his?" Marla laughed, shaking her head. "I should have known."

Apparently everyone knew about Cole's suicidal mission to save himself from full corruption. And they all thought he was crazy for it.

I pulled out my tablet. Again, no notifications from Styx or new assignments listed in my queue. I tapped on the Look Up a Spirit feature, like I had with Victor in Kay's shop.

Holding up the device to take Marla's picture, I said, "You need to cross over. Here, let me—"

"And what if I don't want to go?"

"Then you'll have to spend your afterlife wandering the living plane, unable to interact with anyone or anything. It's a miserable existence."

"You sound like you know about it quite well."

I only nodded. Really, she had no idea, but I wasn't going to give her a speech.

Maybe it was time to try a different tactic. Marla was all about trading and getting the best deal, right? I had the ability to do what she wanted, and she had the information I needed about the herb. This way, in the end, we could both win.

"I'll get you to the afterlife," I began, "if you tell me where the herb is. No games. Just an even trade."

She stared at me for a long moment. At first, she seemed impressed I had come up with a deal she couldn't really refuse, but then, that admiration quickly switched into skepticism. Maybe she thought I had the upper hand in this ultimatum, and maybe I did. But her distrust in me showed clear on her face. I didn't blame her. I wouldn't trust me either.

"Tell me where it is, and I'll help you. I swear it."

"You know how many people have sworn to me and

never pulled through? Pinky promises never pan out in my line of work, sweetheart."

"It will here," I said. Quickly, I held up the tablet and snapped a picture of her. In an instant, her profile popped onto the screen.

Marla Victoria Jones. Age forty-two. Level three witch. Dead on arrival. Cause of death: Unknown.

Unknown? Definitely not true.

And how could an all-seeing, all-knowing cosmic force not know how a person died? I'd never seen that cause of death before.

"Everything okay?"

When I lowered the tablet, Marla was staring at me with great concern.

"Yeah, you're here in the system." I forced myself to smile, but I could feel it wavering at the edges. "Whenever you're ready."

She didn't move, her body rigid.

"I know you're nervous. It's the unknown. But let me tell you, I live in the supernatural afterlife, and it's not too bad to be honest. Slightly boring for my taste." I shrugged. "It takes some getting used to."

"Paradise, boring? Figures." She let out an annoyed breath. "All right, then. Let's get it over with."

I admired her bravery. Not many people accepted what had happened to them so quickly. Like Tristen.

Marla pointed to the stone wall on her right. "It's there. Between the third and fourth shelf. One of the bricks is loose."

After crossing the room, I followed her directions, searching the bricks until I found the one slightly protruding, uneven with the rest of the wall. When I reached for it, my hand passed right through, and I cursed. I was going to have to find another way to get to it.

Hopefully, Marla was telling me the truth.

"Thank you." I pulled out my handy-dandy chalk piece. "As promised…"

Working quickly, I drew the symbols for the spirit door on the floor near her body. The moment the circle was enclosed, the orange glow appeared and the door opened.

She came to my side and stared at it nervously.

"You're going to be fine," I told her, and I meant it. Our time together had been brief, but in that short time, I knew Marla to be a force to be reckoned with. "You did quite well for yourself in life. I'm sure you'll kick ass in the afterlife. And who knows? Maybe I'll see you on the other side."

That got a smile out of her. "It'd be nice to meet you under different circumstances. Over drinks or something. If that's allowed over there. I know I need one."

"It is," I said. "And that sounds good to me."

I'd need one, too, after all of this.

Moving to the edge of the spirit door, she hesitated and glanced up at me. "If it wasn't for you working with Masters, I'd even go as far as to say I like you."

I laughed. Despite all that Cole had said about Marla, I was beginning to like her, too.

Then, sucking in a deep breath and holding it, Marla squeezed her eyes shut, as if she were about to dive into a swimming pool, and jumped through the door.

After smearing the chalk marks and sealing it closed, I peered back at Marla's dead body and the pool of blood she lay in. She had said those two angry-looking men who had come into the shop had been asking about the Breath of Life herb, too. Then, a couple of hours later, a gaggle of Halfling demons attacked her in her shop.

Who knew about the demon cure besides us? And were these Halfling attacks because of it, or did someone just want us out of the way? Was it Xaver, maybe because we had the mother of his spawn hidden from him, or was it another demon?

Coincidence?

Too much had happened these past few days for me to believe in coincidences.

CHAPTER

SEVENTEEN

A low groan came from across the room. I spun around to find Cole rocking side to side, his hands shaking as they ran over the burns on his arms and face. He tried to sit up but winced and lay back down.

I hurried over to him. "Cole, I don't know what happened. My power burned…"

He waved off my explanation and attempted to get up again. With a loud pain-filled grunt, he was able to pull himself upward to a sitting position.

"I told you to use it." He grunted. "It's on me."

Examining his arms, bright red and cracked in some places, he sucked in a breath. "Looks like you gave me a bit of a sunburn."

I was glad he was able to joke about this. Unfortunately, I didn't find it as funny, especially when I spotted a couple of blisters on the parts of flesh that had been directly hit, like his neck and around his collarbone.

After a moment, he glanced around the room. "Did we win?"

"Sort of. The Halflings are all gone, if that's what you mean. But who knows if they'll be back."

"So, my tan lines are worth it."

God, he was infuriating. I shoved him in the shoulder and stood.

He hissed in pain. "Hey!"

"What I'm saying is that we need to get out of here now before they come back."

"And the herb?" he asked.

"I know where it is, but I can't get to it. I'm a reaper again, a spirit."

Cole pushed himself to stand, groaning.

"For a mercenary, you're quite a crybaby," I teased.

He shot me a look, which I ignored.

Then, I remembered what Marla has said about the healing ingredients she had for his burns.

"You're going to have to help yourself because I can't touch anything anymore on this plane. I'm useless." Quickly, I told him where Marla had hid the herb and the two things we needed to treat his burns.

I let him lean on me while he got the things we needed, thanking whatever higher power that I could at least touch him. Five minutes later, we were out the door again, back into the early morning air and under a lightening sky.

The drive back to the motel was a slow one. Concern knotted my stomach at every bump we hit in the rundown Jeep and every turn we made. If I could have driven the metal box, I would have, especially because Cole's evident pain was heart-wrenching to watch. Guilt weighed heavily on me knowing that I had caused him some of that pain, and there was nothing I could do to help him.

It didn't matter if he told me over and over that he was okay. I could see the pain on his face.

The moment we got into the room and shut the door, he pulled off his shirt and collapsed onto the bed.

"You did quite a number on me," he said with a small chuckle.

I hadn't wanted to use my light power; he had told me to.

"Why do you think my light affected you more this time than last?" I asked.

He reached over to the side table, scooped the concoction of aloe and crushed seeds, and began rubbing it on the red marred skin on his arms and chest.

I tried not to look at his naked torso, all hard lines and sculpted muscles, especially as he spread the shiny, waxy goo all over his skin. But I was failing miserably.

The parts that had been covered with clothes weren't too bad, but the backs of his hands, neck, collarbones, and some of his face were severe. As if someone had thrown boiling water on him, and for some reason, it was still steaming.

Even with all the wounds, he was still a sight to behold.

I commanded my raging libido to settle down.

"I'm not sure why it affected me more now," he began, still smoothing the aloe on. He moaned in relief. Within seconds, the blisters disappeared and the redness to his skin lightened. "It could be because this new power of yours is getting stronger…"

"Or…" I pressed, noting the wavering in his voice.

"Or I'm getting more like them."

Them meaning the Halflings.

"I was forced to use my Hellfire at Wyatt's. Every use

pushes me closer toward my demon side now." He rubbed his forehead in worry. "We need to get the rest of the cure."

Agreed.

"I've been getting this terrible pain in my head whenever I use the power, so I think I may need one of your magical guns. Do you have an extra? If things switch back for me and I become alive again, that is."

My light was too unpredictable to be using, especially if I could hurt Cole again in the process. As much as he annoyed me, I didn't want to blast him back to Hell.

Not yet anyway.

I might be able to use that as a threat in the future, if he got me mad enough.

He scoffed and continued lathering on the aloe. "You with a gun? I don't think that's a good idea."

"And why not?" Annoyance pinched at me, and my gaze dropped to his waist, where his pants rode low on his hips. My throat thickened. The silky aloe glistened across his skin in the dim light of the room, and all I pictured myself doing was running my tongue along every inch of him.

His sexiness didn't make him any less of an asshole. I had to remember that.

"I saw you fighting back there," he said. "A bit reckless if you ask me."

I crossed my arms. "Just because I use my hands to fight and don't rely on a weapon all the time doesn't mean I don't know what I'm doing."

"I didn't say that." He held up his hands in surrender. "It's just an...*unreliable* technique, in my opinion. And not my style."

My anger flared. "Oh, you mean shoot first, ask questions later?"

"Hey, it's worked well for me this far." His tone grew sharper.

"That's why you were on my assignment list, and I found you unconscious in the alley?" I retorted. "Besides, if I recall, I saved your ass twice. Actually *three* times. Without me—"

He let out a quick, skeptical laugh and jumped from the bed. "That's not what the claw marks across my chest and the burns on my shoulder say."

"I don't need your help, you know. I don't need to be here." I whirled on my heel and headed for the door, but my temper swung me back around to face him. "No wonder you're used to working alone. Who could stand you?"

He blustered, closing the distance between us with two large strides. "You're no fairy princess yourself."

I had never wanted to strangle someone so badly in my life. Every part of me burned with fury, and at the same time, I couldn't help noticing how sexy he looked with the muscles tensing across his chest and arms from anger.

Something sparked in his stare, intensifying the normally cool blue to a more vivid cobalt. Was the demon part of him coming out again, or did he normally look this intimidating and breath-takingly hot when he argued with someone?

I should be scared of this man. Who knew how close he really was to turning into one of the hellion things and dragging me into a pit?

The conflict raging inside me only heightened my frustration, but I met his gaze straight on, determined to show him that I was not the type of woman who backed down.

I pronounced every next word out of my mouth with gusto. "Go to Hell."

The moment those three words left my mouth, he pulled me into his arms and silenced me with a kiss.

The rage died the moment Cole's lips claimed mine, his aggression transforming the kiss into something wild and mind-blowing. It was unlike anything I had experienced before—at least that I could remember.

As his tongue danced with mine, every hormone in my body ignited white-hot. It had been so long since I had been touched like this, alive or not. The way the heat of him radiated off his skin warmed me to the bone. I was burning all over.

It made me feel...*alive*. But not like before when I had been given only a taste of life again. Something much more than that.

Heart drumming, breath heaving, skin tingling. The feeling of his body pressed against mine. It was a new but familiar sensation at the same time, but somehow amplified.

My head whirled from it all.

All I knew for sure was that suddenly I wanted nothing more than for him to devour every inch of me with his hands and mouth, all while stripping each other naked and doing my share to make him beg for mercy.

Wow, he had gotten my libido to go from zero to a hundred quick. But I didn't care. I wanted him.

All of him.

"You're infuriating." I unbuttoned his fly and slid his zipper down so I could touch him. His cock all but burst out of his jeans as if the tight denim couldn't contain it anymore. When I took hold of him, I was shocked to find that he wasn't only rock hard and ready, he was more than a handful.

Glancing down, I saw how big he really was and bit my lip.

Oh, this was going to be fun.

He growled when I started stroking him—actually *growled* —an animalistic, guttural sound that made the hairs on my arms rise. Like the Halfling demon creatures we had just fought. But at the same time, it lit something else inside me, a heavy need clutching at my core.

As he buried his face in my neck and ran his tongue along the curve of my collarbone, I shuddered all over.

Should I be concerned a half-demon had such an effect on me? Probably.

Did I care at the moment? Absolutely not.

I'd worry about that later. Along with all the other shit I had hovering over me.

He undid my jeans swiftly, and when he pushed his hand inside to touch the most private part of me, I moaned. I rose onto my tiptoes so he could slide a finger deep inside, and his palm rubbed my clit.

His skin was fiery hot, warming me with every stroke. Fireworks exploded behind my closed eyelids as the heat spread through me. My body wanted him inside me, but the last ounce of sanity screamed that was a bad idea. Everyone knew you never merged work with pleasure. You never got involved with a coworker. It would only make things complicated and slow us down. Kay didn't have time to waste.

Before I could shove him away, Cole grabbed my thighs and moved us both across the small room. He dropped me on the dresser, knocking me back into the lamp in his haste. When it hit the ground, the bulb popped, cloaking the room in darkness.

Fuck it. It wasn't important anyway. Not when my body was shaking with desire.

Cole didn't seem to notice either. His kisses became harder as he grabbed the top of my jeans and yanked them down. They barely made it all the way off before he was spreading my legs and pushing himself in between them.

Shit. His aggression was hot as hell.

Who didn't like it rough once in a while?

His hands were everywhere. All over me. Tangled in my hair, squeezing my breasts, running along my waist. Eventually, both hands ended up on my ass, his fingers digging in enough to bruise.

"Fuck." His husky voice vibrated against my neck. "You feel so good."

"What about your burns?" I asked him.

"That aloe stuff really helped."

I somehow doubted that, but when his kisses traveled along my shoulder, I realized I didn't care. I was tired of waiting. "Well, shut up and get on with it already."

He was part savage beast, and it made me wonder what it would be like to have him deep inside me.

I didn't have to wonder long it seemed, because suddenly, Cole was jerking my body onto the edge of the dresser and sliding himself into me, filling me to the brim. We groaned in unison.

Gripping his hips, I encouraged him to move faster, and he did, not really needing my instruction. He slammed into me, withdrawing almost completely before driving himself back in. I wrapped my legs around his middle and locked them in place. Every thrust hurt at first but then added to a wave of pleasure that was growing bigger and bigger until it became too much to handle and I was riding the orgasm high and fast.

"Oh yeah…" A low rumble came from the bottom of his throat, but Cole didn't slow.

The sound of our bodies pounding against each other was enough to make my head fog. The dresser underneath me crashed against the wall in time with every thrust, and it wasn't long before my body was climbing again toward another climax.

Faster. Faster. Faster.

He was relentless.

This time, when I came undone, he did along with me.

We stayed like that for a while, his face buried in my neck as I clung to him, both of us breathing hard.

After a few moments passed, he whispered, "You make me feel so…*human*." His breath tickled my skin. "How stupid is that?"

It didn't sound stupid at all, because in all honesty, I was thinking the same thing.

My heart was pounding against my ribcage. Sweat dripped down my spine. Everything tingled, and there was a deep ache between my legs that I loved. But I was the farthest thing from human. I wasn't even alive.

And he was half-demon, forever inching closer to the corrupted blood taking over fully.

Okay, maybe it did sound silly when I thought about it, but the fact that Cole could not only see me, but we could touch each other, even in my spirit state, gave me a piece of life I felt like I was missing for so long.

"I'd settle for ironic instead of stupid," I said.

He snorted a laugh as he pulled away from me, rebuttoning his pants.

"That's a nicer way to put it." Red kissed his cheeks, and I couldn't help but wonder if it was from the sex or if he was a bit embarrassed by what he'd revealed to me. Cole wasn't exactly an emotional guy.

He ran his fingers through his blond hair, an attempt to regain his typical blasé front. "I'm sorry about the lack of foreplay. It's not really my style."

I slid off the dresser and fixed my clothes. "I'm not complaining, am I?"

And if I was being honest with myself, I didn't care—not in the least. When I glanced at him again and saw how he was looking me over hungrily, desire reignited in my chest. Heat spread across my skin.

"Maybe next time," I teased.

"You got it." He gave me a wolfish grin. "For you, I'll make an exception."

That was a promise I was looking forward to.

Cole plopped onto the bed, settling against the pillows, and placed his hands behind his head. His muscled chest glistened with sweat and aloe, and it took everything in me not to join him on the bed and try for a round two.

Readjusting my tank top, I moved toward the room's small mirror. When nothing appeared in the reflection, I frowned. All the giddiness I'd been feeling drained out my toes, leaving me empty.

Spirits didn't cast shadows or reflections.

The reality of what I really was smacked me across the face. No matter how Cole had made me feel in the moment, the truth was that I was still dead. I could never have a relationship of any kind. Once this mission was over and Kay was safe, I had to return to the afterlife and my job at Styx.

And if this cure worked for Cole… Well, he would want to live his new life as normally as possible.

When I turned around, I found Cole fast asleep in the same position, mouth slightly open and a soft snore rolling past his lips. So peaceful.

So *alive.*

My heart tugged in my chest. As much as I might have wanted to be, I knew I couldn't be a part of this world the way I wanted. Only a passing phantom. That's all I was. It'd be foolish to think anything else was possible.

Suddenly feeling too confined in the small space, I walked through the motel room's door and left Cole alone with his dreams.

Hopefully they were ones that didn't include me in them.

CHAPTER

EIGHTEEN

Not knowing where else to go, I headed toward the oldest part of Fairport, to the cemetery. It had started as a small space of land, occupied by the graves of some of the first settlers. Some were as old as the eighteenth century. As the colonist town grew over the decades to the city it was now, the cemetery gained more and more land, expanding to over a mile in every direction. Most of the first graves were decimated by time and nature, but some stone markers still stood, a stark contrast to the new, shinier marble tombstones on the opposite side that sat on top of fresher bodies.

With days until the solstice and me as a spirit now, I knew I couldn't collect the Holiest earth tonight, but the least I could do was find the grave with the oldest marker and hope that was the one that was going to save Kay and help Cole. That way, on the solstice, we could return and scoop it up without a problem.

As I approached the cemetery's iron-gated entrance, I was halted by what was before me. The ground on the other side seemed to shimmer with a range of different colors. Reds, blues, greens, and golds hovered just above the grass, like wisps of rainbow smoke.

Not spirits. I would be able to see them if they were souls. But waves of pure energy that were collecting on this Holy ground. I had seen this before but only on the solstice, when the living and nonliving planes were at their closest. The fact that the solstice was still days out and the veil was thin enough for this to happen was very concerning.

Not good. Not good at all.

"It's true."

A male's voice had me spinning around, fists out, ready for a fight.

There stood a stranger with a long face, pointed nose, and dark hair in a ponytail. He was unknown to me, but he smiled as if he knew me, making apprehension slither up my spine.

He wore a finely tailored plum-colored suit and polished shoes, looking very important and equally expensive. Both felt out of place here in front of a cemetery, even though it was creeping closer to midday.

He held his hands up in surrender. "I'm sorry for startling you," he said, his voice as smooth as silk. "When I heard we may have had an actual A-lister on the main floor, I had to come see myself."

I had no idea what he was talking about, but if he could see me, that meant one of three things. He was either dead, part or whole demon, like Cole, or a Medium, like Kay.

Not one of those options were good for me.

"Who are you?" I asked, unclenching my one hand just in case I had to unleash my light. "More importantly, what do you want?"

His eyes flashed a brilliant, unnatural red.

A demon. A full-blood.

"Xaver?" I stepped back, every muscle rigid.

The demon in the human's body rolled his eyes. "You insult me. Of all my brothers, you pick the most uncivilized one to assume I am."

"I don't know many of you, and the ones I have met don't exactly have the best manners."

His smile was slow and deliberate. "Well, I'm not quite like the others," he said. "Let me introduce myself. I prefer to be called Monnie, but the proper name for me is Mammon. Have you heard of me?"

"Can't say I have."

Was he trying to be my friend? What a bizarre introduction. Definitely not like the one I had with Xaver. But despite his heavily spread charm, the tension in my body didn't ease.

"How about the Seven Deadly Sins? Greed?" He held his hands out to the sides, as if welcoming me to marvel at him. "Here I am."

A prickle of warning zoomed up my neck. I didn't know much about demons, but everyone knew the stories of the Seven Deadly Sins. What I didn't know was that the sins were actually demons.

And now I was standing face-to-face with one of them. An original sin demon.

Greed, who wanted to be called Monnie. Pronounced like "money."

You've got to be kidding me. Did he think he was funny? I fought the urge to roll my eyes.

He was waiting for me to do something. Whether it was marvel at his presence, comment on his cleverness with his name, or run for the hills, who knows. Unimpressed, I just stood there, hands raised and ready to blast this cocky S.O.B. back to where he came from if I needed to.

"Are you proud of that? Really?"

He sighed and dropped his hands, disappointed. "Don't have much of a funny bone, do you?"

"What do you want?" I shot back, growing more annoyed.

"Jade, right? That's what you're going by now?"

What the hell was that supposed to mean?

"Yes, well," he went on, "I've come topside to help you, actually. I've heard you are in quite a bind."

"I don't want your help," I snapped.

He held up a finger. "Why don't you hear me out first. I'm sure I can change your mind."

Not wanting anything to do with Monnie, I turned around and marched away. Turning my back to a powerful, full-blood demon probably wasn't one of my smartest ideas, but nothing about Monnie screamed trustworthy. I needed to get away from him, and fast. The grave dirt would have to wait until another day.

Maybe going for this walk by myself hadn't been such a good idea.

"Your Medium friend may want you to reconsider," he called, and I halted at the mention of Kay.

Guilt bubbled up, as it always did when I thought of Kay and the trouble I had put her in. I hadn't even gotten that far down the sidewalk before spinning around to face him again. That got a pleased smile from the demon.

"There," he purred. "A little bit of your time. That's all I'm asking for."

"Talk fast."

"That's why you're here, isn't it? At Fairport's oldest

cemetery? You're looking for the next piece of the demon cure. To save your friend."

How did he know any of this? Had he been following me?

Unease skipped through me. I didn't like this; I didn't like this one bit.

Monnie took his chance and closed the distance between us. "I can help you save her."

The red color of his eyes flashed for a second before turning the human's normal brown again. Whoever Monnie had taken control of, I felt bad for them. No one deserved to unknowingly surrender control over their own bodies, especially by a demon.

And he was expecting me to trust him? Just like that?

Despite my gut twisting in warning and all the sirens going off in my head, I heard myself asking, "How?"

His grin spread wide. "I won't only tell you, I'll take it a step further," he said. "I'll give you the key to the cure."

"And what do you want in exchange?" No one ever did anything for free, and something told me there was no way Monnie, the demon of Greed, was going to do anything for free.

Shrugging, he said, "Nothing much. Just…a kiss."

I almost choked on my tongue. "Excuse me?" He couldn't be serious. What kind of weird, pervy request was that?

"That's my price. My information for a kiss."

I said nothing as I considered his offer. *Was* I considering it? I guessed so. Finding out how to save Kay's life had been my main priority since the attack in her shop. Her time was limited to find a way to help her, and we weren't even sure if our interpretation of the cure was the real one. I promised her I'd do everything to save her. And I would.

What was a kiss? Nothing really. A quick two second peck and that was all.

Wasn't much of a sacrifice on my end.

"That's really all you want? A kiss?" I asked. "And you'll give me what I need to save Kay."

"That's all."

"No tongue, do you hear me?" I said, firmly. "Two seconds, max."

His perfectly shaped eyebrows arched. "That's only if you don't beg for more."

I resisted the urge to vomit. Probably one of the hardest things I'd ever had to do in my afterlife.

"I expect payment up front," he said and puckered his lips.

I hesitated. What if he didn't hold up his end of the bargain? I mean, I wouldn't be losing much if he did decide to leave after, right?

"I'm waiting," he chastised, pursing his lips out farther. "Just a little kiss."

Taking a deep breath, I told myself it would be over in seconds. It wasn't like he was asking me for a limb. I needed to suck it up and do it. For Kay.

Closing my eyes, I leaned forward and pressed my lips against his.

A zap of energy surged between us, ricocheting from my head to the tips of my toes and back again. I leapt back, stunned, and when I opened my eyes again, I was staring at the hideous red eyes and gray face of the full-blooded demon, Mammon. Similar to Xaver, he had a protruding brow and pointed ears, but unlike him, Mammon had an oversized mouth jam-packed with sharp teeth.

I gasped, backpedaling. But as quick as the image appeared, it vanished, replaced by the suave and collected man I had been talking to all this time. He was staring at me with a puzzled look.

"What did you see?" he asked, intrigued.

It took me some time to find my voice again. My heart felt like it was stuck in my throat.

"You," I whispered, and rubbed my lips together. They still tingled from the electric charge that had passed through me. "I saw you. The real you."

"Interesting…" When he smiled again, I thought about the huge mouth with hundreds of pointy teeth—what really lay underneath the human façade. "I wonder if that's because of what you are."

"A reaper?"

To my surprise, Monnie laughed so hard, his head snapped back and his shoulders bounced. His laughter boomed loud enough to wake the dead.

"You're joking, right?" he said. "You have to be joking."

When I said nothing, his laughter died abruptly. "You're not joking."

"I'm not."

"You don't know what you are?"

"I'm a reaper," I said, growing more and more skeptical about his intentions here.

"I can't believe they didn't tell you."

Who was *they*? And tell me what?

"You bear the angel mark," he said and pointed to the strange branding above my heart.

The what?

"This?" I pulled down my tank top a little, just enough to expose the symbol and not slip a nip. "This is just a tattoo. One I'm guessing I got when I was alive."

His eyes widened in shock. "You really do have no idea."

Now he was getting on my nerves. What did he know that I didn't?

"Are you going to tell me, or just keep dicking around?" I snapped. "Angel mark? What the heck is that?"

"Quite the opposite of *heck* actually. You've been touched by one of those halo-wearing freaks." He gestured to the mark again. "There. They've branded you."

Hadn't Wyatt and Sean said something about seeing the mark in ancient texts? Some that talked about higher beings? Could Monnie be telling me the truth?

"What does that mean exactly? You said you knew what I was." My heartbeat was speeding up now. "What am I?"

"Oh, sweetie," he said with fake sincerity, "I would love to tell you, but that's not my place."

"Bullshit. Like you care about that."

"You're right. I don't," he said. "I'm all for breaking some rules. But"—his voice dropped low, ominous—"the answer to that question will cost you a lot more than a measly peck on the lips. And it's a price I doubt you're willing to pay."

I was about to press him for more information, like what that price would actually be, but I stopped myself. As much as I wanted to know who and what I was, deep down, I knew I had already kept this interaction going for long enough. And something told me he was right—the price he would ask of me would be too much, and I wasn't willing to risk anything else for a demon.

If Monnie was telling the truth, the tattoo on me was called an angel mark, which apparently meant I was touched by an angel. The only angel I knew was Azrael. I wondered if this had anything to do with him.

Either way, I had more information than I had before. Maybe I could go back to Sean and Wyatt and ask them about it. Having an actual name to go on might help in the search.

I'd find out the answer I'd been looking for on my own. Later.

For now, I needed to get the secret he'd promise to tell me for the cure. That was more important.

"Fine," I said. "You got your stupid kiss from me. Now it's time for you to hold up your end. What else do I need for the cure?"

He tugged at the jacket of his expensive suit, readjusting it. "Yes, well, it's obvious you know what the Holiest ground is. That's why you're here, isn't it? And the Breath of Life is the smoke from an ancient herb, which I'm assuming you also know…"

He was stalling. If he had any connection in the underworld, he most likely knew Cole and I had battled a group of Halflings in Marla's shop and could gather why we were there in the first place. Hell, he may have even been the one to send the Halflings. That bone-chilling thought reminded me that I had to tread very carefully with this demon.

"Hell's fire is obvious." Monnie clicked his tongue, pausing again for dramatic effect. "So, it's the Blood of the Damned I must be talking about."

"I know what that is," I cut in. "That one's obvious, too."

"Is it though?" he said. "Or maybe with this, the less obvious answer is the right one."

I growled, "Out with it, Monnie."

"Right." He chuckled. "I apologize."

"You're probably thinking the damned blood is the blood of the one affected, the one you're trying to save. In your case, the Medium. But actually, the blood must come from the one who *inflicted* the damnation. Where the curse began. The blood you need to make the curse reverse is—"

I gasped. "From Xaver."

"Precisely." Monnie smirked. "The one who impregnated your friend in the first place."

Oh shit. This mission just got a whole lot harder.

We didn't have time. How was I going to track down the full-blood Xaver *and* get a sample of his blood? There was a chance he was still possessing Laurence's body, but who knew where he was right now. Tracking him down could take weeks. Months.

Maybe Cole knew a way to track other demons. Or maybe Wyatt and Sean had some kind of book on summonings that we could try.

And what did that mean for Cole? Did he have to find the demon responsible for knocking up his mother? His demon father?

Did he even know who that was? That was a better question.

"And as the second part of my end of the bargain, I'm going to tell you how to find my brother," Monnie said. "It's easier for us to come topside nowadays, and because of that, he's going to be looking for and collecting his conquests."

Conquests with a S. So Xaver had many women out there in the world carrying his children? Gross.

"If he hasn't already, he'll come for the Medium," he continued.

"He can't get to her. She's somewhere safe."

"Are you sure about that?" He smirked. "There aren't many things that can hold us back."

Fear laced up my spine. All this time, I assumed Kay was protected at the vampire club. I cursed. Had I made a mistake trusting in Cole's judgment—a mistake that could cost Kay her life? What if Xaver had already snatched her from Andre and had dragged her into one of those Hell pits?

I had to go to Red. I had to check on her and make sure she was okay.

Spinning around, I forgot all about Monnie, my thoughts pinned on getting to Kay as fast as possible. I only got a couple of steps, before the Greed demon called out to me again.

"Don't you want to know what's going on here? Why the veil is thinning and creatures like me are going topside without the solstice?"

I ignored him, even though my head was screaming to

stop. Was he just trying to waste my time, or did he really know the answers I needed? Also, did I trust him to tell me the truth? Most likely no. I was better off getting to Kay and making sure she was all right.

There was a whoosh of air, and suddenly, he was standing in front of me. I skidded to a halt.

"I think you should," he said.

Trying to sidestep around him, he met my movements toe for toe to block me.

I clenched my fists, my anger growing.

When I was about to curse him off, he held up his hand to stop me. "All right, *reaper*. I'm going to give you this one for free. Only because, believe it or not, I feel bad for you."

Monnie glanced at the cemetery, where the ground still shimmered with energy, and then back to me. His eyes flashed red again to reveal the evil within, and leaning in close, he whispered three words that made my heart seize in my chest.

"A war's coming."

Then, he was gone.

CHAPTER

NINETEEN

I headed straight for uptown and the vampire club called Red. It took me some time to get there, but it wasn't like I could hitchhike or grab a taxi. Jogging at a decent pace was the most I could do, and since breathing wasn't a requirement when you were dead, I managed it okay.

When I reached the club, I slipped past a huge, angry-looking bouncer guarding the locked door. It was still too early for them to be open for business, so my guess was they just had him standing there for security reasons. An extra pair of eyes, especially since vamps didn't do too well in the daylight.

Inside was quiet. Dead, for lack of a better word. No one

tended to the bar. No girls danced in the hanging cages. No one sat at the tables along the stage. Not a soul around.

Was it still sleeping time for these vamps? Guess so. That was good for me though. Then I could find Kay and not worry about running into Andre or one of his workers. They wouldn't be able to see me, of course, but if I needed to sneak out Kay, it'd be better without them around.

Glancing up at the second floor overlooking the main club, I realized that if I were a vampire needing a place to sleep, behind a wall of tinted black glass was the winner. Unless there was a dungeon in the basement. But that was a bit melodramatic.

Even for Andre.

I climbed the modern-style staircase and walked into a large lounge area with a circular black leather couch and red carpeting. Off the lounge was a long hallway lined with doors. All closed. Most likely all locked.

But that wouldn't be a problem for spirit Jade.

Approaching the first door, I listened for any movement or sounds inside. When I heard nothing, I stepped through.

It was an office. The entire wall behind the desk was made of darkened glass, making the club below visible with a slight shade to it. I could bet money this was where Andre did his work and where he observed his customers and employees down below. Something told me the glass was bulletproof, too.

Unlike the rest of the club's modern decor, the desk was as wide as the room itself and made of solid wood that looked as heavy as an elephant. Grand, vintage, and very out of place among all the straight lines, red paint, and smooth metal accents.

Oh man, I bet that desk held some secrets in its drawers. Curiosity itched at me. What did a centuries-old vampire keep during his long lifetime?

That was a question for another day. I had to find Kay and get her out of here.

I phased into the adjoining room and wasn't surprised to find a bedroom as grand as the desk in the office. A huge four-poster bed made of mahogany and draped in red fabric sat in the very center of the room. No windows or glass at all in here, but there was a stone fireplace that was alive and giving off so much heat, I could feel the caress of warmth, even in my spirit form.

If I were going to decorate for a vampire, this room would be how I would do it. It looked like something straight out of Dracula's castle. The only thing it was missing was the coffin and gas lanterns on the walls. I guess some habits were hard to break.

As I crept toward the bed, I noticed a shape underneath the thick quilt and a wave of blond hair. I didn't need to get much closer to know it was Andre. His handsome, pale face and golden hair were the only parts sticking out of the blanket as he lay unmoving—barely breathing—on his back. He was so still, he reminded of a corpse or Sleeping Beauty, stuck in some kind of magical sleep trance. Yeah, maybe that was a better comparison. Less morbid.

He definitely reminded me of a princess with his sharp, regal features and long straw-colored hair.

I chuckled. He probably wouldn't have liked being called a princess.

Andre's eyes snapped open at once and jerked upright in bed so fast, I choked on my laughter from shock. His icy stare locked onto me, and I froze.

But he couldn't see me. Right? I hadn't shifted unknowingly again, had I?

I didn't think so. He shouldn't be able to sense me, yet he was sitting upright in bed, his gaze locked on me across the room.

I shivered. When I had first visited Red with Cole, I could have sworn Andre had been watching me then.

He shot out of bed and was in front of me in half a second. I jumped back out of reflex.

With eyes narrowed, Andre studied me. Then, he swiped his hand out, across my stomach, his hand going through me completely. He rubbed his fingers together as if expecting something to be there.

That's when I realized he was completely naked.

My breath froze in my chest. Forget the princess comment. There was nothing princess-like or dainty about *that* package. Even without the stiffness of arousal, his cock was thick and large enough to please any woman. His body was a lot leaner than Cole's wider frame, but I wasn't complaining. He was just as enjoyable to ogle over.

As he began to circle the place where I stood, examining the air through hooded eyes, I didn't move. Didn't breathe.

The way he was looking at me made delicious shivers race throughout my body, and for a moment, I wished he were looking at me that way because he could see me. Like he saw me as something new and exciting he wanted to try out.

But I couldn't just stand here all day. There were only a few hours left before it was nightfall and the vampires in the club would be getting up. I needed to get Kay out of here before then to avoid questions or any issues.

Sidestepping around Andre carefully, I hurried across the room and drifted through the wall into the next room. It was plain and matched the rest of the club's modern décor. A single bed and a red leather couch were the only furniture in the room. My guess? This was where the VIPs came to spend a little extra money for more time with one of the dancers.

Or this was where the vamps brought their victims for a late-night snack.

Either way, ew.

I popped through the next two rooms, which were exactly the same as the last. It wasn't until I reached the very last room that I reached my destination. Kay was sitting on the couch, face in her hands. She hadn't seen me come in, so I approached quietly.

"Kay?" I whispered so as not to spook her.

Her head shot up, her eyes sparkling with hope at my voice. "Oh, thank God it's you!" She jumped to her feet, rushed over to me, and flung her arms around me, squeezing me tight.

When Kay pulled away, her brows were pinched in confusion. She stared at me like that for a long moment, saying nothing. It took me a moment to realize why.

She had hugged me. She had been able to touch me.

I'd gone solid again.

Reaching out, she poked me in the shoulder to double-check, getting me right in the boney area so it hurt.

"Hey now. Watch it."

"That hurt?" she asked, but then her voice rose. "That hurt! And I can touch you!" She wrapped her hand around my wrist and shook it hard for good measure.

I jerked away and readjusted my leather gloves just in case.

"Careful. I still have a deadly touch," I said. "Don't want to make that mistake."

Her eyes widened, as if she were still processing the hug. "How… What happened to you?" She waved her hand over my body, not touching this time. "Are you alive?"

"No," I said, but then quickly added, "I don't know actually. I do bleed, though, when I'm like this, but I keep switching back and forth randomly. I have no control over it."

"I can't believe this! It's what you've always wanted, Jade."

Her grin radiated, and for the first time since this entire shit-show started, happiness flickered inside me. Kay just had that effect on people. Even me.

Yes, she had completely ignored the other things I'd said —the more negative parts about the flashing from spirit to alive and it being uncontrollable—but her joy for me was genuine and comforting.

"Have your memories come back, too?" she asked.

I shook my head.

Her smile faltered a bit, but she kept it on. "Maybe that comes next. Then you'll finally know who you are. Wouldn't that be amazing?"

It'd be everything I'd ever dreamed of. To know everything about my life that had been stripped from me after death, who and what I was, and to live my life again, exactly how I wanted to? Forget amazing; it would be a miracle.

Kay grasped my arm, gave it three hard squeezes, and laughed. "It seems like we've both had a little too much excitement in the last couple of days."

When I glanced down at her stomach, I remembered why I had come here in the first place, and guilt smacked into me like a tidal wave. I forced myself to meet her eyes again, my throat suddenly drier than the Middle Eastern desert in the summer months.

"Yeah, it's been interesting," I managed to get out.

"What have you found out? Do you know a way to fix me?"

I quickly told her about everything Cole and I had been through while she was here at Red, the demon Halfling attacks, finding the box and cure at Wyatt's, the run-in at Marla's shop, and the ingredients we still needed. I skipped the whole bit about sex with Cole and made sure to leave out my unexpected meeting with Monnie the demon.

"But as for what is going on with me, I have no idea. It's been happening randomly since the attack at Wyatt's, and there's no one I can talk to about it until we get this demon thing sorted out."

"No other"—she struggled to find the word—"r-reaper buddies you can ask?"

I shook my head. "The afterlife is just as messed up as this one. My boss is nowhere to be found, and my mentor is trying to sort everything out. Looks like I'm on my own here."

"Well, maybe this is a good thing. Maybe this is your second chance to get your life back."

"Not sure about that. It's been happening on and off for a while. I can't control it. It's like a malfunctioning light switch," I replied. "But that's not the only thing. Do you remember the white light I zapped Laurence with back at your shop?"

She nodded.

"Not only do I have the 'touch of death,' but now I can blast demons back to Hell with the light. Which is new."

"Is it a reaper thing?"

I shrugged. "No clue. But it's come in handy more than once these past couple of days."

"So why did you come here?" Kay asked.

"For you." How to explain this to her without freaking her out? "You're not safe here."

"I thought that was the entire reason I was here. To keep safe."

"Now that the veil is thinning between worlds, demons and spirits and God knows what else are running amok. There's nothing holding them back anymore, and they don't have to wait until the solstice. Xaver is looking for you and whoever else he managed to knock up, and will drag you back to some Hell dimension until that baby comes."

Kay turned pale.

"I need to get you out of here. I was able to kick Xaver's ass before, and now that I'm more in control of this new power, I think Cole and I can protect you more than these vamps."

Even though horror stayed planted firmly on Kay's face, she nodded, seeming to understand.

"We have the herb, Cole's fire, and a place on Holy ground to perform the ritual. The only part we're missing is the blood of the damned," I said.

"I can give you some of my blood. As long as it's not a lot."

"See, I thought it meant your blood, too, but that's not the case. It couldn't be that easy, right?" I let out a nervous laugh. "Unfortunately, it means Xaver's blood."

"So, we need the demon."

"That's right."

"But we're running from said demon because he wants to capture me and force me to have his demon baby."

"Exactly."

She began to pace across the room with quick, frantic strides. "You know what that means?"

I glanced about the room, not quite sure what she was implying.

"We need to trap him," she said bluntly. "Use me as bait."

"No, no." I held up my hands. "There's no way I'm putting you in even *more* danger."

"What other choice do we have?" she said, voice rising in a mix panic and certainty. "He wants me; we need him. I can lure him out."

I hadn't even thought about that. It made sense, but I hated that it did. I didn't want to use Kay as live bait for a full-blooded demon. She already had this demon baby growing inside her, and her life was on the line. It felt wrong.

So, so, so wrong.

Kay stopped pacing, her expression firm. She had made up her mind. "If we don't get this demon's blood, I'm dead."

I winced at the word.

"I'm not an idiot. I know my fate. This is what we need to do to save me, so let's do it."

I admired her bravery. Especially with everything she was going through already.

She walked over to me and placed her hand on my shoulder. The heat of her touch warmed me. She had always been so kind to me, even when I didn't think I deserved it.

"I trust you, Jade," she said with a soft smile. "I know you'll keep me safe."

My own smile wavered. I was glad she was so confident in me. That made one of us at least.

There was a hard knock at the door loud enough to make us both jump. Then a booming voice.

"Madame? Who is in there?"

The thick French accent told me it was Andre. Dammit. He couldn't know I was here.

I waved at Kay, telling her to answer him.

"Er—it's just me. I was talking to myself," she said, her voice shaking.

The door handle rattled against the lock.

My pulse skipped. I glanced around the room for a place to hide.

Could I even hide from a vampire? Something told me no.

I closed my eyes. *Turn back. Turn back!*

The door shot open so hard, it hit the wall, denting the plaster. Andre, now fully dressed in his normal tailored suit, looked directly at me. Four other vamps filed in behind him, three men and a woman.

Recognition flashed across Andre's face as he stared at me, and he hesitated. But the other vampires rushed at me.

My first instinct was to shove Kay back. She fell onto the couch just as a blur slammed into me, throwing me onto the bed. Vamps moved fast, way faster than demons. They could barely be seen. I rolled out of reach just as another blur grabbed for me.

Another whoosh of air nearby, and I spun, lashing out with a foot. The blow connected with one of them, and the vampire grunted as it flew back and hit the wall. Plaster from the wall exploded behind his head, but instead of being knocked out like any normal human would, his thin features only contorted in rage.

"Stop!" Kay yelled. "She's my friend! She's come to help me."

But her pleas fell on deaf ears. Again the air moved, giving me warning. But I wasn't quick enough this time. Sharp nails raked across my cheek. I gasped as the scent of blood whiffed past my nose.

For a moment, the room was still. Completely still.

Blood. Vampires. My gut twisted. I was in deep trouble.

Snarls sounded all around me, and when I scanned the room, I saw the four vampires circling me. Their eyes had changed color, the irises and whites completely consumed by blackness.

Bloodlust.

I glanced at Andre, who was still standing in the doorway —the only exit—his icy gray eyes pinned on me. He hadn't been lost to the bloodlust as easily as the others. If anyone could stop these other vampires, it was him.

At least I thought so.

As the four vampires stalked toward me, I readied myself to use the white light if I had to. Did it work on vampires? No idea. But that didn't mean I wasn't going to give it a try. No one was going to be sucking on my neck tonight, that was for sure.

Again, I looked toward Andre. Maybe there was a way I could grab Kay and blast our way through the door.

All hope vanished when Andre's eyes turned pitch black, too. He was gone.

He ran at me, the others closing in at the same time. Kay screamed for me, but I didn't have time to do anything else but dodge the hands grabbing for me. I swung a fist and hit Andre's jaw. He paused, touching the side of his face in surprise.

I wrestled with one of the male vamps, pulling his long mop of hair and throwing him into his friend's path. They hit each other with enough force to rattle their teeth.

Then, Andre came at me again.

As I tried to jump out of the way of the third hungry vampire, Andre's shoulder slammed into my chest. The strength behind the blow knocked me off my feet and stole the breath from my lungs. I hit the carpet with a grunt. Colors danced before my eyes. Then the weight of a fully grown man hit, his body pinning me to the ground.

I stared into Andre's beautiful and terrifying face, his eyes soulless and his canines slowly extending past his bottom lip.

Not my neck. Not today.

I bucked my body, but it did nothing to move him. He even chuckled, and that only made my blood boil. When he grabbed both my wrists and pressed them into the floor on either side of my face, making my neck completely accessible, I kicked out as hard as I could. My boots did nothing but slip against the carpet.

Kay's frantic cries rang above the chaos. "She's my friend! Stop! Please!"

Andre seemed lost to his hunger now, like he hadn't heard a word.

The other vampires stayed back to allow their boss first taste.

No way.

I summoned the power to my hands again, took a deep breath, then released it. The white light shot out, hit Andre square in the chest, and catapulted him across the room. He smashed through the glass wall and disappeared as he fell to the floor below.

As if snapped from a dream, the four vampires ran to the window.

I didn't wait another second. Snatching Kay by the hand, I half dragged her out of the room, down the staircase, and toward a back door labeled *Emergency Exit*.

I kicked it open. A siren blared.

Briefly glancing over my shoulder, I shoved Kay outside and noticed Andre rising to his feet slowly. Half his face was burned from the blast, the flesh pink and glossy, with bits of glass sticking out. Just in those few seconds, his skin began to knit back together before my eyes.

Yikes. Looked like I made a fast enemy.

No need to stick around any longer. I pushed the heavy door open and rushed into the early night.

Kay and I ran down the street in silence. Only until the tall city buildings began to change into the cobblestone roads and brick-faced homes did we slow down. No one was following us, at least that I could see, so I let Kay rest for a few minutes. Sweat dripped from her forehead, and her chest heaved.

With her hands on her hips, she said, "Can you believe I used to be a competitive runner in high school?" She gasped between words. "I used to be able to run for miles without a wheeze."

I scanned the area and realized we were close to Kay's shop, but still some ways away from the motel. We needed to tell Cole about what had happened at Red. But more importantly, I needed to tell him about Xaver and the final part of the cure. If Kay was willing to offer herself up as bait to lure Xaver in, that meant we needed a plan.

And weapons. Lots and lots of weapons.

"Can you keep moving? Or do you need to catch your breath some more?" I didn't feel safe staying in one place, but I wasn't going to show that fear to her. "Cole is waiting for us in a motel under the freeway."

Kay's lip turned up in disgust, probably knowing the area wasn't a good one, but she nodded.

We hurried the rest of the way. When we reached the familiar ugly orange door with the crooked number two on it, I paused. Two male voices came from the other side. One was Cole's. I'd know that overconfident, sarcastic tone anywhere. It was the second one that confused me.

I stepped closer and pressed my ear to the door, gesturing for Kay to stay quiet.

"Your job was simple, Masters. Keep her occupied. Whatever it took, remember? Yet I find out you have her chasing demons all over the city. And her powers have triggered."

"It would have been nice if you told me about that," Cole shot back to his guest, sounding annoyed. "You could have made my job a lot easier. How was I supposed to know she was going to stumble across some ancient text and find the demon cure?"

A warning prickled up and down my spine. They were talking about me. They had to be. But that meant Cole was working with someone else to keep me running around, distracted?

Fury surged. I was an *assignment* for him? All of this— everything, even the sex—had it been part of the job?

My next question was why? Why me, of all people? It didn't make sense.

My fingertips glowed white. Energy crackled across my

skin like tiny lightning bolts, unable to be contained by the leather gloves I wore. I gasped.

The Greed demon, Monnie, had said I had been touched by an angel; that was what my tattoo had been about—I was branded by them. Had he been telling the truth? Could that be what this was all about? *Me?*

But I was a no one.

Wasn't I?

I stared at my hands, still prickling with power.

Just then, Monnie's final words to me resurfaced in my head, replaying in an ominous echo that left me icy cold all over.

A war's coming.

Whatever was going on, it was way bigger than just me. It had to be.

"Things are in motion now. They must sense the change," the other man said. His voice was a booming presence with his anger, much more overpowering than Cole's.

Wait a minute. Recognition twitched through me. That voice… I knew that voice.

Cole let out an exasperated sigh. "What is she, anyway? I think I have the right to know."

There was a crash inside, as if something had been thrown. Maybe a side table or television.

"She's the one that can ruin everything I've worked centuries to build," the man barked. "Keep her away from this. Do you understand? Stick to the script. Or I'll end whatever's left of your pathetic life for real and send you straight to Hell. No stops. Got it?"

Every muscle in my body tensed as the realization hit.

I knew that voice because I'd heard it every day during my year as a reaper.

It was my boss, Azrael.

CHAPTER

TWENTY

I needed to get out of here. If I was really Cole's job, I
needed to get as far away from him as possible.

But God did I want to kick down that door and
punch those two square in their faces.

It took everything in me to spin around and head back
down the street. Kay stayed close at my side. Her silence told
me she had heard the same thing I had but was too nice a
person to bring it up right away, seeing how angry I was.

Even though I'd heard it with my own ears, I was having a
hard time believing what had just been revealed. All this time
—my job, my afterlife—had been a lie somehow? How long
had Azrael been planning this? Had I been a part of some
larger plot all along?

What was Azrael up to? I had a feeling it had something to do with the veil between worlds thinning before the solstice. But what did that have to do with me? Why was I such a risk to this plan?

So many questions. None with even a hint of an answer that I could think of. None of it made sense.

All I knew for sure now was that the entire moment in the alleyway with Cole had been staged. Which made sense in hindsight. It had felt off when I found him not on the verge of death but only knocked out.

Did Simon know about any of this?

I wanted desperately to say no. When I had met him on the street the other night, he had seemed genuinely confused and concerned. He hadn't given off any hidden intentions.

But then again, neither had Azrael.

Who knew who else was part of this larger plot. I couldn't trust anyone. Except Kay.

Poor Kay. She had been dragged into this because of me. Because of what I was.

I had felt responsible for this before. Now, I was sure everything that had happened to her was my fault.

We trudged downtown for a while in silence, until it dawned on me that I wasn't sure where to go. Especially to keep Kay safe. We were running out of time. The solstice was two days away. It would be our only time to perform the cure.

Xaver, Azrael, Cole, Andre. Who weren't we running from at this point? There was nowhere safe. Cole was going to be searching for me soon. We needed a place to lie low for a while. A place to regroup and make a plan.

But where?

"Is there any way we can stop at my place?" Kay peeped up from beside me. "I would kill for a shower and maybe some new clothes."

I wanted to smack myself in the forehead. Of course. It was so easy for me to forget about living necessities. If Kay wanted something as simple as a shower and some new clothes after everything she's been through, I could do that.

"We have to be quick though," I said. "I don't want to stay in one place for too long. For your safety."

"Agreed."

"Wait, before we go." I reached into my back pocket for the small Styx Corp tablet Azrael had given me on my first day of work. The green light flashed, telling me I had a message waiting for me. Anger coursed through my veins at the thought of him using it as a way to keep tabs on me all this time. A tracker or maybe an audio recorder.

Not anymore.

Gritting my teeth, I threw it onto the ground as hard as I could. The glass splintered, and the blinking green light died out. I stomped on it several times with the heel of my boot. That was more for my own self-satisfaction. Pieces of glass and plastic flew all over the sidewalk.

Only when it no longer looked like a tablet did I feel a little better.

I kicked the remaining parts into a nearby sewer and grinned.

Fuck you, you son of a bitch.

When I looked up, I found Kay staring at me with worried eyes.

"You okay?" she asked.

I straightened myself up. "Better now, I think."

"Do you want to talk about it?"

Too sweet. Why was she always so kind? Especially to me. The one who probably deserved it the least.

"Maybe another time," I told her. "Let's go."

We turned down the next block toward Chestnut Street and Oh! Kay's Pastries. Kay lived in a small one-bedroom apartment above the shop. As we came up to the storefront, I noticed the broken windows had been boarded up with plywood. Sorrow filled my chest at the sight of the destroyed store. I glanced at Kay, who sighed heavily.

"That's what insurance is for, right?" she said with a wavering smile. "It'll get it fixed."

As we walked around to the side of the building to her apartment's entrance, we stopped short. Laurence sat there on the steps in front of her door, his head in his hands.

"Laur—"

My hand shot out to stop Kay from moving and talking. The last time I had seen Kay's sorcerer boyfriend, he had been possessed by Xaver and had tried to kill us all. Now he was just sitting here on her stoop, waiting for her to get home?

I didn't trust it.

Gesturing for her to stay put, I crept closer to Laurence. He looked up slowly, his gaze skipping me and going straight for Kay.

He leapt to his feet. "Kay! Oh my God! I've called you hundreds of times. I stopped in. I've circled town, but I couldn't find you anywhere!"

When he went to her, I placed my gloved hand on his chest and pushed him back. Since he hadn't been expecting it, or hadn't really seen me, he plopped back onto the step he had been sitting on.

He looked up at me in confusion. "I'm sorry. Have we met before?"

"Sort of," I answered.

It sounded like Laurence. His jittery mannerisms were like the Laurence I had observed Kay with for over a year. Right down to his hokey Hocus Pocus T-shirt. More importantly, the twisted, ugly demon face didn't spring up when I looked him in the eyes. So maybe this was Laurence —real Laurence.

I had to make sure. I didn't trust anyone. Not anymore.

Laurence glanced over my shoulder to Kay, who was hugging herself, seeming unsure and probably a bit cold from the nipping bite of the cool night.

"Kay, it's me. Really me this time. I'm so sorry for what I did to you. And the shop. I'll help you fix it. I'll pay for it all." He was rambling. A very Laurence thing to do, especially when he was nervous. "I couldn't control myself. You have to believe me. I could see what I was doing, but I couldn't stop it. That thing—"

"Demon," I corrected.

He pushed a hand through his hair. "Demon? Well, shit."

Kay still hovered behind me. "How do we know if it's really him?" she whispered to me.

"It's me," he said, standing. "I swear."

We both knew swearing meant nothing.

If only I had some of Cole's Holy Water to test on him.

"Can you touch him with your light? See if it affects him?" Kay asked.

"Only if you want real Laurence possibly blasted into the next town," I said. "I can't control it like that yet."

"Blast me? What? No." Laurence's expression turned desperate. "Kay, it's me. Can't you see?"

"I don't *see* the demon," I told her. "I could see it before, but I don't see it now. It may be him. Xaver could have willingly left his body."

Kay stepped around me. Before I could stop her, she said, "Fine, then tell me. What did I want to name the shop before I settled on Oh! Kay's. Only Laurence would know the answer to that."

Laurence smiled gently. "You wanted to name it Abigail's

Kitchen. After your grandmother who raised you and taught you how to bake."

With that, Kay jumped into his arms. He embraced her, allowing her to cry softly into his shoulder, as he repeatedly told her he was sorry.

I didn't interrupt. After everything they both had been through—and were going to still go through—it was probably overdue. My chest ached for them.

When they finally parted from each other, sometime later, I said, "We should go inside," and ushered them up the staircase to the second-floor apartment. I made sure to lock every door after me.

"There's no need for that," Laurence said as I pushed one of Kay's heavy side tables in front of the door. Kay went straight for the kitchen to fetch drinks from the fridge.

"There are protection spells all over this apartment. I wanted to make sure that if Kay came back, she would be safe from everyone." He frowned. "Even me, if it came down to it again."

"No offense, but I'd feel a little safer if those spells were coming from a level three sorcerer. Maybe even level two." I closed the blinds to both windows in the living room.

"I've been working on it," he countered. "How did you know I was a level one sorcerer anyway? Better yet, who are you? Has Kay been with you this entire time?"

Guess I was the one thing he hadn't seen while Xaver had possessed him. Maybe it was because I had still been in my spirit state and only Xaver himself had seen me.

I was about to open my mouth, but Kay beat me to it. "This is Jade Blackwell."

She placed three glasses of what looked like orange juice on the coffee table. That was just like Kay. Even in such dire times, she was a sweetheart, thinking about everyone else. Manners for miles.

Laurence's mouth dropped open at the mention of my name. "The spirit Jade Blackwell?" He gasped. "The one who's been helping you this past year, who you had me look up towns and names online for?"

"And I appreciate that," I said, and I really did. "But yes, it's me."

"How—How can I see you right now? Aren't you a spirit?"

"Specifically, I'm a reaper," I said. "I help souls pass when it's their time and help them over into the afterlife."

"That's why she's been so good at helping me keep those pesky ghosts away," Kay said with a smile.

Laurence collapsed on the small blue sofa. "Wow, a reaper. I didn't know they even existed."

"That's how it's supposed to be," I replied, "but things have become extra screwy in the past couple of days. On top of the whole you being possessed by a full-blooded demon and getting Kay pregnant with its spawn…"

Kay's eyes widened in horror, and I wished with everything I had that I could have sucked those words back into my mouth and swallowed them back down.

"Wait, what?" He glanced at Kay's stomach. "You're—"

Maybe I should have let Kay explain that one.

She drew in a deep breath to compose herself. "Like Jade said, a lot has happened these past couple of days. I'll fill you in."

And she did. Quickly and efficiently, too. She told him about everything, including my newest powers, and how we had to somehow get Xaver's blood to save her with a ritual.

When she was done, Laurence swallowed a bunch of times, as if he were doing all he could to keep the vomit from coming up. His face paled. "So now we have to find the very demon that impregnated my girlfriend and almost killed me?"

"To be fair, he tried to kill all of us at some point," I said.

Laurence launched himself up and started pacing across the room. "Even better!"

"It's how we're going to help Kay," I said. "I have all the other ingredients. We just need Xaver's damned blood on the solstice, and we're good to go."

When I turned to my friend, I noticed her looking a bit flushed. "Why don't you go take that shower, Kay?" I offered. "Laurence and I will keep watch, and then we'll head out when you're done."

She nodded and disappeared into one of the rooms down the hall. Not even a minute later, the water to the shower turned on.

"You really should do a better job at keeping her relaxed," I said to Laurence. "She's been through enough already. We have to stay positive for her."

"So what now? Do you have a plan?" he asked.

"Not exactly… Not yet anyway, but we can't let Kay see how scared we are for her. It'll only make things worse."

He sighed. "Okay. You're right. I just can't believe I did this to her." He dropped his head into his palms again. "I'm the worst boyfriend ever."

"I wouldn't say worst…"

Even though he wasn't exactly my boyfriend, Cole Masters's name sprang to mind.

As I looked over at Laurence, still whispering to himself and hiding his face, sympathy twisted within me. The guy thought he had sentenced the woman he loved to her death. I'd be distraught, too.

I wanted to comfort him, but I wasn't the best at emotional situations like this. I never knew what to say or do.

If anything, I was just awkward.

I reached out to touch his shoulder, but then thought better of it and pulled away.

Fumbling for the right words, I said, "Er—you know, if I really thought you and Kay weren't good for each other, then I would have stopped your relationship a long time ago. I had plenty of opportunities."

Slowly, he lifted his chin, and a small smile tugged at the corners of his mouth. "Well, that's good to know."

"Hey, all it would have taken was one little touch." I fiddled with the glove of my right hand. "And lights-out forever."

God, I was bad at this.

Well, at least I was being honest.

"Keep that in mind for the future," I said.

He swallowed hard. "Heard the threat loud and clear."

"Good." I smiled. "What we need to do now is come up with some plan on how to get Xaver here without getting anyone else hurt. Especially…"

The fine hairs on my arms rose, followed by a layer of goose bumps. White light bounced across my fingertips, like electricity, even with the leather gloves on.

Something wasn't right.

Laurence must have seen the panic in my face because he jumped to his feet, knocking the coffee table and spilling the glasses of juice all over the white carpet.

"What? What is it?" he asked.

My head whipped toward the bathroom, my heart dropping to my toes.

Kay.

Her bloodcurdling scream confirmed all my fears.

CHAPTER

TWENTY-ONE

Forgetting about everything else, I sprinted to the bathroom and grabbed the doorknob. Shaking it multiple times revealed it was locked.

"Kay! Kay!" I screamed over and over before stepping back, ready to kick the door down with my boot.

Laurence was beside me suddenly, whispering words in an old language and gesturing toward the lock. A spell.

There was a soft click, and I shouldered the door open just in time to see Kay cowering in the bathtub with a towel clutched to her nakedness, the water from the showerhead spraying all over, and the small window busted open with the huge red-eyed demon Xaver trying to squeeze inside. He growled ferociously, his clawed hand swiping for Kay who was just out of reach.

Laurence started muttering more spells frantically, but I didn't want to stand around and see if any of them worked. I threw myself at Kay and tried to tug her out of the tub. Xaver swiped and his talon met my upper arm, slicing through the flesh like it was paper. Blood bubbled up instantly.

For a minor wound, it stung like hell. Like a giant papercut.

Xaver's smile was all toothy and monstrous. "She *bleeds*." He seemed too excited to have found this out.

Without Cole and his backpack of tricks, the only weapons I had were my hands. The white light and the death touch.

I quickly pulled off my glove and snatched Xaver's arm. His boney fingers wrapped completely around my wrist, his claws biting down. Pain sliced through me, more blood springing up.

My death touch wasn't working on him.

Guess that made sense. I couldn't kill a demon. He was already sort of dead, wasn't he? Demons didn't have souls, either.

"I was mistaken," Xaver drawled, his voice grating across every nerve. "Not only a reaper, but something more."

His gaze fell on the tattoo on my chest, and for the first time, fear flashed in his eyes. "I never thought I'd see one of you again."

I needed to summon the white light. That was the only thing that had worked on him last time.

But before I could reach down and pull the power out, the demon used our grip on each other to throw me across the small bathroom. The back of my head slammed against the mirror, shattering it, and the motion flipped me over the vanity sink. My vision blurred, and every bone in my body spiked with agony. I landed in a puddle on the floor.

So much pain. Even with all the fights I had been in these last few days, I still wasn't used to the shock pain brought me. After a year of feeling almost nothing at all, it was crippling. But I couldn't stay down. Not when Xaver was so close and Kay was in danger.

I pushed myself up on shaky elbows, my stomach retching from the movement.

"Stop muttering your nonsense, sorcerer!" Xaver shouted at Laurence. "You're not strong enough to do anything. Your silly little protection spells couldn't even keep me out."

Suddenly a small fireball shot across the room, hitting Xaver square in the face. He screamed and fell back, disappearing from the window.

I glanced at Laurence, who still had his hands up, breathing heavily. He looked as shocked as I was that whatever he had done had worked.

"Awesome work," I said, pushing myself to my feet. Touching the back of my head made me wince, and when I looked at my fingers, more blood glistened there. Damn. Xaver had got me good.

"I-I didn't know I could do that." Laurence gasped. "That's a level two spell!" He laughed and punched the air. "Yes! Take that, demon scum!"

I turned to Kay, who was ghostly pale and shaking.

"Are you okay?" I asked her, which in hindsight, was a stupid question. Of course she wasn't okay. She had just been ambushed by a demon. Again. This time in her own home.

Despite all that, she nodded. "He didn't touch me," she whispered. "You guys came just in time."

I helped her stand up with my gloved hand and shut off the shower's water with the other.

Clutching her towel, Kay turned to Laurence. "I didn't

know you surrounded my apartment with protection spells. When did you do that?"

Laurence's cheeks reddened. "The moment I realized I loved you. After our lunch date at the harbor. I reinforced them again before you guys found me on the steps."

"Not to be a downer, but why didn't they work?" I asked.

"The best protection spells fortify the structure they're placed on, but it has to be an enclosed structure. Closed doors. Windows. That's what keeps the spell at its strongest."

"So, when I opened the window to let the steam out from the shower…" Kay began.

"It weakened the spell," Laurence said, but then smiled at her. "But that's okay. He's gone now. You're safe."

"Not without some blood spilled." She tossed me my leather glove, and I slipped it back on. "Are you okay, Jade? That was quite a landing."

Rubbing at a stiff muscle in my shoulder, I replied, "Eh, I haven't spilled blood in a long time. I have a lot to catch up on."

"Well, just to be safe…" Kay reached for the window to close it.

A gray-skinned hand reached through the opening and seized Kay by the arm.

"Kay! No!"

But it was too late. Xaver yanked her out of the window, leaving us only with the echo of his laughter.

I rushed over and peered outside. "Kay! Kay!" But she was gone. Vanished.

Not knowing what else to do, I ran out of the apartment, my heart pounding harder than it ever had before. Laurence was right behind me as I circled the building, but there were no signs of Kay or the demon.

"What do we do now?" Laurence cried out, searching the surrounding area.

"I'm thinking. I'm thinking." I paced in front of the boarded-up store. My head was still throbbing from the fight with Xaver in the bathroom and now from the new panic of losing Kay to the monster.

Come on, Jade. Think.

We needed to rescue Kay. That was a given. But how to find her…

Something resurfaced from my memory—something Kay had said a long time ago about Laurence and doing a spell to find out who I really was in life.

"Laurence!"

He jumped. His nerves were obviously shot.

"Do you know how to do a location spell?" I asked.

"Uh, I've been practicing. It's the highest form of level one magic there is, so I haven't perfected it yet."

"Didn't you say the fireball was level two magic? Shouldn't that mean you're level two now?"

"That fireball was extremely lucky. And it was small compared to what it should have been. I've been tinkering with the spell, but I'm not there yet," he said. "As for moving levels, that's not how it works for witches and sorcerers. You move to the next level after passing a test held by the Magic Council."

What the hell did I know? These weren't the types of questions you asked people. Especially ones you just helped die to cross over.

"Level one is mostly defensive magic. Protection spells, concealing and levitation spells. Counter curses. Stuff like that. Level two is more offensive, and they don't really tell you what's in level three. Not many of us get that far."

"Do you think you can perform a location spell to find Kay?" I asked. "Or even Xaver?"

She was bound to be wherever he was. After everything,

it was doubtful he would let her out of his sight again. Even more so since he knew I was involved in this.

"Maybe," Laurence said, "but I would need a piece of her…"

"Er—what?"

"Like a lock of her hair or a clipped fingernail. Something for the magic to know who it's looking for."

There had to be something in her apartment. "Go back upstairs and snag her hairbrush or something."

"Good idea." He was gone in the next second.

I took the moment alone to really take in what was going on. Did I trust Laurence to do the spell? Did I really have a choice? If Marla was still here, I could have asked her, but it was doubtful she was even done with her afterlife orientation and readjustment. It would be some time before she was sent to her dimension and settled in. And even if she was, the afterlife wasn't really the safest place for me right now, was it? Azrael could find me a lot quicker on the other side. The dead were his "thing" after all.

Nope, I was stuck with level one Laurence.

"Jade." Laurence's harsh whisper came from around the corner.

I followed it to find him sitting on the stoop again, a piece of paper laid out on his lap and Kay's brush in his hand. "What's up?"

"You can't blame me if this doesn't go right, got it? I'm doing all I can."

I opened my mouth to say "Well, no shit" but stopped myself. In the time I had known Laurence, one thing was for certain: he had enough self-confidence to fill a grain of rice. He was always doubting himself and his magic. Maybe that was contributing to his mediocre spell casting?

Didn't magic come from within, or some philosophical nonsense like that?

It was worth a try.

"Laurence, look at me."

He did, and the worry in his eyes spoke volumes. My mind blanked. Dammit, I was awful at this stuff.

What would Kay say to him if she were here? Something encouraging and gentle, no doubt.

Be gentle, Jade.

I took a deep breath, trying to channel my inner Kay. "You can do this, Laurence. Don't get in your head. It's your own worst enemy."

"I *know* that." His voice rose in annoyance. "You don't think I know that? I have to get this right. I have to. For her."

"Listen to me here. There is no pressure." He went to cut me off, but I held up my hand. "I know other ways to find her, but I want you to do it because I know you can. I just saw you conjure a fireball without being a level two sorcerer. That's unheard of."

Man, the lies were just rolling off my tongue now, but the sudden glint of hope in Laurence's eyes kept me going.

"I know you love Kay, and she loves you, too. That connection is what we need. It'll strengthen the location spell."

It sounded as if that would work, but who knew if it made any difference at all? I wasn't going to tell him that, though.

He plucked a couple of hairs from Kay's brush and pulled off the necklace he'd been wearing. It was a white crystal wrapped in wire and then threaded with a rope. Holding the hairs in his palm, he muttered a few words in Latin, then placed the top of the necklace over them and closed his fist so the crystal could sway freely over the paper.

That's when I noticed the paper wasn't blank. Laurence had scribbled a large blob-like object with small random dots inside. It took me a second to realize the sketch was supposed to be Fairport, and the dots were all the major landmarks in the city. The harbor, city hall, cemetery, the war memorial, and Oh! Kay's, where we stood now.

He said a few more words, and the crystal began to sway like a pendulum. It rocked back and forth by an invisible force and then around and around, skimming the crudely drawn map for a place to land.

But it never did. It just continued to swing.

I waited a few moments before saying, "What's it doing?"

"I don't know," he said, frustrated. "It's not supposed to take this long."

Another minute of the necklace swinging, and he slammed it down. "It's like it can't reach her." He sighed. "I'm sorry, Jade. I thought I could do it, but I obviously can't."

"Hey, stop that. You did great," I said. "Maybe the map isn't big enough. Maybe she's somewhere—"

"What?"

My stomach clenched painfully. I knew exactly where Xaver had taken Kay.

"The spell didn't work because of you," I said as dread set in. "It didn't work because Kay is no longer on this plane."

Laurence's face fell in horror. "What do you mean?"

"Xaver brought her to Hell."

He leapt to his feet. "What!"

Monnie had said Xaver would probably do something like that—bring her to a Hell dimension until she gave birth, where she couldn't be reached by anyone. How could I have forgotten something like that?

"We need a way to summon a demon," I said in a rush, my mind and heart racing too fast. "Is there a spell for that?"

"Not that I know of. Maybe a level three?" He put the crystal necklace back around his neck.

There was no way for me to get to Marla to ask her.

Maybe I could find another level three witch or sorcerer

and force them to perform a summoning spell, if that even existed. But I didn't have time to go knocking on doors and ask every single person what kind of supernatural they were. There would be a lot of confused humans in the mix, too.

Who else did I know who could help us?

Wait… Maybe humans were just what I needed.

"Do you have a car?" I asked.

He pulled his keys out of his pocket, looking extremely confused, and pointed across the street. "The blue Toyota there. Why?"

"Let's go. I'll fill you in on the way." Sprinting toward his car, I waved for him to follow. "I'm driving."

CHAPTER

TWENTY-TWO

Why had I insisted on driving Laurence's car? Because I wanted to, mainly. It'd been a long time since I had done such a basic human thing, and I wanted a crack at it. I couldn't be as bad as Cole. But after missing the exit I needed to get off at and having to circle back around again, I realized I probably should have taken the passenger seat.

I wasn't awful. If anything, I was driving a little too slow, just stuck to the basics—steering, gas and brake pedal, blinker—and stayed away from all the fancy buttons on the dashboard.

When we pulled up to Wyatt and Sean's trailer, I threw the car into park and climbed out. Laurence did, too.

"Where are we?" He took in the junk cars and scrap metal all over the property and small trailer in the middle, boarded up and marked with strange symbols. It looked like they had added a few more since my visit with Cole.

"Some friends." Wow, I sounded like Cole, didn't I? "Let me do the talking here, okay?"

Laurence nodded, appearing thankful more than anything else.

"Throw some protection spells around the house, will you?" Even though I knew most of those symbols were meant to keep out certain creatures, we could use all the protection we could get.

Their German shepherd, Angel, barked from inside the trailer, but instead of Wyatt and his gun meeting us at the door, I spotted his suspicious glare through a boarded-up window as I walked up to his porch.

"Uh, hey, Wyatt. It's me," I said with a little wave. Why did I feel like even though I couldn't see his shotgun, it was still pointed in my direction?

"Who's that?" the old man asked, nodding toward Laurence, who was walking around the trailer, hands up and chanting. "And what is he doing to my house?"

"That's Laurence. He's a sorcerer. He's placing more protection around your house."

Wyatt snorted.

"Can I come in? I have something to ask you." When he didn't move, I added, "Please. It's important, and I'm on a strict deadline here. Lives are at stake."

He still seemed unimpressed. "Lives are always on the line," he said. "Where's Masters?"

The mention of Cole's name brought back the anger. And surprisingly, sorrow. I hated that part of it. It meant Cole had managed to worm his way into my heart somehow.

"Not here," was all I said. Wyatt had known Cole longer

than I had, so telling him the truth about our split could make him not want to help me. "He might meet us later."

Not a total lie. Cole would come back here eventually, and hopefully when that happened, I wouldn't be around. He had to be looking for me by now, realizing I hadn't just gone to a vending machine or to grab a slice of pizza.

Wyatt nodded toward the front door. "Stand on the welcome mat."

An odd request, but okay.

The mat, which had a faded Christmas tree on it, looked normal enough, so I did as he asked and waited. Nothing happened.

Then the creaky storm door opened to reveal Wyatt and the shotgun at his side. "All right. Come in."

"What was that all about?" I asked, stepping inside.

Angel rushed toward me, pushing her large head under my hand so I could pet her. I scratched her behind the ears.

"Demon trap under the mat. Just in case." Wyatt set his gun down against the wall and walked over to his armchair. Angel took her place at his side. "So, why're you back here?"

"I need a way to summon a demon. From Hell."

His eyes widened. "And why in the world would you want to do that? They need to stay in Hell. We shouldn't be helping them get out."

"Xaver, the one who impregnated my friend, kidnapped her and took her into one of the Hell dimensions so I can't reach her," I said. "Is there a way to summon him?"

Wyatt slumped in his oversized chair and sighed. "There is, but it's extremely difficult. And messy."

Messy?

"We're going to need blood. A lot of it, too."

Oh. Messy. It made sense now.

There was a knock at the door. I turned to see Laurence standing there. He gave a little wave.

Angel barked, ears perking up, until she was shushed by her owner. Then she curled by his feet.

Wyatt gestured for him to come in. He did, proving he was also demon free.

Just like I had when I first entered the human's home, he marveled at the mountains of books and papers and strange symbols covering the walls, floors, and windows.

"I have some wild cats in the area," Wyatt said. "Sean has a few bowls out back where he leaves food for them. Maybe if I snag two or three…"

Woah. I was not going to sacrifice Sean's cats. No way. Just like I wouldn't do anything to hurt Angel.

"What about using a person's blood? Would that work better?"

"Yes, actually. And a supernatural's is even better. Has the energy and magic needed for the incantation."

I knew what I had to do. But before I could say anything, Laurence stepped forward.

"We'll use my blood. I volunteer it," he said.

"Absolutely not," I shot back. "You don't need to do that. I'll do it."

"Do you even have blood?" Laurence asked.

I showed him the dry blood on my wrists from where Xaver's talons had sunk in. "It seems like it."

"Can you even…*die?*" he asked.

That was a good question. I definitely could feel pain in this "alive" state. I could bleed.

But I was technically already dead.

There had to be a risk. The question was, did I really want to find out what it was? If I died while on this plane, my soul could be lost forever. Stuck between worlds. Or maybe I would just go to a Hell dimension for trying to cheat death. Anything was possible, and that was scary.

"I'm not going to die," I said to convince myself as well as Laurence. "Did it once, don't feel like doing it again."

"We'll need a good amount of blood," Wyatt interjected. "You may feel sick after or even pass out."

"I'll be fine." Maybe if I said it enough, it'd come true. But I was shaking a bit on the inside from my nerves. I clapped my hands to fake enthusiasm. "All right. When are we doing this?"

"Midnight," Wyatt said. "Sean should be getting home soon. Then we'll prepare."

Just before twelve, we gathered the things we needed for the summoning on a small folding table behind the trailer. A bowl, a candle, a dish towel, a knife, a jar of dirt, and a belt. That last item threw me, until Sean explained it was for a tourniquet.

And of course, there was a first aid kit to sew me up afterwards.

Even though we had everything we needed to pull Xaver out of his Hell hole, we didn't have much of a plan for what came after. Well, besides a bunch of guns.

I suggested we dip the bullets in Holy Water for two reasons: to give them a little more kick and because we didn't have Cole and his bullets here. We were on our own, but the good thing was that it was four against one.

One mediocre sorcerer, two humans, and a reaper-thing against a full-blooded demon. Our odds didn't sound as good when I said it that way.

Wyatt set out the bowl and lit the candle beside it. Besides the flickering motion sensor on the back of the trailer, the candle was a weak light in the dense darkness. Sean beckoned me over to the table.

"Are you sure about this, Jade?" Laurence asked, nervously swaying side to side.

More certain than I'd ever been in my afterlife. Kay was my closest friend. I had the ability to save her. And that was just what I was going to do.

I nodded and held out my arm.

Sean wrapped the belt around my arm above my elbow and pulled it tight. Then, Wyatt took the knife, pressed its sharp edge against my skin, and sliced my forearm open. The pain was instantaneous and severe enough to make me gasp. As my blood spilled over, Sean moved the bowl underneath to catch it all.

I watched as the lifeforce I didn't even know I had drained from me. Besides the pain in my arm, nausea roiled in my stomach and sweat beaded on my forehead. I swayed on my feet.

"Woah." Sean was quick to steady me. "Don't go down on us, Jade."

I bit the inside of my cheek to force myself to stay awake and focused on what we needed to do. But when I glanced at the bowl again, now halfway full, my head fogged.

"She's going to pass out." Laurence's voice was a distant hum. "Surely we have enough by now?"

"A little more," Wyatt whispered gruffly.

The seconds felt like hours, but finally, the belt loosened on my arm and pressure was applied to my wound with a towel. Something pressed against my lips, and when cool liquid splashed against my tongue, I realized it was water.

"Drink," Sean said gently, and I did.

It was as if the water flushed away the haze. Not completely. I was still woozy from the blood loss, but things were becoming clearer.

Sean had the first aid kit ready and began stitching me back together.

After having my forearm slashed open, the stitches were a breeze. I barely felt them at all. Sean was quick and efficient with his care, and it wasn't long before I was sewed back up and bandaged.

While Sean had been working on me, Wyatt was preparing his makeshift altar. He sprinkled the dirt he had collected earlier from his yard into the bowl of my blood.

"Xaver, demon of the underworld," he began, talking directly to the mixture, "we call you to the earth with this blood offering."

The wind picked up around us, turning up the dirt and whipping through the tall grass. The trees farther back on the property, though, didn't rustle. The mysterious, unnatural breeze only touched the area around us.

Wyatt dunked his hand into the bowl and threw a handful of the blood and dirt onto the ground in front of the table as he spoke. "Rise, Xaver. Rise!" His voice grew more aggressive with every command and wave of his hand. "Rise! RISE! RISE!"

The ground underneath our feet trembled violently, causing the items on the table to teeter. Wyatt and Sean scrambled to hold the things down. Laurence struggled to keep his footing.

Despite the pain in my arm, I pulled off my gloves and readied the gun Wyatt had let me borrow for this special occasion—ironically, the same one I had grabbed during our first encounter with the Halflings. At least it felt familiar in my hands. I'd also loaded it with Holy Water bullets for a bigger punch.

Sean had a similar gun, and he wore a sheathed machete on his hip for backup. Laurence was relying on his defensive spells mostly, but just in case that didn't work, I had slipped a hunting knife I'd found amongst Wyatt's mess into his back pocket.

"RISE!" Wyatt continued to yell into the darkness. "RISE!"

The air crackled and snapped with power, and the wind became an unruly tornado, throwing up my hair and tossing dirt into the air. I squinted as it smacked against my face and bit my exposed arms and shoulders.

Laurence yelled against the torrent, hands up to block the gale, "Is it working?"

"Oh, he's coming," Wyatt called back and grabbed his shotgun. "Get ready, everyone! The bastard's not going to be too happy we ripped him from his home."

Then, everything stopped. As if on cue, the blustering winds, the charged energy in the air, the tremors underneath our feet, all stopped, followed by nothing but complete stillness.

It was as if the world itself was holding its breath. The sudden silence after such a flurry of noise and activity was eerie.

A strange prickling sensation rocketed up and down my spine, and when I looked up, I was staring into the glowing red eyes of the full-blooded Hell demon Xaver.

CHAPTER

TWENTY-THREE

T he demon threw his head back and roared, his thunderous voice filling the forest and shaking sleeping birds from their nests. Smoke radiated from his gray, cracked skin as if it were burning, and the pungent scent of sulfur and hot coals wafted through the air.

He was a massive beast, as tall as the trailer behind him, with two horns jutting out of his forehead and twisting at the peaks, like a deranged half-bull creature. He even had the cow-like snout with big nostrils. Two fangs poked out of his bottom lip. The two legs he stood on resembled a goat's, hairy and hooves and all.

I hadn't been able to get a good look at him in Kay's apartment, but it was safe for me to say he was ugly as sin.

He lunged at me, only to have his feet planted in place. Seeming confused, he looked down.

He was standing in a demon trap, one I had drawn in spray paint before we'd started the summoning.

His face contorted in fury. "You summoned me here?" he barked. "You spilled sacred blood for me?"

The word "sacred" threw me for a second, but since blood was one of the keys to keeping humans alive and demons didn't exactly bleed or live like they did, I guess that made sense.

"You have my friend," I said, trying to keep my shoulders pulled back and my spine straight even though my head still whirled with the blood loss. I locked eyes with him to mimic strength. Fake it until you make it, baby. "I want her back. Bring her back."

He laughed. Actually laughed at me, his voice a horrible grating sound, like nails on a chalkboard.

I ground my teeth together, and my anger coiled tighter inside me. Really want to piss me off? Laugh at me. That was the way to get you on my shit-list mighty quick. I aimed my gun, wanting nothing more than to blow his face off and shut him up for good.

His laughter got louder. "You think that human weapon will hurt me?"

I was hoping it would.

My finger hovered on the trigger. Someplace in the back of my head, a tiny voice whispered that shooting him right away might not be the best idea. Only he could bring Kay out of the Hell pit, and if I got him angry enough, he wouldn't exactly want to bend to my will.

"She's *mine*." Xaver's gaze hardened. "She's carrying my spawn. She doesn't belong to this plane anymore."

A fiery ball hurled across the yard and hit Xaver in the center of his chest. The skin there sizzled.

"Bring back my girlfriend, asshole!" Laurence shouted, hands up with another small fireball hovering between his fingers.

Xaver's gaze swept across the yard and spotted Laurence, Wyatt, Sean, and their weapons for the first time. But instead of fear, his expression only reflected amusement.

"More human weapons?" he bellowed and laughed again. "And you with your puny fireball spell…" He pointed one talon at Laurence. "You think fire will kill me? I was made from fire!"

His laughter grated on my nerves. My finger itched on the gun's trigger, but before I could make a move, three more fireballs were launched Xaver's way and hit him in the shoulder and side of his face. He howled in pain.

Laurence's face was all determination.

Xaver growled and leapt Laurence's way, only to find his feet were still cemented in place. That only enraged him more.

"Here's the deal, Xaver. We have you trapped and will be keeping you that way until you give us Kay." When I said it that way, it sounded like we had the upper hand, didn't it? "So, I suggest you do the smart thing and bring her to us now. Or you're going to be living a very lonely existence here in a human's backyard."

A sickening grin curled up the corners of his mouth. "I have all of eternity," he said. "The Medium girl, on the other hand, does not."

Oh shit. There went our leverage.

"How about you give us the girl or we'll kill you?" Wyatt shouted up at the demon, shotgun at the ready. For an old man, he was no joke. But could you even kill a demon? Was that even possible?

"You can try," was all Xaver said.

The gunshot popped off, the echo ricocheting throughout

the woods around us. Wyatt's smoking barrel told me it was him who'd fired.

At first, Xaver didn't move. The bullets had buried themselves in his stomach, but no pain showed on his face. For a moment, I thought he had been right and we were screwed, but then his skin bubbled and blackened around the wounds.

Xaver peered down at it, shocked. "Holy Water?"

"There's more where that came from," Wyatt replied. "We may not be able to kill you, but we can make living hurt like hell." He raised the shotgun again. "Now, give us the girl."

Xaver's glowing red eyes bore into the human standing off in front of him, as if he couldn't believe what he was witnessing. Then, amusement toyed with his beastly features. "You'll need to let me out of this trap first."

"Fuck no," Wyatt yelled immediately.

"No way," followed Laurence.

Xaver turned toward Sean. "How about you, pretty boy? You want to be a good kid and let me out?"

Another loud bang of a gun, this shot skimming the side of Xaver's neck. Instantly, the skin sizzled.

In one swift motion, Wyatt popped the empty shells out and reloaded. "Don't test me, demon."

I admired his need to protect his son, even if Sean was more of a man than a boy. There was no doubt in my mind he knew his way around a weapon, too. Especially growing up with a father like Wyatt.

I wasn't proud of myself, but in that moment, I wished Cole were here. He would know what to do in the situation we were in. Better yet, he would have something special in his backpack that could maybe save the day.

Who knew where he was. Probably still at the motel or roaming the streets of Fairport trying to find me for his contract with Azrael. I ground my teeth at the thought.

Fuck him. I didn't need him. Or his stupid backpack.

"Let him out," I said.

Every head whipped my way. It felt as if I were pinned into a corner. What other option did I have? Every second counted now. Tomorrow was the solstice. There wouldn't be another time to summon Xaver to collect his blood and perform the cure ritual.

"Are you out of your mind?" Wyatt said in a harsh whisper. "The first thing he's going to do is come after us."

"We'll keep our guns on him the entire time. If he tries anything funny, blast him."

"I don't know about this, Jade…" Laurence said. "There has to be another way."

"What if he runs?" Sean added.

I eyed the demon before us, who was grinning wide enough to show every single pointed tooth.

"He won't run," I said. "Not when he hears that I have a deal for him."

"A deal…?" Xaver's pointed ears perked up at that. What was it with demons and deals? I thought that was just a rumor. "What kind of deal?"

Cautiously, I approached him and the demon trap. Like I did with the spirit circles, I smudged one of the outermost lines with my boot, deactivating the magic binding him to the spot.

I held my breath, praying I wasn't wrong about this and my promise of a deal was enough to keep Xaver earthbound. More importantly, I hoped I hadn't just signed everyone's death warrants by letting a powerful demon go.

Slowly, Xaver stepped out of the trap. His gaze stayed locked on me the entire time.

Okay, light power thing. Whatever you are. Get ready. I might need you here. I called to the white energy inside me, praying I would somehow be able to control it this time and it would listen to my pleas.

Laurence held his fireball, and Wyatt and Sean aimed their guns.

Xaver crossed the yard until he got to a flat, grassless area. Then, he held out his hand and pressed his claws into his palm. Black goo flowed from the self-inflicted wounds onto the ground.

Was that...his blood? Gross. It looked like tar. Smelled like it, too.

Walking in a small circle, he let the sludge spill.

The dirt in the center quaked before falling away completely, leaving a bottomless crater in the earth.

I stepped back. The last time a hole had opened up in Wyatt's yard, a bunch of Halflings had crawled out and tried to kill us.

Instead, Kay floated up from the pit and hovered there in midair, out of reach.

"Kay!" I called, but she didn't flinch. The bath towel was wrapped around her naked body, and her eyes were closed and her head lolled to the side.

Dead?

My chest constricted in terror, but then her chest moved, still breathing as if she had been placed in some kind of dreamless sleep, and I relaxed. But only a little. She was still in danger.

As I started toward her, another body rose out of the ground and hung suspended next to Kay.

Blond side-swept hair. Model-like features. Oversized jacket and the tattered backpack hanging off his arm.

My heart plummeted.

The demon had Cole, too.

CHAPTER

TWENTY-FOUR

I shouldn't care.

I *didn't* care. Nope. Not at all. Not even a little. Cole had been working against me the entire time. I had been his *job*. His mission. A part of some cockamamie plot with Azrael to keep me distracted and out of the afterlife while he did who knows what.

Keeping secrets. Telling lies. Manipulating me. Using me.

That made him a grade-A asshole in my book.

But even as I went over it again in my head, my insides twisted at the lie.

It shouldn't bother me in the slightest that he had been captured by a demon and was now hanging above a Hell pit, but it did and I hated myself for it.

I'd had sex with him, too. Had that been all part of this charade, a way to gain my trust completely?

I wanted to punch myself for that one. How could I be so stupid?

The moment I had seen him rise out of the ground, my chest had constricted with a new kind of fear. Dammit! I barely knew the guy. Why hadn't I just done my assignment, like Simon had said, and not gotten involved? I could have avoided this entire thing.

Now, seeing the two people I cared for the most dangling feet above a Hell pit, my stomach was in knots.

"Let them go," I shouted, my voice shaking. Power buzzed across my skin, jumping across my knuckles like an electric current. I curled my hands into fists, scrambling to think of a plan to save them. If I blasted Xaver back to Hell, would Kay and Cole disappear, too? I could lose them forever.

What was I going to do?

Think, Jade. Think. How are you going to get out of this one?

I scanned the backyard, looking for something that could give me a leg up or trigger an idea. I not only had Kay and Cole's lives to think about, but I had Laurence's and Wyatt's and Sean's, too. Whatever I did, it had to be enough to protect them all from Xaver.

Annoyance pinched Xaver's ugly features. "So, what's this deal?" he pushed. "You said you had a deal for me. Out with it, then."

Deal?

Oh. I had almost forgotten I had offered him a deal to get to Kay. Problem was, I didn't actually have one. It had been just something I'd said to get one step ahead of him. I'd been hoping it would have bought me some time, and instead, it had revealed Cole as Xaver's other captive, causing more of a mess.

But maybe there was a way a deal could get everyone out of this alive. If that was what he wanted, that was my only option.

What could I offer a demon? I had nothing.

"Well?" Xaver growled.

"Let them both go, and crawl back into the hole you crawled out of. Leave us all alone." I rolled my next words on my tongue. I had to save my friends. They were all I had.

Xaver waved his hand, and Kay and Cole's unmoving bodies began to descend back into the crater.

Panic clawed up my throat. "Wait, wait!"

They continued to fall.

What was I going to do?

Cole's blond hair disappeared past the ground line.

"You can have me!" I yelled, my heart hammering. "Take me in their place!"

Xaver's eyes widened in surprise.

The gravity of what I had just offered hit me like a ton of bricks, but instead of regretting it, certainty flooded me. Yes. This was what I had to do. The choice was easy.

But would my soul be enough for not only Kay and Cole's, but for Laurence, Wyatt, and Sean's, too? I was a nobody. All I had going for me was being a newbie reaper and this new white light I had. Would that be desirable to a demon?

I had to hope so.

"Me in in your little Hell hole forever in exchange for them." I added more force this time to show him I wasn't playing around. "All of them."

I didn't trust demons. There was nothing to assure Xaver wouldn't spin around and grab the other three after the deal was done.

Xaver's gaze roamed over every face in the yard, and he

frowned, as if I had spoiled his plans. When his eyes landed on me again, his expression twisted into something devious. Animalistic and unnatural.

"You're willing to give up yourself and your eternity for these…blood sacks?" he asked.

"I'm not negotiating," I said, staying firm. "That's my offer. Take it or leave it."

He scratched his sunken cheek with one talon, pretending to be in deep thought.

To mock me and my deal? Or was he actually considering it?

The tense moments dragged by, every second like a painful prick to my skin. I didn't have a plan B. If this didn't work, I didn't know what I was going to do.

"Jade…" Laurence's whisper came from behind me. "Are you sure?"

Absolutely.

"Is there another part of this plan we should know about?" Sean asked.

Nope. This was all I had.

"We could just light him up," said Wyatt, his hold never wavering on his shotgun. It was still aimed and ready to go at any second. "Sounds good to me."

I stayed locked on Xaver, waiting for his decision. Even though I was shaking on the inside, I had to keep the façade of complete calm on the outside. Maybe if I made it appear like he was getting the better end of the deal, the demon would take it.

Glancing at the tops of Cole and Kay's heads peeking out from the Hell pit, anger tugged at me. I didn't like gambling with lives, and I was growing tried of whatever game Xaver was playing.

"Going once," I said, holding up one finger. Testing him.

When he didn't even flinch, I put up two fingers. "Going twice."

Disbelief flashed across his face. This wasn't a joke. I meant business.

"Deal," he said finally and snapped his fingers.

Kay and Cole floated out of the pit again. Once their feet touched solid ground, their eyes fluttered open, as if waking from a deep sleep.

"Wha-what's going on?" Kay asked, rubbing her forehead.

Laurence hurried over to her and hugged her tight.

"Laurence?"

With Kay in his arms, he mouthed the words, "Thank you" to me over and over.

I smiled. "Get her out of here," I whispered. "Wyatt and Sean will help you with the cure."

Sean nodded and moved closer to them. "We will."

When I turned back around, Cole was staring at me intently. There was heavy conflict behind his eyes. I doubted he knew I had been behind the motel door listening in to his conversation with Azrael. This was something else.

"Jade… I…"

I shook my head. "You don't need to say anything. It's done," I told him. "Just please make sure you help Kay with the ritual. Promise me."

"What did you do?" He glanced back at Xaver, who was grinning broadly. "No. No, you didn't." When his head whipped my way again, his eyes were wide. "You didn't make a deal."

"She did. And it's done." Xaver huffed. "Come on. Let's go, reaper."

"Wait, Jade. No…" Cole reached for me, but I stepped back. If he touched me now, I might lose my nerve, and I couldn't afford it.

The wounded look he gave me was enough to make me second-guess everything, so I looked away.

"There has to be something else we can do," he said. He swung his backpack around and ripped the zipper open. Fumbling through the contents, he mumbled to himself angrily.

It was a wasted effort, though. We both knew it.

"What?" Kay chimed in. Her gaze passed from Xaver to me. "What's going on? Jade?"

"She traded her life for ours," Cole said, still searching through every one of the bag's pockets.

"All of ours," Sean added.

Xaver growled in irritation. "Come on, reaper. Or the deal is off."

I tossed my gun onto the ground and stepped toward him.

"Jade, please!" Cole sounded desperate now.

His pleas stabbed at my chest, and I didn't know why. Maybe it was because I would never know the secrets of my life before dying now. Or maybe it was because I knew, deep down, I would miss the friends I'd made. All the things I was never going to experience.

I had to do this, though. I had to. To save them all.

Meeting Xaver's stare, I said, "Let's go."

I was ready now.

He gestured to the Hell pit. "Jump on in."

After walking over to the edge of the crater, I looked down, seeing nothing but darkness. The distinct rotten-eggs smell of sulfur wafted up, and I gagged. An eternity of that smell? Yuck. That sounded like Hell, all right.

One last glance over my shoulder, and I saw all my friends—new and old—standing there, watching me in silence. Wyatt saluted me, but all I could offer him in return was a sad smile.

I was never good at anything emotional. Especially goodbyes. So, instead of facing the sorrow in their stares, I turned around and confronted my fate, telling myself I was doing this for all the right reasons. This was the right thing to do.

Sucking in a deep breath of clean night air for the last time, I closed my eyes and jumped.

CHAPTER

TWENTY-FIVE

Everything stopped.

Why wasn't I falling?

When I opened my eyes, I was stuck above the pit, hovering in midair. Frozen in place. I waved my arms and legs about, ready for the drop, but it didn't come.

Xaver shouted something in a foreign tongue. He was angry. It was obvious from the blaze in his eyes. Something was happening, and it wasn't his doing.

A ball of bright light whizzed across the darkness, illuminating the night and capturing every eye. It circled Xaver, who swiped at it like a pesky fly, before it flew my way at full speed.

What the—

The orb crashed into me. Like I had been hit by a sack of bricks, all the breath left my lungs. Whiteness exploded, and I was suddenly soaring through the air, away from the Hell hole.

I landed hard, several feet away, rolling several times before stopping with my face in the dirt. Gasping for air, I hauled myself to my knees. My ribs screamed in protest, and every inhale was sharp like sucking in glass shards. They were probably bruised. Possibly broken.

Struggling to my feet, I searched the sky for the thing that had shot me out of danger but only saw darkness.

Had I imagined the flying speck?

I must have.

But then how had I ended up all the way across the yard?

Unfortunately, I didn't have time to mull what had happened around because Xaver let out another one of his terrifying, animalistic roars, and the ground beneath my feet shook so hard, I almost lost my footing.

When shadowy shapes appeared at the pit's edge, my insides iced over with dread. The blackness began to concentrate, gaining more density, more horrifying features, and by the time the dozens of creatures lifted themselves out of the ground, it was clear we were in deep, deep shit.

Halflings. More than I'd ever seen before.

And they were crawling out of Hell at an alarming rate.

Inside the trailer, Angel barked ferociously. Kay screamed as the Halflings rushed for them. Cole whipped out his gun from his bag and began emptying the magazine. One by one, Halflings flew back from the impact of his bullets, screeching so loud my ears rang, but as a single creature withered away, another five would take its place.

More gunshots blared, this time from Wyatt and Sean's weapons.

My pulse banged against my eardrums. There were too

many of them. Even with the rapid fire of bullets. Everyone was forced to take steps back as the creatures drew closer.

I had to do something. I had to help.

As I raced around the crater, toward my friends, I kicked one of the Halflings back into the hole. My gun was gone, thrown away after my deal with Xaver, so I had nothing to fight with but my fists and feet. Lucky for me, I was pretty good with them.

"Get the girl into the house and barricade the door!" Wyatt yelled above the commotion. He reloaded his shotgun and fired again.

Laurence didn't need to be told twice. He scooped Kay up like she was a child and ran up the stairs into the trailer.

Smart move. With all of Wyatt's protection symbols and Laurence's extra spells, the trailer was the safest place to be. Getting everyone in there would be ideal but unrealistic. Then we would just be trapped. Put in our own cage.

No. We had to fight this fight. Now that the deal was off and things were a mess, Xaver would keep coming after Kay —maybe all of us—if we just put him back where he came from. I couldn't let that happen.

It was time to find out if a demon could really die.

Wasting no time, I leapt onto a nearby Halfling's hunched back. It flew forward, bringing me with it. We landed with a thud. When the Halfling twisted to throw me off, I wrapped my arms around its neck and squeezed hard. My hope? To cut off the thing's breathing. But when its bucking and squirming only increased, I realized these demonic creatures probably didn't need to breathe air, like I hadn't.

I needed a new tactic.

"Jade!"

When I looked up, I spotted Cole through the throng of bodies pouring some liquid on the blade of Sean's long knife. Then he threw it at me when such precision, it landed perfectly stuck in the dirt by my arm. I grabbed it and plunged the blade into the Halfling's back, then dragged the knife down its spine when it tried to throw me off again.

Black tar spurted from the wound, and the creature collapsed.

Holy Water. Cole had doused the knife in it.

Standing, I twisted the weapon in my hand. Not a gun, but it would work just fine. Now I was ready.

"Bring the reaper to me." Xaver's voice boomed over all other noise. "Kill the rest."

About a dozen pairs of eyes whirled on me. Some Halflings even let out a deafening squeal before charging me like a stampede of angry bulls.

Fear commanded my feet to run, but my muscles clenched in protest, pinning me in place. As the Halflings closed the distance, I could smell the stench of decay and sulfur wafting on the breeze.

Claws reached out to grab me. I swiped out with my blade.

A bright light shot between us, making the creatures skid to a halt. I blinked. I couldn't believe what I was seeing. It was the orb I had seen before—a solid ball of white light, the one that had collided with me and saved me from the pit.

It zoomed back and forth, creating a barrier in front of the Halflings. A few of them reached out, curious, but the moment their skin came in contact with the mystical glow, the creatures disintegrated. Poof. Gone. Just like when they were blasted with the light from my demon-blasting power from my fingertips.

I stared at the white light, dumbfounded. "What are you?" Not a spirit, that was for sure. I knew spirits. This was something else. And it had saved me. Twice.

Of course, the thing didn't answer me. I hadn't expected it to. But I was grateful for its interference.

I awkwardly waved a thank you to it and spun around. To my horror, Cole, Wyatt, and Sean were now battling hand to hand with the other group of half-demons. The old man was using his shotgun as a bat, smashing the creatures in the head if they got too close, while Sean was shooting off his handgun like a pro.

An unseen force slammed into me from the side, claws latching into my collarbone. A Halfling and I jetted backwards onto the folding table, and the thing collapsed under our sudden weight. Everything prepared for the summoning went flying, and the bowl of blood spilled all over us, soaking my shirt and pants and coating the demon's face in dark red. Pain spiked up my spine and throughout my chest where its nails dug in deep.

Before I could even think to retaliate, the Halfling let out a piercing wail and jumped off me. Its grayish skin blackened as if it had been sprayed with Holy Water and began peeling off the bone, reminding me of wax melting down the sides of a candle.

The creature ripped at its flesh, pulling it off in chunks, and screaming.

Like my blood was burning him.

That wasn't normal. Was my blood acidic to these demons? It sure seemed that way. Maybe it had something to do with the light power I now wielded.

Whatever it was, I'd take it.

I scrambled up to see another beast rushing toward me. I kicked out, and the sole of my boot met the bend of its knee. There was a terrible popping sound before it collapsed, clasping its leg and squealing like a distressed pig. Taking the opportunity, I gripped the knife and stabbed it into the Halfling's chest, where the heart *ought* to be. It wiggled in agony, black goo bubbling out of the wound, before slumping into an unmovable heap. Dead.

I glanced over my shoulder to see the one that had snuck up on me and had been affected by my blood was nothing more than a puddle of tar in the soil.

Yuck! Had my blood really done that?

I shivered. What *was* I?

Movement whizzed past my right. Another half-demon determined to take me to Hell. I twisted last minute, spinning my blade at the same time and catching the monster across the stomach. The sharpness sliced through the skin and muscle with such ease, it wasn't until its rancid insides started spilling out that it realized what had happened.

I took a second to catch my breath and scan the scene before me.

The yard was littered with bodies, all Halflings, and I praised our luck. There were still many more creatures to fight, and they were relentless, doing everything and anything they could to get to Wyatt or Sean or me.

A sudden blaze of fire lit up the darkness, painting the yard in a brilliant orange and yellow. When I turned, I found Cole throwing blasts of fire toward the enemy, taking out groups of them at a time and pushing many of them back into their hole. His laughter rang in my ears. It sounded haunted, maniacal, and very unlike him.

My chest tightened, remembering the last time Cole was forced to use his fire ability while fighting the half-demons, and the demonic twist I had seen in his face. If he kept tapping into that dark part of him, he would lose himself completely. Become one of these disgusting creatures that dwelled in Hell and followed full-blooded demons for the rest of eternity.

He continued to trudge forward, the fire shooting from his palms like a human flamethrower and forcing the Halflings back into the crater where they had come from.

The scorching heat slapped against my cheeks and face, making me step back.

"Cole! No!"

His head whipped toward me, and the flame extinguished. But it wasn't Cole I saw looking back at me. The eerie red eyes and over-stretched smile told me he had gone too far this time.

Oh no, Cole... Why did you use it?

Cole tilted his head to study me. Curious.

"Grab her!" Xaver's command shook me to my very core. "Bring her to me!"

Cole didn't move. Only stared at me, brows rising as if he were considering his options.

Okay. That was a good sign. Maybe he wasn't completely gone yet.

"Cole, don't. It's me. Jade," I said, hating that I was actually pleading with him now. "You're still in there. I know you are. You need to listen to me."

Still, he just watched me, his red eyes searching my face for something familiar.

"He's gone, Jade," Sean shouted as he whipped a Halfling with the back of his gun, sending it reeling back. "He's one of them now."

"No!"

He couldn't be. Not yet.

I wasn't ready to have to kill him, too.

"Cole, listen to me," I said with more vigor. "We need you here to fight. We need you—"

He charged me.

Oh no.

My first thought was to turn and run. So that was what I did, spinning around and bolting as fast as I could to the trailer. But the idea must have come a second too late because Cole was on my heels immediately. When his body slammed into mine, we were propelled forward, rolling and tumbling. Every one of my wounds screamed, but it was nothing compared to my heart, which was pounding at an unnatural rate.

I twisted and thrashed against Cole's hold, which clamped down on my wrists instantly. His knees pinned me down as he straddled my middle. Trying to buck him off did nothing. He was too strong like this, and all I could do was stare up at his eyes and wonder if the Cole I knew was still reachable inside him. Somewhere.

"Cole...please." I struggled against him, but his grip bruised. My only option was to wriggle my hand free somehow and use one of my gifts. Either the reaper's death touch or the white light.

Both could bring his death.

I didn't want to kill him, no matter what I had said before. Not to mention the white light would leave me weak. Then Xaver could easily take me to Hell without a fight.

It looked like I didn't have a choice. I would have to take my chances with the light power and pray I had enough energy to continue fighting afterward.

Reaching deep down, I found the power buzzing inside me, as if it had been patiently waiting for release. I didn't have to do much to pull it out; it sprang to the surface with ease. Raw energy crackled across my knuckles.

"I'm sorry, Cole," I whispered as my fingers began to illuminate.

"Don't." Cole's voice was quick and sharp, and it took me a second to realize what he had said. "Not yet."

I blinked. "Cole?"

He gave a small shake of his head. His eyes flashed from red to calming blue and back again.

"You need to strike him with your power where he's the

weakest," he continued, his voice feather light. "It's the only thing that can kill him."

Letting the power settle again, I nodded, understanding. If Cole was telling the truth, then I would only have one chance at this.

A warning niggled at the back of my head that this might just be a lie. A way to get me to Xaver quietly and without a fight. But what other choice did I have? I had to trust him.

"Get up," Cole said.

When he shifted his weight off me, I hurried to my feet. He clutched my wrist, careful not to touch my palm. He tugged me across the yard, the remaining Halflings creating a walkway for us as we passed through. They snarled and snapped their jaws at us. I threw them dirty looks.

When we reached Xaver, the demon grinned broadly.

"I'm here," I shot. "Recall your hellions. They aren't needed anymore."

"There won't be any more deals," he barked. "You took advantage of my kindness and ruined that option. I won't let it happen again."

His kindness? I almost laughed out loud. Had I missed that part?

"Hey, I didn't call for any backup. I don't know what that thing was that came flying in."

Cole inched me closer to Xaver and the Hell pit, and my pulse kicked up a notch. What was stopping him from just throwing me in? Maybe Wyatt was right, and I had played right into Cole's plan. Had I made a major mistake?

I locked my knees, refusing to get any closer. He shoved me forward.

He was trying to push me into the pit. He had tricked me again.

"Now I will take you and all your little blood bags to Hell," said Xaver. "My Halflings have been bored for some time and would love some new playthings to torture for eternity."

When I peered up, I noticed the blackened spot in the center of Xaver's chest, where one of the blessed bullets had landed. The skin around the area had festered away, creating a small hole surrounded by his sticky, tarlike blood.

If I got close enough, I could punch my fist through his flesh and expel my power. Blasting him from the inside out.

Sounded like it would work in my head. I didn't have another plan, so let's hope I was right with this one.

But since Xaver towered over me, I needed to find a way to get up to his level. Or bring him down to mine.

"Well, here I am," I said. "Come and get me."

To my surprise, Cole let me go, just in time for Xaver to reach down and grab me by the waist. He hauled me up to face him, the stench of his rotting breath making my stomach churn.

"The first thing I'm going to do is cut those pretty hands of yours off, so they can't do any more damage. And then—"

I lashed out with a closed fist straight for the center of his chest and called for my light at the same time. It whipped through me like a tornado, wild and finally free. In an instant, white wisps of power surged out of my fingertips.

"You mean like this?" I said, satisfied.

Whiteness exploded inside him, the light bursting out of the other bullet holes in his skin, his eyes, ears, and mouth. It was so bright, my eyes burned. I could barely look at it.

When the light consumed Xaver completely, drowning him in brightness, he let me go. I dropped to the ground onto my knees.

Like discharging a bomb, the whiteness expanded suddenly, illuminating the entire yard in a blaze.

I squeezed my eyes shut and held my breath.

A few seconds later, when darkness pressed against my

lids again, I opened my eyes. Xaver was gone. As was every Halfling. All that was left was a distinct ringing in my ears.

"You did it." Cole was by my side, his voice almost childlike in his excitement. "You killed him and blasted all those fuckers back to Hell!"

I smiled up at him. I had done it, hadn't I?

His eyes had changed again, mostly their normal color but also rimmed with red. He hadn't been completely changed into one of those creatures, but he had come pretty close. If he opened himself up to that part of him again, there was a good chance he wasn't coming back. His familiar grin was welcomed, though, even if I didn't know who he was. Not really.

He took my hand to help me up, but the moment I tensed my muscles in my legs to push myself upright, exhaustion swept me up in a merciless embrace. This time, I couldn't fight the darkness when it called my name and dragged me under.

CHAPTER

TWENTY-SIX

As the lull of sleep entwined me like a serpent, images floated to the surface of my mind.

I was a boy no older than six, looking at my face in the reflection of a river's shallow edge. My skin was the darkest shade of brown and perfectly smooth in my youth. Although I knew from some distant memory I had been told to stay away from the waters that had been flooded from a recent heavy rain, the desire to jump in and ride the current was overwhelming. Especially since I was being teased a lot from the other village children for not knowing how to swim. At least, that was what they claimed. I thought I could swim just fine. And I was determined to show them they were wrong.

But the moment I stepped my muddy bare feet into the icy water, the world around me shifted. The forest vegetation and river were lost to a blur of colors.

When the picture before me reformed, a crowd of angry faces stared back at me. Men, women, and even children sneered my way. Some cursed, calling me a harlot and witch in another language. Something hard struck the side of my face. I cried out as sharpness sliced across my cheek.

A rock? Someone had thrown a rock at me?

When I tried to tug at my wrists, I found them bound behind my back and tethered to a pole. Even more horrifying, I was sitting on top of a pile of wood and straw.

These people were going to kill me. And watch my death for entertainment.

As a scream crawled up my throat, the faces before me blended together, and the scene changed again.

This time, I was running. My bare feet flew over a forest floor, my breathing coming out in short, frantic bursts in the frigid night air. I kept glancing over my shoulder. A giant lumbering man followed me, and it seemed no matter how fast I ran, he was closing the distance. There was something in his hand, too. Something long and solid. A branch? A bat? Who knew what he'd grabbed this time in his drunken rage.

Like with the other visions, bits and pieces of information came floating back from the recesses of my memory. This man wasn't a stranger. He was my stepfather, and like he did when he drank too much, he wanted to do things to me that weren't allowed. But now that I was older and getting stronger, I fought him. Mostly, I ran or hid. But that made him mad, and his anger had turned physical. Brutal. Deadly.

The absolute fear churning inside told me that this night wasn't like those other nights. This time, if he caught me, he'd kill me. If I could just get to our neighbor's house down the hill, I could ask for help. I could be safe.

In my panicked thinking, I misjudged my next step and tumbled down, down, down the steep angle of the hill. Everything spun. Sticks and rocks bit into my skin all over. It felt like I was falling for eternity, but then I suddenly stopped.

Everything hurt. My fingertips on my right hand were numb. The pain radiating from my shoulder down was excruciating—dislocated, I assumed, but I knew despite all my pain, nothing would compare to what my stepfather would do if he caught up to me.

I looked up at the glowing lights and smoking chimney of my neighbor's house like a beacon from God. So close. Salvation was just a few feet away.

I just had to get up and knock on the door.

The crunch of boots by my head tensed every muscle in my body. The pinching, sour scent of liquor confirmed all my fears. And his voice sent chills all over my skin.

"I tol' you not to run," he slurred, but I could make out the threat to his words just the same. It was my fault. Everything he did was *my* fault.

A scream bubbled up my throat, but before any sound escaped, the scene went black again.

Then, like rapid fire, faces passed in front of my eyes. Women, men, children of all shapes, skin tones, sizes, and ages flashed across my mind in quick succession, like someone was flipping through one of those old flip books or clicking through a vacation photo reel too fast to really see the pictures. Who were all these people? And why did they feel familiar to me?

Why was I seeing them at all? That was the biggest question.

Was this like the old saying? My life flashing before my eyes? But I was seeing other people's lives instead. Not one or two. Dozens—no hundreds, all flying by in rapid succession.

I didn't understand. What were they trying to show me?

"Jade?"

My name floated to my ears from a distant place. A voice I knew, too. It was a kind, gentle voice, but one ebbed with concern. Like a mother coaxing a child to their side. Or a friend.

Was this another vision?

"Jade, please wake up."

No. Not a vision. This was real.

Recognition tingled at the nape of my neck. Friend. It was a friend talking to me now.

Kay?

"Is she dead?" Another voice chimed in—a male's, also familiar. A bit shaky with nerves but sweet nonetheless. His name snapped forward. It was Laurence. "Can reapers…die?"

"I-I don't know," Kay whispered.

The memory of the night with Xaver and all his Halflings crashed into me like a semitruck, bringing back all the aches and pains to my limbs and head. Nausea rolled through my stomach, and every inch of me was weak with exhaustion. Something as simple as opening my eyes was a struggle.

"Jade, wake up. This isn't funny." This voice brought with it a wave of emotions. Conflicting ones. Desire was one that surprised me. There was also relief. Hurt. But anger, mostly.

Suddenly, a hard pressure seized both my upper arms. The feeling of fingers digging into my flesh grew clearer, more painful, as the man shook me hard.

"Get up, Jade. Dammit. Get up!"

Masters. Cole Masters.

As his name shot across my mind, my eyelids snapped open.

Blue eyes rimmed in red stared back at me, and instantly every worry line around his lips and brow softened. The one side of his luscious mouth curled up for a model-worthy smile that could have made any normal woman swoon on the spot.

Lucky for me, I wasn't a normal woman by any means. And I definitely wasn't a fool. Cole had betrayed me. I remembered that part, too.

I sat up, perhaps a little too quickly because my head spun. Holding my forehead, I waited until the earth stopped swaying.

"Woah there. Give it some time," Cole said, as if nothing had happened between us—as if he hadn't been using me for a paycheck all this time. But I guess he didn't know I had discovered his little plan, did he? To him, I was still blissfully ignorant. Trusting.

Boy, was he going to be sorry.

"You just blasted a full-blooded demon to bits and sent his Halflings back to Hell. It's expected for you to be a little lightheaded."

Damn, he was good at this faking-concern thing. Move over, Tom Cruise. Cole was gunning for an Oscar.

I shook off the grasp he still had on my arms. He moved back to give me space, but suddenly, Kay was there, touching my face all over.

"Good, you're still h-here with us. Not a spirit." She pulled me into a fierce hug. "I'm still iffy on all the rules when it comes to this reaper business, but I felt like I lost you. Really lost you. I couldn't sense your soul while you were out of it and…"

For a minute, it felt like I had lost myself, too.

When Kay pulled back, she sniffed, her eyes misting over.

"Hey, I'm okay," I told her. "I'm here."

She smiled. "Hormones, I guess."

I took my time to stand, ignoring the pain clinging to my body. Cole and Kay stood, too.

"So," I began, rubbing the side of my face, "what did I miss? Where's Sean and Wyatt?"

"Good question," Laurence said. "We just came out of the trailer after we heard the explosion and saw the coast was clear. We haven't seen them."

I glanced at Cole, who shook his head.

Angel's loud barking shook the silence of the night.

Laurence sighed heavily. "Dang dog. We tried keeping her inside when we left, but she snuck out."

More barking in the distance, closer to the woods where the light of the trailer didn't quite reach.

I headed that way.

"Where are you going?" Laurence called out behind me.

"I bet you wherever she's barking is where Sean and Wyatt are, too."

"She's got a point." Cole said, and then a scurry of footsteps followed in my wake.

At the edge of the woods, three shapes came into view. As expected, there was Angel, whose bark turned into a low whine the moment she saw me, and two shadowed figures huddled together at the base of a tree.

It wasn't until I was a few steps away that I noticed the blood trailing onto the ground and Sean had something draped across his lap. Soft sobs came from Sean as he stared down at the frail-looking man cradled in his arms. His father. Wyatt. Lying deathly still but with eyes open.

Blood dribbled down his chin, but his lips moved, his words coming out too gurgled and soft for me to hear. Whatever he was saying, Sean could hear him, though, and he leaned in closer as the tears slid down his face.

My heart clenched. I knew what I was witnessing here. I

was all too familiar with it. Wyatt was dying. From the looks of it, he might have pierced a lung or two and he was slowly drowning in his own blood.

Sean seemed to know it, too. Because even though Wyatt tried to smile up at him as he whispered to his son, the tears kept flowing.

Oh, how I regretted following Angel's barks. I didn't want to see this. Even though I'd only known the two for a little while, I still cared for them. Watching Sean hold his father like he was frailer than a newborn and shaking with grief was heart-wrenching.

My feet started pedaling backwards, but then Kay's gasp reminded me they had followed me here. Sean's head snapped up, and when he saw us, desperation clung to his watery gaze.

"Cole. Jade," he choked out. "Please. Do something. Anything. Help him. Please."

Cole hurried to Wyatt's side and examined him, looking for a way to save his life, but I already knew the truth. He wasn't going to survive this. His body was already shimmering, his soul readying to leave the body.

When Cole realized he couldn't help, he glanced over his shoulder at me. "Jade," he whispered. "What can we do? There has to be something."

My voice lodged in my throat, and tears prickled the backs of my eyes.

What could *I* do?

Nothing. There was no way to cheat death. Unfortunately, I had learned this many times during my year as a reaper. If I didn't deliver the death touch, the soul would leave the body on its own, like it had with Marla. Without a reaper to direct it, the spirit could be lost, forced to wander a world it was no longer a part of forever.

And that also meant Wyatt would have to keep suffering

until he passed. Drowning was a terrible way to die. I couldn't let that happen to him. But to kill a friend? To kill a father in front of his own son? How could I do that?

"Jade, please…" Sean's desperate tone stabbed at my chest. "Don't let my father die. He's all I have left…"

I glanced down at Wyatt. His body shimmered again, warning me he didn't have much time.

"Sean, I—"

Wyatt's lips moved again, but this time no sound emerged. Blood leaked from the side of his lips, and he coughed, splattering more of it all over Sean's shirt.

I took a deep breath. As much as I hated to do this to Sean, I had no other choice. To secure Wyatt's afterlife and make his passing easier, I'd have to touch him. Even if it killed me to do it.

"All I can do is help him cross over," I said. "I can assure his soul is put where it needs to be."

Sean shook his head frantically. "No, no, no. There has to be another way. A spell. An incantation. Something. Pop, you know! You have to know. Tell me what to do. You can't leave me. You're all I have left."

The ghostly glow pulsed around Wyatt's body. The soul was readying to break free.

"He doesn't have much time, Sean…" I said. "I'm sorry."

Sean glanced at Cole, who only nodded solemnly.

"It's what Wyatt would want," Cole whispered.

Then, through his sobs, Sean agreed.

I knelt beside them, and with my eyes closed, I lifted my hand to Wyatt's neck. I said a small apology to him for allowing this to happen before pressing my palm against his bare skin.

Immediately, Wyatt's spirit rose out of his earthly body, looking like a more polished version of himself. Brushed and newly braided hair, a clean plaid shirt, jeans, a shiny oversized belt buckle, and a big leather cowboy hat to top it all off. He stood beside his son, who didn't see him, and smiled my way.

"I know it was hard for you to do that," Wyatt said. "But thank you. It was getting a bit too tight in there."

Cole didn't notice Wyatt standing in front of him, either. He and Sean only stared at Wyatt's chest, looking to see if another breath would lift it again. Behind me, Kay gasped, obviously seeing Wyatt's spirit form.

"Ah, the little lady can see me, too, huh?" Wyatt said, and tipped his hat her way.

"She's a Medium," I replied. "I think I told you that before."

"You probably did." He tapped the side of his head. "Old man memory."

Sean and Cole stared at me.

"Are you talking to him now?" Sean asked, seeming amazed.

I nodded.

When Wyatt reached for Sean's shoulder, his hand passed right through, and he sighed, turning to me. "I was never afraid to die, you know. I just thought it would be the cigarettes that did it."

Despite the sadness of the situation, his wittiness still rang true.

"What is he saying?" Sean asked. "Can you tell me?"

"He says he thought it would be the cigarettes that killed him," I repeated.

Cole sputtered a laugh. "That's Wyatt all right."

A flicker of a smile touched Sean's lips. "Is he okay?"

"Better than okay," I said.

"Not a single ache in my bones!" Wyatt twisted and stretched his arms like an athlete might do before a run to prove his point. "I don't remember the last time I've felt like this."

"What is he saying?" Sean pressed.

I looked at Kay. How did she deal with this back and forth? It was annoying.

"Make sure you bury me with my hat on," Wyatt said. "I need my hat. It's part of me."

I repeated that part for Sean. His smile widened.

"You got it, Pop," Sean said to the area next to him where Wyatt stood.

Reaching for the chalk in my back pocket, I waved Wyatt away from the others, deeper into the woods.

"What's going on?" Sean asked. "Where are you going?"

"I have to help your father cross over."

"Already?"

"Tell him it's time to be strong. It's time for me to find his mother and be with her again," Wyatt said firmly, but I caught a glimpse of a tear in his eye.

I did.

Sean sniffed and nodded.

"Oh, and take care of Angel, and she'll take care of him, too."

I passed the message along. Sean patted the dog's head. She continued to whine nervously at his side.

"I love you, kid. I'll see you soon—but not too soon, you hear me?"

As if Sean had heard him, he said, "I love you, Pop," to the emptiness beside him.

"It's time to go..." I whispered, and together, Wyatt and I walked into the privacy of the woods. I walked until I found a tree with a wide enough trunk and drew the symbols for the spirit door. When the lines glowed orange, signaling the opening of the door, Wyatt turned to me.

"I know what you're thinking, and don't you dare," he said.

That took me off guard. "What do you mean?"

"Don't feel guilty for this. Me dying wasn't your fault in any way."

I blinked. Was I really that predictable?

"I can read it on your face," Wyatt explained. "I know that look, and there's no reason for you to feel that way. It was my time."

"After you're processed, I'll come look for you. Make sure that whatever afterlife they give you, you're comfortable."

He waved that away. "Eh, I'm sure I'll be fine. But I'll never turn down a visit."

"I'll bring beer. The expensive kind. Arrogant Bastard is what it's called, right?"

He winked. "You got it. Just like me."

Wyatt stepped closer to the shimmering door but paused. "One more thing," he said. "The box. The one my wife found with your tattoo symbol on it? You can have it. Maybe it can help you find out who you are in some way. Maybe Sean can help you, too. The kid's smart. And he knows all that technology stuff."

"Thanks." I didn't know what else to say. Even though I knew quite well that his soul's "life" didn't end here, I couldn't help but feel like I was losing him somehow. My chest ached terribly.

"I know everything about supernaturals. I made it my life to know. Yet I've never met anyone like you before." Wyatt offered me a warm, reassuring smile. "Whoever or whatever you are, Jade, you're something special. Something this whole damned world and all its damned people may need."

I was about to protest such an outrageous statement, but like a parent, he tsked the excuse away.

"Take my word for it," he insisted and tapped the side of his nose. "I am an expert in this area, after all."

I couldn't help but chuckle at the crazy old man. "Goodbye for now, Wyatt. Thank you for all your help."

"See you soon," he said, and with a tip of his hat, he stepped through the spirit door and disappeared into the afterlife.

CHAPTER

TWENTY-SEVEN

I stood there for a while, staring at the radiant orange glow of the spirit door against the inky darkness of the night. I had done the right thing, hadn't I? There was no way I could have saved Wyatt's life. Especially when his soul was pulling away before we had found them near the woods. But even with all the facts, I couldn't help but feel I should have done more.

Dying shouldn't bother me still. I knew what happened after death. Souls lived very happily and comfortably, just on another plane. I knew this, but whenever I delivered the death touch, a part of me pinched with regret and sorrow for the person's life I was ending.

Simon had always told me that feeling went away the

more people I reaped, but for me, it didn't. Why couldn't I just be like Simon and do my job? Not feel anything? Death was just another part of the process. Everyone had to do it. There was nothing to be sorry about. At least that was what Simon had tried to drill into my head during his mentorship, yet it never stuck.

With death, there was still loss, wasn't there? Sean had lost his father, the only person he had left in his life to love and be loved by. He had already lost his mother. Cole had lost a longtime friend and confidant. Hell, maybe even a fatherly figure. And even though I'd only known Wyatt for a short time, I felt the sting of his departure, too. It hurts still.

Maybe I wouldn't ever be able to void myself from grief when doing my job. Maybe I was defective that way.

All I did know as I stared at the spirit door pulsing with some ancient power I didn't understand was that I wished I could have saved him.

Now, I had to go back, look his son in the eye, and tell him it was done. He'd never see his father again. Not until his own death, anyway.

Using the palm of my hand, I smudged the chalk markings on the rough tree trunk, closing the door, and began my short walk back to the group. Kay's comforting words floated from the edge of the forest, and when I approached, I saw her rubbing Sean's shoulders and assuring him that I knew what I was doing, and if his father ever decided to visit the living world, she'd have no problem channeling for him. Of course, she didn't know spirits crossing over without a reaper guide was a rarity, but I wasn't going to ruin their moment together. It seemed Kay's soothing touch was doing its job and calming Sean. Why hinder a good thing?

Besides, maybe once this whole mess was over and I returned to the afterlife, I could find a way to pass Wyatt between worlds for some kind of earthly visits. A spirit vacation, if you will. It had never been done before, as far as I knew, so there was a good chance it was against the rules.

But I had never been someone to follow the rules, now had I?

This was all based on the idea that I was safe to return to home and work, that is. I still didn't know why Azrael had hired Cole to track me down and gone through this elaborate dance to keep me "distracted" and away from demons. I had never wanted anything to do with demons in the first place. Whatever his reason, it had something to do with this white light I possessed and the marking on my chest.

It was almost as if he didn't want me to find out what they were.

Who I really was.

Maybe I'd lay low for a little bit. Not go back into the afterlife until things blew over or I figured out more about myself.

Sean turned to me the moment I stepped out of the concealment of the trees.

To my surprise, he said, "Thank you, Jade. I'd rather it was you who got to help him cross instead of anyone else."

"You're welcome," I replied with a small smile.

I glanced around, finding Laurence and Cole were gone. So was Wyatt's body. I could put two and two together there, and I didn't blame Sean for not being able to take part in the burial of his father. I still hated that we couldn't have done anything for Marla's body. All I could do was hope that when the police came to the residence the next day on a suspected break-in call, they would take good care of her. Maybe call family and let them know.

"We'll stay over here tonight with you, if you want," Kay suggested. "Or you can come over to my apartment. I have a pullout couch and tons of food in the fridge. Angel's invited, too, of course."

Sean scratched the dog behind the ears. "Thanks, Kay. I appreciate it."

A couple minutes later, Laurence and Cole trudged back through the darkness. A floating ball of light hovered in front of them, illuminating their way. Must have been another one of Laurence's level one spells. Pretty useful.

"We made a temporary marking with two sticks that we found. He's by his old Buick like you wanted," Cole said.

"Okay." Sean looked up at me. "You know, he used to say that when he died, I better not make it a big deal. He didn't want the wake and lavish coffin and all that. He would say he didn't care if I put his ashes in a coffee tin and set it on the mantel." A hiccup of a laugh escaped. "I figured his beat-up old Buick was a better place. Could you ask him if that's okay when you see him?"

I didn't know what to say, so I just nodded.

"Did you find his hat?" Sean asked the two men. "He must have lost it during the fight."

"Yes. He has it again." Cole walked over and grasped him by the shoulder. "Let's get out of the dark. We can talk more inside."

"Good idea," Kay chimed in and began walking toward the trailer.

As the group strolled ahead, I slowed my pace, lingering at the place where the crater had opened up and the Halflings had crawled out of. Just like before, the ground had rematerialized over the hole, the earth zipping back together again as if nothing supernatural had happened at all.

The ground there was still muddied and darkened by the tarlike blood Xaver had used to draw his Hell circle. I needed his blood, didn't I? For the ritual to save Kay and possibly Cole? And Xaver wasn't alive anymore to get it.

Would it matter if I collected whatever I could from the ground and used that? Hopefully not. There weren't any other options at this point.

Before I got closer, I examined the sky for any glowing orbs suddenly appearing out of nowhere. No glowing light balls. Nothing but twinkling stars and swaying tree branches. A rather peaceful night, despite all the chaos that had happened earlier.

Maybe I would never know what that thing was that had saved me from selling myself to a demon. Maybe I could find something more about it in some of Wyatt's books or the box he'd gifted to me with the angel mark. Or I could just let it be and be thankful that it had intervened when it did.

I mentally added it to my Things to Do list for another time. I still had this night to get through and tomorrow to prepare the ritual for Kay. Then there was the whole mess with going back to the afterlife and Styx Corp.

Yeah, my plate was kind of full right now.

The sound of someone approaching stiffened my spine. "Er— Jade?"

I turned to see Cole walking towards me as the others entered the trailer and shut the door.

Oh boy. This wasn't going to be good.

"Came to collect your bounty?" I asked. The instant shock and confusion on his face was priceless, and I soaked it in—a little too happily, I'll admit. When he didn't reply, I added, "I know. You don't need to keep on lying through your teeth. I know our entire meeting wasn't accidental. I know I'm one of your assignments."

He blinked, obviously not expecting this conversation yet. Or this bluntly. But since we were all almost dragged into the deepest pits of Hell only moments ago, now felt like a good time to lay it all out.

At first, I thought he might deny it and try to go on with

the ruse, but to my surprise, he said, "How did you figure it out?"

"Honestly? I was suspicious from the beginning. But I didn't know fully until I overheard you talking with my boss in the motel room."

He rubbed the side of his face. Then after a few seconds, he sighed. "Yes, Azrael hired me to keep you away from the afterlife plane until the solstice. He was adamant about it but didn't tell me why, other than he had business to attend to. Apparently, your friend getting attacked by Xaver wasn't part of his plan. I didn't think much of it because it seemed like a good reason for you to stay on this side of the spirit door, but once Azrael found out you were caught up in demon business, he wasn't too thrilled. As I'm guessing you heard."

I had. But what I didn't understand was *why*.

"What was he paying you?" I asked.

"It was more like the other way around. He threatened me," he said. "Said that if I didn't do this, he could speed up my change. Make me a Halfling and deliver me personally to the full-blood responsible for me."

"Can he do that?"

"Hell if I know. I've worked with a lot of supernaturals in my day but never with an actual angel. And not just any angel. The Angel of Death. I wasn't about to risk it."

Okay, I could understand that somewhat. I had worked for Azrael for a year, and I still didn't know what power the angel really possessed. He was the only one I had ever met, too, so there wasn't anyone else I could compare him to.

"I'll tell you this, though. He put me in a death-like sleep pretty quickly before you came and found me in the alley. And the dreams I had... Bizarre." He went on. "Why do you think Azrael wanted to keep you away from the afterlife, anyway? Or out of demon affairs? What does it matter to him?"

"That's what I'm still scratching my head about, too. I have no idea. He was the one always telling me to stick to my job. Not get involved in human stuff."

"Be a mindless worker bee, huh? And when you couldn't stick to that, he tried finding another way to keep you busy," Cole said. "Seems like he needs you out of the picture for some reason."

"But why?"

Cole shrugged. "It must have something to do with your light power thing. And that you can read ancient dialects. I mean, that tattoo on your chest and the box can't be a coincidence. Neither can that glowing ball of light swooping in to rescue us. It all has to mean something. Azrael must be scared of you."

I almost laughed out loud at that one. "Scared of m-me?" I sputtered. "He's the Angel of Death, for Pete's sake. Why would he be worried about me? I'm just one of his reapers."

"Not just a reaper, Jade. You can't be."

I shook my head frantically. "I don't know what the hell I am, but it can't be anything crazy enough to be a threat to an ethereal being."

"I saw you make a full-blooded demon explode from the inside out. *And* send all his hellions back to their hole."

He was right. I had done that. But what good was power if I didn't know the cause of it or how to use it properly so it didn't drain my energy whenever I needed it?

"You're a force to be reckoned with, Jade," he said. "You just have to learn how to control that power of yours and—"

"This, coming from a half-blood who almost turned Halfling on me because he couldn't control himself from using his corrupting Hellfire."

He held up his hands in surrender. "No judgment there."

"And besides," I began. "I don't like what you're hinting at."

"What do you mean?"

"I'm not one of your magical weapons that you store in your backpack. I won't be used as one."

One eyebrow lifted, like he was impressed. Had I read his mind? Had he been thinking about using me in that way for his mercenary work?

At this point, I wouldn't be surprised.

How had I felt anything for this man before? Now I was seeing the real Cole Masters. The clever, ruthless, work-driven assassin, and I wasn't liking who I was seeing at all. He was something else.

I gritted my teeth. "So, you obviously weren't doing your job efficiently enough. Azrael sounded mad when he visited you in the motel."

"Oh, he was," Cole said. "I had every intention of doing the assignment. It was probably one of the easiest jobs I've ever had. And his threat was read loud and clear. A specialy trained supernatural bounty hunter babysit a woman for a few days? It was almost insulting."

"Wow, thanks."

Asshole.

He held up a hand. "Then I met you and saw the power you had, saw the way you blasted Xaver out of the store, and I kind of got it. You weren't just a reaper like he said you were."

"Was Azrael the reason you could see me in my reaper spirit form?" I asked. "Did he do some kind of angel voodoo on you to make that possible?"

"No, actually he didn't do anything. I still don't know why I could see you."

Still another mystery I had to figure out.

"When I brought you here and we discovered the demon

cure—the very thing I'd been searching for most of my life—I got a bit sidetracked. Azrael's mission suddenly didn't matter anymore. You were the key I had been waiting for to get this demon part of me off my back."

"As flattering as that is, Cole, it doesn't excuse the fact that you lied to me all this time," I said. "I trusted you."

"I never asked you to trust me."

Ouch. Good point. But ouch. That had been all me. Me and my naivety.

It still was a douchey thing to do.

"I have to admit, I expected you to be madder if you somehow found out the truth," he said. "You knew all this time, and you still saved me from Xaver?"

I had expected to be angrier, too. It had come so quickly before, but now, all that fury and feeling of betrayal had fizzled out. Maybe it was because I found understanding in his explanation. He hadn't asked me to trust him. I had done that on my own, and it had been a mistake. I couldn't fault him for that. He was just doing his job, one he had been threatened to perform. If I had been put in that situation, could I say I wouldn't do the same? Especially when my assignment was a complete stranger?

The answer was a common sense one. Of course I would take the job.

Cole let out a long, dramatic sigh. "Even so, I should say thank you. For saving my life, that is. And for what you did for Wyatt."

"I liked him," I said, which was the wholehearted truth. I would have said the same thing about Cole, but now, I wasn't too sure how I felt about him. I didn't know him. That was for sure. "He helped me a lot. I owed it to him, too."

Cole ran his fingers through his hair nervously and stared out into the darkness. "I definitely owed him more than a quick, shallow grave burial and a cross made of some dead branches. I'll miss that son of a bitch."

"Yeah…"

We stood like that for a while, saying nothing.

In the stillness, I pulled out the velvet bag I had gotten from Marla.

"What's that for?" he asked.

I walked over to the place Xaver had once stood, bent down, and scooped as much of the blood-soaked dirt into the bag as I could find. Just in case. The magical bag held about three pounds of the stuff, even though it was the size of a silver dollar.

"What are you doing?" Cole asked.

"We need Xaver's blood for the cure. I'm hoping the fact that it's soaked in dirt won't matter much."

"Xaver's blood? Why do we need his blood?"

"We need the blood of the one originally damned. The one responsible for giving the curse. For Kay, that's Xaver."

"How did you find this out?" he asked, brows pinched. "I thought it was just 'damned blood.' Like mine."

I hesitated. I didn't want to tell him my information had come from another demon. And not just any demon. One responsible for one of the Seven Deadly Sins.

"I'm not sure if it's true, but I figured we'd try all options. Can't be too safe, right?" There. Didn't actually answer his question but didn't lie either.

"Right…"

Tying the drawstrings, I closed the bag and put it in my back pocket. "We should get back to the others and figure out what we need to do to get this right. It's a big day tomorrow. For all of us."

That was an understatement, wasn't it? My anxiety kicked up a notch, knowing that realistically, we only had one chance to save Kay.

Possibly Cole, too. Who knew how much longer he had before the demon side of him took over and he was lost completely? He had come pretty damn close to that point before.

Too close.

CHAPTER

TWENTY-EIGHT

As the fiery pinks, golds, and blues painted the sky, Sean, Cole, Laurence, Kay, and I gathered in Fairport Cemetery under the bare branches of an old oak tree. After consulting a few lost spirits, we discovered the first grave here predated the Revolutionary War and wasn't actually marked by a headstone at all. A family—a husband, wife, and their three children—had all been buried beneath the giant oak after a fire had wiped out their entire farm and claimed their lives. So, under the crooked, naked-looking thing was where we had set up the ritual altar and laid out the other ingredients.

Because I couldn't help but notice that Kay looked a little paler today, a little more sickly, I was more than thrilled today was the solstice. Who knew how much longer she would be able to hold on. It was something I hoped we never had to find out.

We had all spent the night in Wyatt's and Sean's trailer, partly to review the instructions for the demon cure and discuss our plan, and partly to reminiscence about a great man we were all going to miss. Cole and Sean loved telling stories about Wyatt's life. Each one had us hooting with laughter, especially the tale of the one time Wyatt had joined Cole on one of his missions. After being shot in the arm, he'd decided his butt was better off behind a desk, reading a book and searching for information than on the front lines.

Could have fooled me, the way he came out guns blazing to fight the Halflings and Xaver. But Cole assured me that when his property or family was threatened, that was just the way Wyatt was. As for a job in mercenary work—not so much.

With the Breath of Life herb, Xaver's blood, and a scoop of dirt from the Holiest ground, or in our case the soil near the oak tree's roots, all on the makeshift altar Sean had set up, we waited eagerly for the setting sun to hit the horizon. According to the cure I'd found in Wyatt's wife's box, the sun's positioning was just as important as the ingredients. And we would only have a few seconds to throw all the pieces together for the magic of the ritual to work. Cole stood at the ready, hands out, for his part in it.

"Are you sure about this?" I side-eyed him, my heart beating abnormally fast for someone who was supposed to be dead. "You seemed pretty far gone after using your Hellfire during the fight. I can't have you turning into one of those Halfling creatures here."

He shrugged, and while his calmness was relaxing at other critical moments, now it was just annoying. "I came back, didn't I?"

"Well, yeah, but…" Why did I care, really? If he used his Hellfire again and became a Halfling, he'd be out of my hair forever, wouldn't he? I wouldn't have to worry about Azrael using him anymore. He'd be in Hell, and I'd probably never see him again.

Problem solved.

Right?

Fear gripped my muscles, canceling out that idea. As much as I didn't want to, I did care still. A little. I'd seen those hideous half-demon beasts up close and personal—I'd fought them—and knowing that they had once been people just like Cole was horrifying. And having to serve a full-demon's every beck and call? No one deserved a fate like that.

"Jade, I'll be fine. I won't let it corrupt me. I'm stronger than that. Give me some credit." His blue eyes bore into mine with the confidence and certainty I couldn't muster up myself. Yet the red lining around those naturally cool irises made worry gnaw at me again.

"Besides," he added after a second, "it's not like there's anyone else here who can add the last ingredient we need. I'm the only one with the power to manipulate Hell's fire. I'm the only one you got."

"He's got a point, you know," Sean said.

"Shut it, you," I threw back at him. "You're not helping."

Sean made the motion of zipping his lips shut and throwing away the invisible key.

"Uh, Jade." Kay's fragile voice came from my left. She stood with Laurence's arms wrapped around her for comfort. "The sky."

I glanced up past the harbor to see the sun was taking its position on the ocean's edge. It looked like I didn't have time to contemplate this one any longer. We were out of time.

"All right. Let's do this, then. Everyone say a prayer."

Sean began to combine the ingredients together while

reciting the ancient language I had gone over with him the night before. I had found more information in the box, and surprisingly, everything had been conveniently laid out for the person executing the ritual. Simplified. Organized. As if the author had had their future audience in mind. Almost like it had been done that way on purpose.

We had been lucky that I somehow could read the language everything was written in. Extremely lucky. But after everything we'd been through, we needed some good karma to help us out. Damn, I'd even go as far as to say we deserved it.

Sean beckoned Kay and Cole over. He lit the Breath of Life herb with the white candle and blew the smoke over the two of them. Then he doused the flame in two waiting bowls of dirt.

As he did all this, I went over the instructions in my head, making sure we didn't miss any steps. I had read that slab of skin over a thousand times, had even come across a small faded note in the corner saying to add Holy Water before consuming. But that extra little tidbit had made me nervous. What if there were other notes that had faded with time, parts we were missing? This was Kay's only chance to survive the pregnancy and birth. If this demon baby didn't take her out in the coming weeks, there was no way she'd survive the delivery. No one had.

The amped up magic in the air slid across my skin, raising every hair on my body. Normally on the solstice, the veil between the living world and the nonliving worlds were blurred, but since the balance had been already tipped before this night, it felt like the planes were mashed together. Colliding. Unnatural.

It felt like pure chaos.

Spirits of all types and ages flooded into the cemetery, drawn to us and the magic we were playing with. There were hundreds of them, too many to just be the normal haunts who'd passed without a reaper to guide them into the afterlife or ones who had stumbled out of an open spirit door. Those cases were rare, but now I couldn't even count how many souls gathered around us.

It seemed like the veil had been stripped away entirely, allowing spirits to cross over at will.

If that were true, that couldn't be good.

Kay swayed in her spot nervously, seeing exactly what I was seeing.

"Don't worry," I whispered to her, urging her to stay focused. "I'm here." I doubted they would do anything to us—just curious, probably—but if someone got out of hand, I'd have no problem taking them down.

Cole took out a pocketknife from his jeans and sliced open his palm. Not even a flicker of pain showed on his face as he let the blood flow into his selected bowl.

God, I hoped this worked for them both. Maybe Monnie had been wrong about the whole "the blood must be from the originally cursed" or the full-blooded demon that had helped conceive the baby. Maybe we'd be lucky again and any cursed demon blood would do.

Wouldn't that be a miracle?

Working quickly, Cole used his uninjured hand to create a spark of flame between his fingers, just big enough to light a cigarette. He tossed it into both concoctions.

Kay's popped and a small burst of red light emitted, then rapidly turned blue before extinguishing altogether. Cole's bowl crackled, too, but when the light appeared, it stayed red before snuffing out.

Lastly, Sean added a vial of Holy Water to each.

When everything was mixed together, he handed Kay her bowl first. She took it in both hands, said the ancient words she was supposed to, and gulped down a few mouthfuls of the liquid. She gagged a little at the end but managed to keep it all down.

Cole didn't wait to see Kay's reaction before taking his own bowl, repeating the words, and drinking the mixture. He wiped his mouth clean with the back of his hand when it was empty.

For a moment, nothing happened. We stood there, waiting for something to let us know it had or hadn't worked. But we just exchanged worried looks.

Then, Cole drew in a deep breath, but it came back out as a sputtering cough. "Is your throat burning?" he asked Kay. "Mine's burning. Ugh, and my stomach."

I took a few steps toward him as he bent over and started hacking.

"N-No," Kay said nervously, touching her neck. "I feel fine."

"It's the Holy Water," Cole managed to get out between coughs. "It has to be. Whose idea was it to have a half-demon drink the stuff?"

"That's what the cure said," I told him.

"Technically, Kay has a half-demon inside her, too. So, if it was the Holy Water, wouldn't it be affecting her, too?"

"But you feel fine, Kay?" Laurence asked her, never wandering from her side.

She nodded. "I don't feel anything besides a lot of movement from the baby."

Laurence's eyes widened. "But you're only a week or so along."

"The gestation of a half-demon is much shorter than a normal human gestation. In most cases, it only takes three months," Sean said.

"Wow," was all Laurence said, but his expression showed all his fear.

"So, we need this cure to do its thing and work," I said

and glanced over at Cole who was still coughing so hard his face was turning red. Turning to Sean, I asked, "Any idea why Cole's acting this way?"

He shrugged. "There are other rituals I've read about where ingesting the mixture is needed for the spell to work, and in those cases, any ill effects, especially throwing up, is not a good sign."

At the moment, the sound of Cole heaving came, along with a spew of vomit.

"There's our answer," said Sean, looking at Cole. "It didn't work for you."

Cole grumbled and wiped his mouth again. "Tastes even worse coming back up." He flicked his wrist, and a small flame appeared. He snapped his fingers to extinguish it just as fast. "Well, looks like I'm still me. Still half-demon."

"I told you using your blood might not work," I told him.

"Well, my blood is all I have. Xaver wasn't my maker. I don't know what demon was."

"You don't?"

"Do you think I would have let that bastard live another day, knowing what he did to me and my mother? To me, he murdered her."

True. Cole wasn't exactly the forgiving type. Especially when it came to demons. Like everyone else impregnated by a demon, there was no way Cole's mother survived the birth of her half-demon son. He would want revenge.

"Of course no one wants to talk," he went on. "Every demon I've managed to track down, trap, and question won't spill the beans. Those bastards might be hideous, but they're loyal to each other."

"How do we know if Kay's cured? And the baby…" Laurence glanced at Sean.

"Why do you all keep looking at me?" he asked.

"You're the one who knows more about this stuff than anyone else," Laurence said.

Cole started coughing again and gasped. "He's got a point. You know just as much as your father."

"I wouldn't go that far..." Sean mumbled, but a smile was peeking through.

When I had first met Sean, he had gone on and on about how he didn't want to be like his father. This life with supernaturals wasn't for him, yet here he was, in the same place his father would be if he were still alive, helping us all with our supernatural problems. And now, it appeared that he didn't mind it at all.

Actually, there was an air of confidence about him that I hadn't noticed before. Maybe it was just another thing Wyatt had been right about—his son was made for this type of work.

"Have you read anything about a similar case maybe?" Laurence asked him. "What comes next?"

Sean wrung his hands together. After a moment, he said, "Yes, actually. There are other cases where babies are cursed while in the womb. If a counter curse is administered correctly, the baby will be born completely normal. No longer cursed."

Laurence let out a long breath of relief. "Oh, thank God." Then, his face pinched in thought and began to change into complete and utter joy. "Wait. That means—I-I'm going to be a father?"

"If the cure worked, it's very possible," Sean said.

Kay looked up at Laurence and smiled. She looked so beautiful in that moment as the realization of it washed over her, too. After so much heartache, turmoil, and pain, it was very possible that they had something very life-changing and wonderful coming their way. And they deserved it. They'd make great parents. I thought so, anyway.

My gaze swept across the cemetery to see the onlooking spirits were starting to drift away. A few stayed behind, though. One woman stared at Kay with such fondness and love, I wondered if she knew her. That was when I saw the similarities to her ghostly facial features. They shared the same bright, hopeful eyes and rosebud-shaped mouth.

"Kay…" I whispered, nodding the spirit's way. "Look over there."

But the moment Kay's head swung toward the woman, she disappeared.

"What?" Kay asked. "Oh, most of the spirits left. That's a relief."

I was tempted to tell her what I'd seen, but with so much going on, I decided another day might be a better time for it.

Laurence and Kay began helping Sean pick up the altar.

"Don't throw out whatever's left of that herb," Cole said after spilling more vomit into the grass. His face twisted in disgust. "I'm going to need it."

"You're going to try again?" I asked.

"What choice do I have?" he said. "I have to find the demon responsible for cursing me and add his blood to the mix."

"By the next solstice," I reminded him.

"Exactly."

"And what about Azrael?"

"What about him?"

"Technically you didn't finish your job."

Cole waved his hand. "He can come find me again. Then, I'll deal with it. After all this, I promised myself a vacation, but now it looks like Hawaii will have to wait a little longer. I have a demon to catch."

I looked over at Kay and Laurence who were embracing each other tightly and laughing. The happiness radiating off them was unavoidable, and a twinge of jealousy went through me. Of course I was thrilled for them. I wanted nothing more than my dearest friend to live her life to the fullest. A part of me just wished there was a way for me to have a piece of that happiness, too.

It just wasn't in the cards for me. As much as it hurt to, I had to accept that. But maybe learning about my past and the life I had lived on earth could help ease some of that ache.

At least I had done all I could to save her. And so far, the cure seemed to have worked, but there was no way to tell for sure until months went by and she gave birth.

Now it was time for me to get back to my afterlife, my job —whatever was left of it—and try my best to find out what was going on with me and these new gifts. There were still so many questions, like what was that floating white orb that had shown up to save my ass, not once but *twice*, during the battle with Xaver? Why was I suddenly shifting between dead and alive? And the light power—was it connected to my angel mark? Where had that come from? Had I really been touched by one of them?

Oh, and let's not forget what Azrael had to do with all of this. Why had he hired Cole to distract me?

After so much had happened, I was left with only more questions instead of answers. My to-do list was starting to look more like Santa's naughty or nice list. Too overwhelming and long to handle, let alone check off twice. Sheesh. The fat guy had the right idea about keeping his job to once a year.

"I guess this is goodbye, then." Cole's voice pulled me out of my reverie. Like a business partner might, he stuck out his hand for me to shake.

I only stared at it, my hands comfortable in their place in my jean pockets. Had he forgotten that we had not only almost died battling demons and Halflings together, but we had slept together? And not some mediocre, quick sex either.

Yet here he was acting like our encounters this last week were nothing more than part of the job requirement.

He flexed his fingers before withdrawing and rubbed the back of his neck instead. "Well…maybe I'll see you around, Jade."

Then, he turned around, snatched the herb and his backpack from beside the tree, and walked out of the cemetery, throwing a short wave goodbye to the others as he went.

Kay came to my side. "Do you think he'll be back?" she asked as we both watched Cole disappear around the corner. In the unseen distance, his old Jeep whined to life as it started.

I shrugged, but on the inside, I knew the answer. Something told me that if Cole Masters and I ever crossed paths again, it wouldn't be for pleasantries.

The next time we came face-to-face, it was very likely I would have to kill him.

CHAPTER

TWENTY-NINE

When the golden elevator doors of Styx Corp opened, I stepped inside the enormous office space that once belonged to my boss, the Angel of Death himself, Azrael. It was hard to believe that only months ago, I had been afraid to even be summoned to this place. But now, all that fear was gone, replaced with new ones.

Coming to Azrael's office no longer scared me becaus̶ the angel was still MIA. In his place, my old mentor, Simon, sat behind his desk, having been appointed the position in Azrael's absence.

As expected, in the days of his promotion, he had done a hell of a job sorting out the mess Azrael had left behind.

Death assignments were back on track. Everything was organized and working like a well-oiled machine.

Honestly, I never doubted Simon. Everything about him was fine-tuned and orderly. He was made for being the reaper in charge. I had said it since the day I met him—the guy oozed responsibility.

"Jade." Simon greeted me as I walked into his huge office by rising out of his seat. "Thanks for coming."

"Well, you summoned me, and I don't want to get on my new boss's bad side," I said with a chuckle. "I hear he's a real tough ass."

Simon's usual hardened expression cracked slightly and revealed a whisper of a smile.

"So, why do you need me?" I asked. "I've been following the rules this time. Haven't gotten into any trouble. That I know of, at least."

"No, no trouble, which I'm thankful for. But I did want to talk to you about something else."

That set my nerves on edge. After returning to the afterlife, I hadn't known what to expect. Azrael could have been waiting for me on the other side of the spirit door for all I knew. But to my surprise, the afterlife was just how I'd left it. The only difference was that Simon had taken Azrael's place and the chaos behind the veil was trying to be tamed by my other reaper coworkers.

My first trip back to Styx Corp was when I told Simon everything about my adventures with the living. Even about my new gifts and Azrael's strange plot to have a trained assassin watch my every move. I had gone as far as to spill the beans about Xaver and the demon cure, and when I finished my long spiel, Simon hadn't looked the slightest bit surprised.

The man was a rock. Always had been.

"I always knew there was something special about you,"

he'd said when I finished my story, which had been the last thing I expected him to say.

"By special, you mean…weird? Peculiar?"

"Sometimes those are good traits to have. In your case, it seemed it saved lives."

"You aren't mad at me?"

"For not listening to me when I told you to stay out of living affairs?" He faked a laugh. "Oh, Jade. I know you better than that. When it comes to your heart, you'll do whatever it takes. I just wish I had more answers for you. An angel's mark… I'll have to ask around about that one. That's new to me."

Unfortunately, with all of Simon's knowledge and with how long he'd been in the game, he still couldn't clarify any of my questions. The only bit of advice he could offer me was to dive back into my job, and if Azrael returned, we would face him together and demand answers.

It wasn't much, but for some reason, knowing Simon was by my side in this did help some to calm my nerves. So now, when he'd called me into his office this morning, the same worry that usually clung to me didn't this time. Even with his ominous words, "We need to talk."

"I know you miss your friends," Simon began, walking around the desk, down the few steps, and over to me. He still wore his long black frock that billowed behind him whenever he moved. "I've been keeping a close eye on the Medium girl and her progress in her pregnancy."

Staying away from Kay had been the hardest thing I'd ever had to do. Of course, I hadn't strayed too far, keeping a watchful eye from a distance where she couldn't see me just to check in and make sure she was okay. But I hadn't talked to her since the solstice to keep myself in Simon's good graces.

From what I'd observed, everything seemed to be going fine. But now, I was worried.

I commanded my heartbeat to stay steady, but it jump-started on its own. After all this time and even while in spirit form, it still mimicked such living habits. "Is she okay?"

Simon held up a hand to calm me. "She's fine. Actually, better than fine." There it was again—that touch of a smile that curled the corners of his mouth ever so slightly. If I'd blinked, I would have missed it. "She had her baby."

My heart started pounding for a different reason. Excitement filled me, followed by complete and utter fear. "Is the baby…?"

"Completely normal. Yes."

Tears prickled my eyes. I sucked in a deep breath and held it for a few seconds to keep the tears from spilling over.

We'd done it. The ritual had worked. Everything I had done had worked. Kay was saved. More than that, such a terrible, traumatic event had turned into something beautiful for both her and Laurence. They had brought life into this world. Completely demon free.

"I think you should pay them a visit," Simon went on.

I froze. Had I heard him right?

"What was that now?" I laughed in disbelief. "You want me to cross over not on assignment and interact with the living? Is this a test or something? Who are you and what have you done with Simon?"

"No, this isn't a test, and it's me." He reached out and touched my arm gently. To my even greater surprise, his palm was baby smooth and warm against my bare skin. "I'm not a callous monster. Even if you think I am sometimes."

I wouldn't say callous monster… Maybe a tight-ass or a stick-in-the-mud, but not a monster.

"After everything you've been through, and with everything you've done for this woman, I think you deserve a little vacation time." He paused, then added, "That is, *if* you don't interfere with anyone else over there or reveal any more of our secrets. I'm still working on reactivating the censorship to prevent it from happening, but until then, no funny business. Visit your friend and come back. Do you understand?"

I nodded, but my mind was already in what lay beyond the spirit door. Being able to talk to Kay again and meet her new little bundle of joy. I couldn't believe Simon was giving me this chance. It was so...unlike him. Dare I say, rebellious?

"I don't know what's gotten into you, Simon, but I like it." I turned around, ready to speed walk back into the elevator and out of Styx Corp.

"One more thing." Simon's words stopped me cold.

I spun back around to face him. "Yes?"

He held out something for me to take. It was small enough to fit in his hand with a shiny, flat face and two straps coming out of it. When I strolled over to him, I noticed that it was a watch. A fancy one with the Styx Corp emblem glowing silver in the center.

"We've upgraded from tablets," he said as he passed it to me. "I always thought they were too bulky to carry around. These are lightweight and durable. It has all the functions of the tablet so your assignments can be viewed through here, and you and I can communicate if needed."

I hesitated, remembering how I had shattered Azrael's tablet after suspecting my location was being monitored through it. "Can I be tracked through it?"

"Only if you put out a distress signal," he said. "That's a new feature I had added in case a reaping assignment goes wrong, which seems to happen a little more than it should in your case."

Got that right.

"Only then can I, or another reaper, come and find you. To help."

I strapped the flashy new watch onto my wrist. Just the small size of it had me liking it better than the bulky tablets Azrael had given us.

"This is great. Thanks," I said. "But does it tell the time?"

Simon nodded. "I had to pay extra for that one."

Was that...*a joke?* Holy crap. It was like Simon was a new man. Maybe he had gotten laid recently or something. But knowing him, he probably had just reorganized his closet at home to fit the feng shui. To him, it was practically the same thing.

"Death assignments will show up in red, and new assignments will pop up in green."

"Wait, new assignments?" I asked. "What do you mean?"

"With the chaos of the veil thinning, especially during the solstice, many spirits were able to wander into the living world as haunts."

I'd witnessed this myself in the cemetery the evening we performed the demon cure. Hundreds of spirits had stood around to watch us. I had questioned it then, too.

"I know you struggle with separating yourself from the emotion that can come with reaping, so I've put you in charge of rounding these spirits up and bringing them back into the afterlife. Of course, you must still perform some reaper duties, but it won't be as much as before. Edward has agreed to pick up whatever is left of the supernatural deaths to help out."

I couldn't help myself. I leapt forward and wrapped Simon up in a hug.

"Thank you," I blurted out, unable to contain my happiness. To have him change so much just to accommodate me was a wonderful feeling. Especially after everything I had done to disobey him and almost cause him to get Released.

He stood there, his body tense, unsure what to do, but after a few seconds, he softened and patted my back. When I pulled away, he was smiling. This time, it was an actual one, full of pride and admiration. Like a father might give his daughter.

"Go on now. Go visit your friends," he said, waving me off.

Wasting no more time, I turned around and hurried to the elevator.

Stepping inside, we met eyes once again.

"Don't make me regret this, Jade," he said as the elevator chimed and the doors slowly began to close.

I grinned and cupped one of my ears like I was struggling to make out his words. "What was that? I can't hear you over this terrible jazz music."

"Jade, I'm serious," he said, a little louder this time, his concern growing on his face.

"You really need to change this music selection," I shouted back.

"Jade, don't do anything I wouldn't. Jade. Jade!"

The doors sealed shut, cutting off his warnings.

While the elevator descended, I laughed. As expected, the look on his face had been priceless. I didn't know why I enjoyed teasing the man so much, but it sure was fun.

When I reached the ground floor and the elevator let me out, I marched out to the lobby, passing Maryanne's desk. The little troll of a woman popped her head up.

"Blackwell," she snipped, the way she always did.

This time, I wasn't in the mood for one of our usual tit for tats. I had somewhere important to be; I had to see Kay and Laurence while I could.

"Can't really chat today, Maryanne. I'm needed somewhere," I said, still strolling toward the front doors.

She slammed something on the desk so hard, it made me skid to a stop.

"There's a package here for you," she said. "Come get it."

Curious, I walked over and snatched the yellow envelope, surprised at how much it weighed.

As I marched away, I threw a quick "thanks" over my shoulder.

"Your hair looks terrible!" she shouted to my turned back.

I held up a middle finger as I walked through the swinging doors and stepped outside.

As I went down the steps, my interest in the mystery package began to get the better of me. No one had ever sent me anything before.

Making my way to the transportation portal, I ripped the top open and stuck my hand inside. Every muscle in my body tensed at what I felt. Something smooth, cold, and metallic to the touch.

What I pulled out confirmed my assumptions. It was a gun. And it was loaded.

The only other thing in the envelope was a sheet of paper with someone's scribbly handwriting on it, which I had to squint to read.

From what I could make out, it read: *You were right. Sometimes it helps to have some backup.*

What was even more amazing was who had signed the bottom.

Cole.

How the heck—

Weapons weren't allowed in the afterlife for obvious reasons. Who needed a gun when everyone here was already dead? So how had he managed to get this to me? My only guess was Sean. Maybe it was something they'd discovered in one of the old texts? A way to get objects to cross over, too?

I chuckled. Took him this long, but he finally let me get one of his guns.

I played with it in my hand for a bit, testing its weight and fit. Knowing Cole, it was packed with some of his magic bullets, the ones made from iron and dipped in Holy Water, which could stun any spirit or demon. Now, if I ran into any more troublesome characters, like Tristen or Xaver, on my assignments, I had a way to defend myself.

Simon would have a fit if he ever found out, I was sure, but like I always said, what he didn't know wouldn't hurt him. Right?

Making sure the safety was on, I tucked the gun in the waistband of my jeans. I stepped onto the platform and spoke the street name for my apartment on the other side of Fairport's downtown area. As the portal swooped me up and carried me away, for once, my thoughts drifted to the future instead of the emptiness that dwelled in my past.

I felt more like myself than I had in a long time.

Get your copy of book 2: Death Trap

THANK YOU

Thank you for reading Death Wish

Start reading book 2 in the Reaper Reborn Series:
Death Trap

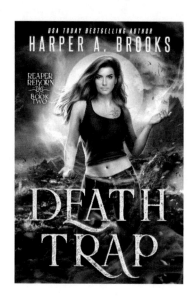

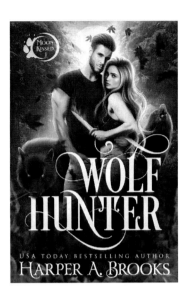

Falling for her target wasn't part of the plan.

Tasha Ward exists as a phantom. Drifting from place to place, she can blend in to the point of invisibility—a trait highly useful for a deadly assassin like her. But after years of perfecting her skills, she wants to be seen.

No… It's more than that. She wants the alpha of the murderous Redcliff wolf pack to look her in the eye as she plunges her knife straight through his heart. Traveling deep into the pack's territory alone, Tasha's prepared for war… until she finally faces the pack's ruggedly sexy leader and does the one thing she's never done before. *Hesitate.*

As the new alpha, Reid Holden doesn't agree with many of the traditions his father believed in. Especially taking a woman to sacrifice once a year. Unfortunately, being on top means he's always a target, and venomous snakes are everywhere. Even in his own family.

Tasha's meant to be another enemy, but Reid is finding it impossible to hate her. It doesn't help that his wolf has already claimed her. She may want him dead, but she might be the one person he'll end up risking everything for.

Sizzling romance meets pulse-pounding suspense in Wolf Hunter, the latest gripping novel from USA Today Bestselling Author Harper A. Brooks!

MORE BOOKS BY HARPER A. BROOKS

REAPER REBORN

Death Wish

Death Trap

Death Match

Death Deals

Death Sentence

Till Death

Christmas Spirits: A Holiday Novella

Halfling for Hire: A Short Story Collection

KINGDOM OF MONSTERS

Cruel Shadows

Necessary Evil

Wicked Reign

SIN DEMONS

Playing with Hellfire

Hell in a Handbasket

All Shot to Hell

To Hell and Back

When Hell Freezes Over

Hell on Earth

Snowball's Chance in Hell: A Holiday Novella

Hell or Highwater: A Holiday Novella

Darkest Sin: Part One (Sin Demons Complete Collection)

Darkest Sin: Part Two (Sin Demons Complete Collection)

MOON KISSED

Wolf Hunter

Wolf Tamer

Wolf Protector

Moon Kissed: The Complete Collection

KINGS OF EDEN

Kings of Eden

Stolen Paradise

Ruthless Lies

SHIFTERS UNLEASHED

Tiger Claimed

Wolf Marked

STAND ALONES

His Haven

Eternally Yours

Monstrous: A Monster Romance Novella

Monstrous Bond: A Monster Romance Novella

Immortal Throne

ABOUT THE AUTHOR

Harper A. Brooks may be a Jersey girl at heart, but now she likes to hideout in the mountains of Virginia with bigfoot and all his little woodland friends. Even though classic authors have always filled her bookshelves, she finds her writing muse drawn to the dark, magical, and romantic. When she isn't creating entire worlds with sexy shifters or legendary love stories, you can find her either with a good cup of coffee in hand or at home snuggling with her furry, four-legged son, Sammy.

RONE AWARD WINNER
USA TODAY BESTSELLING AUTHOR
INTERNATIONAL BESTSELLING AUTHOR

Join Harper's reader group for exclusive content, sneak-peeks, giveaways, and more!

facebook.com/HarperABrooks

twitter.com/HarperABrooks

instagram.com/harperabrooks

Made in United States
North Haven, CT
30 July 2025

71115782R00208